Praise for the Novels of Karen Brichoux

The Girl She Left Behind

"Evokes Richard Russo's *Empire Falls* or Michael Chabon's *Wonder Boys*."
—*Kansas Alumni*

"Brichoux reminds the reader how powerfully the landscape of 'home' can define a person." —*High Country News*

"Karen Brichoux writes with a sorcerer's ease and a voice as stunningly clear as the novel's Montana setting, conjuring characters that feel like old friends, a world as familiar as home."
—Nina Solomon, author of *Single Wife*

"A story that casts the reader into the tangles and relationships of small-town life. As Kat struggles to deal with her past, she develops some wonderful friendships with strong women in the community ... a wonderful story of a woman who struggles through a self-discovery process and accepts the love she embraced as a girl."
—Romance Designs

"A quiet, intense novel."
—*Romantic Times BOOKclub* (4½ stars, top pick)

continued . . .

Written by today's freshest new talents and selected by New American Library, NAL Accent novels touch on subjects close to a woman's heart, from friendship to family to finding our place in the world. The Conversation Guides included in each book are intended to enrich the individual reading experience, as well as encourage us to explore these topics together—because books, and life, are meant for sharing.

Visit us online at www.penguin.com.

Separation Anxiety

"Witty and thought-provoking, *Separation Anxiety* is a fast-paced, feisty exploration into deciphering personal truths. Karen Brichoux writes with such delightful insight, she reaches past the heart and tugs at your very soul. A highly recommended read!"
—Donna Kauffman, author of *Not So Snow White* and *The Cinderella Rules*

"[A] compelling tale of a young woman rearranging her view of the world. Pop this must read into your beach bag this summer, but don't expect to find breezy fluff between its covers as you while away the hours on the sand." —Curvynovels.com

"Brichoux has managed to break away from the standard 'chick lit' fare to offer literature of more substance [and] innovative ideas. . . . Brichoux deserves kudos for her valiant attempts at reinventing the. . . genre known as 'chick lit' . . . an author to watch." —*Lawrence Journal World* (KS)

Coffee & Kung Fu

"*Coffee & Kung Fu* is fresh, lively writing. One of the best parts is its use of metaphor and the elements of folklore gleaned from the Kung Fu universe. After reading Brichoux's debut, you might feel, as I do, that you have not given Jackie Chan his due." —*St. Petersburg Times*

"A young woman's guide to life—as seen through classic Jackie Chan films. Newcomer Karen Brichoux scores a coup by venturing into the cliché-strewn, warmed-over waters of Gen X chick lit and coming up with a bright, fresh, exciting spin on the genre . . . warm, smart, and original: a swift Snake in Eagle's Shadow kick to all the Bridget Jones clones." —*Kirkus Reviews*

"[A] wonderful debut ... charming, witty, and soulful. Readers will delight in the tale of one woman's journey from humorous, melancholic, lonely girl—to confident, self-knowing young woman."

—Jill A. Davis, author of *Girls' Poker Night*

"Thanks to breezy first-person narrative, snappy dialogue, and characters so real you expect to run into them at Starbucks, newcomer Brichoux's literary debut is as vivid as her heroine's close-cropped, bright red hair. A fast-paced, hilarious, yet poignant read—if you liked *The Nanny Diaries*, you'll love *Coffee & Kung Fu!*"

—Wendy Markham, author of *Once upon a Blind Date* and *Slightly Single*

"Absolutely fabulous! A fresh, funny novel about being your own woman. Made me want to run out and rent a Kung Fu movie!"

—Melissa Senate, author of *See Jane Date* and *The Solomon Sisters Wise Up*

"*Coffee & Kung Fu* kicks its way into a different league."

—*Hollywood Reporter*

"Who knew [Jackie Chan films] were so deep? A fun and quick read from a first-time author, this is perfect for a day at the beach."

—*Library Journal*

"A refreshing take on an increasingly crowded genre." —*Booklist*

"Clever and heartfelt turns of phrase.... *Coffee & Kung Fu* is an easy read, well-suited for long weekends or extended beach breaks."

—*Women's Review of Books*

"Brichoux places a fresh and funky spin on a genre often exhausted by generalities and clichés. *Coffee & Kung Fu* is the type of book that you could pick up and read over and over again." —*Cincinnati City Beat*

Other Books by Karen Brichoux

Coffee & Kung Fu

Separation Anxiety

The Girl She Left Behind

Falling into the World

Karen Brichoux

NAL
ACCENT

NAL Accent
Published by New American Library, a division of
Penguin Group (USA) Inc., 375 Hudson Street,
New York, New York 10014, USA
Penguin Group (Canada), 90 Eglinton Avenue East, Suite 700, Toronto,
Ontario M4P 2Y3, Canada (a division of Pearson Penguin Canada Inc.)
Penguin Books Ltd., 80 Strand, London WC2R 0RL, England
Penguin Ireland, 25 St. Stephen's Green, Dublin 2,
Ireland (a division of Penguin Books Ltd.)
Penguin Group (Australia), 250 Camberwell Road, Camberwell, Victoria 3124,
Australia (a division of Pearson Australia Group Pty. Ltd.)
Penguin Books India Pvt. Ltd., 11 Community Centre, Panchsheel Park,
New Delhi - 110 017, India
Penguin Group (NZ), cnr Airborne and Rosedale Roads, Albany,
Auckland 1310, New Zealand (a division of Pearson New Zealand Ltd.)
Penguin Books (South Africa) (Pty.) Ltd., 24 Sturdee Avenue,
Rosebank, Johannesburg 2196, South Africa

Penguin Books Ltd., Registered Offices:
80 Strand, London WC2R 0RL, England

First published by NAL Accent, an imprint of New American Library,
a division of Penguin Group (USA) Inc.

First Printing, November 2006
10 9 8 7 6 5 4 3 2 1

LIBRARY OF CONGRESS CATALOGING-IN-PUBLICATION DATA:

Brichoux, Karen.
   Falling into the world/Karen Brichoux.
      p. cm.
   ISBN-13: 978-0-451-21843-8   1. Young women—Fiction. 2. Missouri—Fiction. 3.
Domestic fiction. I. Title.
   PS3602.R5F35 2006
   813'.6—dc22   2006022897

Set in Bembo
Designed by Spring Hoteling

Printed in the United States of America

For my parents,
who have never forgotten
the joys of childhood

Acknowledgments

I owe a debt of gratitude to my editor, Ellen Edwards, for her suggestions and direction during the birth of this story; and an equal debt to my agent, Kim Whalen, for her advocacy, support, and tireless patience answering questions about the book biz. Additional thanks must go to Claire Zion and Kara Welsh at NAL, as well as to Emily Mahon and the art department. As always, a big thank-you to Jerri and Libby, for friendship; and to Jake, for covering her pool so the mockingbirds wouldn't fall in (it's always nice to meet a fellow traveler!). I also must not forget to express my appreciation to Mac, for eating that three-prong fishhook at the lake and landing us in the vet's office in the middle of the night—from strange things, inspiration is born. And last but never least, I want to thank Dave for damn near everything. You know what I mean.

Chapter 1

"*Once upon a time there was a little girl who lived with her mother and father and baby sister in a little town beside a big river.*"

Beyond the circle of porch light, the crickets chirped an evening song. My mother's arm was warm around my shoulders, almost too warm in the lingering heat of a late-summer day, and the seat slats of the porch swing cut into the backs of my legs. The moon rose red through the harvest dust, and even though I couldn't see them from where we sat, I knew the trees along the Mississippi's banks were gleaming silver in the red moon's light.

"*Once upon a time there was a little girl. And this is her story.*"

In the time-honored tradition of humankind, my mother's stories were oral history, the reality of each story enhanced by the fairy-tale quality of its beginning. But her voice was silenced the year I turned twenty-two, and somehow it seemed—seems—my story ended six years ago when I lost the teller. Life goes on, or so they say, and living stories go on, too. Still, life can be altered beyond expectation, leaving behind a clutter that never quite makes a whole, a story that never quite makes sense even though you pretend it does.

"Let's see that ring!" Mrs. Carlson says.

We're standing in front of the toilet paper at the local Kroger store. My cart has somehow contrived to bump into Mrs. Carlson's cart even though I thought I was doing a pretty good job of not being seen and pretending not to see. The toilet paper is stacked along a wall, and a display stand of corn removers blocks the alternative exit and turns the aisle into a dead end with Mrs. Carlson guarding the only way out. I smile and hold out my hand to show her the ring.

"No diamond?"

"I wanted a plain band."

"I would have thought Colton could afford a diamond. Even a small one."

"It was my decision. He wanted to buy a diamond."

"What's the world coming to when a boy can't even buy his girl a small diamond?"

I reach out for a pack of Charmin and give it a good squeeze.

"I hear your sister is back in town. That must be . . ."

She pauses for dramatic emphasis. When I don't react, she raises her eyebrows and reaches for a twelve-pack of quilted softness.

". . . difficult," she finishes. "Not that your sister is difficult. I mean, it must be different."

I shrug and judge the distance between the shampoo, shelved across from the toilet paper, and Mrs. Carlson's cart. The width of available space is short a few inches, thanks to the store manager's decision to buy bigger carts without widening the aisles, so I won't be escaping gracefully. I feign interest in a particular brand of shampoo just past Mrs. Carlson's cart, clear my throat, and gesture helplessly.

"If I could just . . . ?"

But instead of moving aside, she shuffles backward, keeping me trapped between her cart and the corn removers.

"I suppose it's a good thing that she came home."

I'm concentrating on falling in love with a shampoo at the end of the aisle and working out a geometry problem of angles, curves, two carts, and escape.

"Who?"

"Your sister. It's probably a good thing she came back. A young couple needs their own home. Having her back will make that easier."

I stop my trajectory toward the end of the aisle, stop my feigned interest in softness, volume, and clarification, and really look at my captor's face. She's going fishing. She's hungry for gossip and she's just thrown out the bait to see if I will bite and give her a tasty fish to fry for her next get-together with the coffee klatch that poses as a book club.

"I'm not sure I understand," I say.

"Oh . . . nothing, really. Have you tried this brand?"

An hour later, standing in the warm sunlight of my father's kitchen, I unpack the toilet paper and the shampoo I didn't want.

"Do you like this brand?" I ask my sister.

Saphira is on her way through the kitchen, carrying a basketful of laundry that is, undoubtedly, hers and hers alone. I wonder what happened to Dad's and my clothes—the load I put in this morning. Saphi stops and looks at the shampoo bottle in my hand.

"Not really. It would make a good floor wax. Why'd you buy it if you don't want it?"

"It was a ticket to freedom."

She shifts the laundry basket so it sits on her hip. I dig farther down into the grocery bag and drop a few boxes of tampons and the package of toilet paper on top of her clothes.

"Take these upstairs to the bathroom, will you?"

"Why freedom?"

"Mrs. Carlson."

"My God. So no one has knocked off the old tart in a fit of justified rage?"

"She's not so bad."

I feel compelled to defend Mrs. Carlson and feel angry that Saphi has made me feel compelled to defend the old . . . tart.

"She's got a nose three miles long."

Saphi leans forward and sniffs the air like Jackson Dover's spaniel.

"Ah, I smell gossip hiding in this store."

"It wasn't like that," I say, setting a box of tissues on top of the TP in her basket. "She actually had battle maneuvers laid out and she trapped me in the only dead end. I wouldn't be surprised if the rack of corn removers was part of a strategic plot."

Saphi snorts, and for the moment that it takes our laughter to mingle, I'm fifteen years old and she's ten; our world is still revolving and everything makes sense. The moment lasts only a moment before it winks out and is replaced by the present.

"We don't need tissues upstairs," Saphi says.

"The box in my room is out."

"So carry it upstairs yourself. It's your box."

"The tampons aren't yours, either, but—"

She takes the blue boxes out of the laundry basket and sets them onto the table, effectively ending any argument I might have made.

"There."

"Saphi—"

Dad wheels into the kitchen, and I cut my frustration off at the knees. Saphi shifts the laundry basket off her hip, and I feign industriousness by rummaging in the lower depths of the paper grocery bag for the celery and tomatoes.

"Just leave those out," Dad says as I open the fridge. "I'll make my world-famous chili for supper."

I set the vegetables on the kitchen counter and take a deep breath before turning around, hoping the additional oxygen will help me fool him into thinking that Saphi and I were not on the verge of reenacting the Battle of Verdun over the kitchen table.

"Sounds great."

He glances at my face and then at Saphira's. I'm sure my smile mirrors hers—Raggedy Ann smiles sewn onto blank faces. His eyes register quiet frustration with two adult daughters who are more childish now than they were as children.

"I'd better take these clothes upstairs," Saphi says. "I'm looking forward to trying your chili."

She kisses the top of Dad's head on her way out, but she leaves the tissue and tampon boxes on the table. Dad looks at me and sighs, rubbing his fingers along the arm of the wheelchair.

"Augustina, your sister's been through a lot. Take it easy on her."

———

"Once upon a time there was a little girl who moved to a small town beside a big river."

The small town was Stoic, Missouri, and if the town's people did not always live with indifference to pain and sorrow, as the name might imply, at least the town kept up with its neighbors that bore illustrious names from history. Carthage, Sparta, and Troy. Paris, Hannibal, and Seneca.

Warren Fletcher was a Methodist seminary graduate, and the small Methodist church in Stoic offered him a job and a salary just big enough to cover living expenses and the hospital fees for a second child soon to make her appearance in the world.

"Was I naughty?" I asked Mom, on a warm summer night several years later when crickets chirped and the moon rose red. I leaned into her side and watched Dad bounce a nearly two-year-old Saphira on his knee. I already knew the answer to my question, but this was the time in the story when I asked, "Was I naughty before Saphira was born?"

"You were awful," Mom said, laughing. "Positive that the baby was out to end your life. Fortunately, Beaver kept you in line."

When we moved to Stoic, I was five years old and unaware of much beyond the two facts that I was about to become a member of a two-child household and that Stoic was a fascinating place to explore and get into trouble. My main source of comfort during the trials and tribulations of being five, newly replanted, still friendless, and soon to be the oldest in a family of two children, was a dog of indeterminate breeding named Beaver—so named because his tail was wide and heavy, and he used it to slap the water when swimming after a ball. Unlike his temperamental human sidekick, Beaver had only two main emotions: joy when chasing after a ball, and deep sighs of sorrow with his lot in life when no ball was being thrown.

Beaver's relative placidity helped even out my alternating moods as we explored the unfamiliar square footage of Stoic. The town sat on the banks of the Mississippi River, and even though it had never been a stopover for steamboats, the local chamber of commerce did a good job of fooling the out-of-state tourists into thinking otherwise. The river was a continual source of mystery, and I was determined to solve it, giving Mom fits by taking Dad's compass (not that I knew how to use it), a bottle of water, and my pony-shaped backpack and setting out on river navigating expeditions. With innate doggy knowledge that what I was doing was wrong, Beaver refused to be my accomplice in crime, and instead ratted me out to the authorities. My last attempt at lone river exploration found me in the center of the field across the road from our house. The sky was an endless bowl above me and I was utterly lost. Enter Leviathan. A gigantic animal with huge ears walking in my direction.

"And he had big, nasty yellow teeth," Mom said years later, holding her index fingers next to her mouth and embellishing the story for my benefit as we sat on the porch and Dad bounced toddler Saphi on his knees.

"What did I do?"

"You screamed. And you probably wet your pants."

"I did not! Did I, Dad?"

Beaver and Dad looked at each other. Beaver wagged. Dad looked up at the beadboard ceiling above us.

"Certainly not!" he said, contriving to look like a pastor in need of forgiveness for telling a lie.

When he wasn't rescuing me from Jackson Dover's mules, Dad spent part of the early days in Stoic setting up his tiny church office just east of the Sunday-school rooms and the other part setting up the heavier household things for Mom. Mom washed all the dishes as she unpacked them, so they would be clean when they went into the glass-fronted cupboards in our new kitchen. Beaver and I helped by being underfoot. After a few weeks, life fell into a grand routine.

Then Saphira was born.

———

"Take it easy on your sister," Dad repeats.

It's not an order, just a plea. I struggle to hold in the frustration that wants to come boiling up and ask when someone is going to take it easy on *me,* but the last years have taught me the virtue of keeping my frustration to myself. Guilt from hasty words wears sharp spurs and rides your shoulders forever. If my temper is threatening to boil over, I can go outside and kick a tire or something to turn down the heat, but spoken words are permanent. Before, I might have complained to Dad about life's unfairness, but now I just smile at him as I heft the twenty-four-pack of diet cola into the fridge.

"I'll try, Dad."

He tosses me a bag of tangelos. The distraction on his face means that he's searching for a source—a safe, nonfamilial source who didn't just carry her laundry upstairs—that might explain the weary lines I can feel crease my face.

"Did you have a difficult time with that kid? Dillon?"

"Devon. No, he's fine." Devon is one of Stoic's many high school and homeschooled students I independently tutor in the fine art of using the English language. I drop the tangelos into the crisper. "He's never going to be much of a writer, though."

"You never know," Dad says. "You may have inspired him. Someday he may pick up a pen and say, 'My tutor said I would amount to something,' and go on to write the great American novel."

"Given the state of literacy in this country, he just might."

Dad digests this as he puts away some canned food. In the old days, the days before the accident, the days when the sun still seemed to collect in the sparkle of my father's eyes, he would have had a snappy comeback for my little joke. I wait for it, hope for it, wish for it—

"He just might," Dad says.

I try to smile. Devon just might say, "I blame that woman—

the one who told me copying passages directly out of the book was plagiarism—for my homicidal rampage." Anything else is pushing it.

"It's hot," I say out loud, folding the last paper bag and putting it away. "I'm going to put some shorts on."

"Aren't you supposed to have supper at the Morleys' tonight?"

"Thanks. I'd forgotten."

———

"Your dad wanted to name the new baby Sappho," Mom said as the crickets chirped beyond the porch and the moon rose higher and began to lose its redness in the cleaner atmosphere.

"After the Greek poet," I added, not that I knew anything about Sappho's poetry back then; it was simply part of the story.

Mom pushed the floorboards with her toe, setting the swing into motion.

"And I looked up at him and said—"

" 'Warren Fletcher, you will not name our baby after a dead Greek lesbian poet. I don't care how historical she is,' " Dad said in a creaky falsetto.

"I did not."

"Well, something like that, anyway."

He winked at her, and she rolled her eyes.

I silently wished she'd said something like that when he suggested naming me Augustina, after Saint Augustine. The name Augustina lends itself to certain abuses, primarily the nickname "Gusti," which is not amusing when yelled across the playground to the accompaniment of loud farting noises.

I was at the hospital when Mom nixed the Sappho name and remember Dad rubbing his chin and saying, "Well, how about Saphira, then?"

Mom was either asleep or too tired to argue, so my baby sister was named after a woman struck down by God for lying about how much money she and her husband made in a land deal. I think Dad just wanted to have another "-i" nickname in the family. I'm sure it tickled his sense of humor to imagine future evenings when he would lean out the door and yell in a blaring singsong, "Gusti! Saphi! Time for supper!" while all the adult neighbors gawked, the children snickered, and dogs howled. Actually, he usually said, "Gusti! Saphi! Time for suppi!" which may have had more to do with the snickering than our nicknames.

Driving home from the maternity ward to a "Dad dinner" of frozen waffles, fried eggs, and bacon, I realized I was going to have to share him from now on, share my protector and confidant. Fear came on with the setting sun, and I thought about the way the shadows crept and crawled across my bedroom floor as the oak tree outside my window twisted in the wind and the glow of the streetlight.

"Do you love me as much as the baby?"

It was an embarrassing question, especially for a five-year-old, one who should definitely have been old enough to not ask in such a shaking, pathetic voice. I wouldn't have asked such a question in the morning light, but with the sun sinking faster and faster behind our house, I couldn't stop myself.

"I will love you just as much as the baby. But I will love you for who *you* are even more."

"Because I'm older?"

"Because you're the only version of you."

That sounded good. I wasn't quite sure what he meant, but I figured it probably meant that he loved me more at the moment.

"Can I sleep in your room tonight?"

Sometimes, when Dad was gone, Mom would let me sleep on

a mattress on the floor beside her bed. She tried to let me sleep in the bed once, but discovered I "kick like a horse" in my sleep. I was content with the mattress on the floor and listening to someone else breathing in the room. I was content knowing I was safe from all the terrors the night could hold as long as one of my parents was nearby.

Dad looked at me and then looked at the fast-setting sun.

"Shadows getting you down?" he asked.

I nodded.

"If you sleep in your room, I'll stay with you and sing until you are asleep. Deal?"

Dad knew all kinds of blues, jazz, and folk songs. I later discovered many had been carefully edited for five-year-old ears. It wasn't until I was in high school that I figured out a "backdoor man" didn't fix hinges and ripped screens.

The night Saphira was born and lay nestled in her pink flannel at the hospital nursery, I fell asleep clutching Beaver—who never paid the slightest bit of attention to the experts who said mannerly dogs did not get up on furniture—and listening to Dad's tenor voice charm the shadows away.

Chapter 2

"Oh, Augustina. You can't put that in the dishwasher."

I look down at the plastic bowl in my hands and cringe.

"I'm sorry."

"It's clearly marked," Lorraine Morley says.

She taps the bottom of the bowl where raised letters clearly mark the bowl as not being dishwasher safe.

"I'm sorry," I repeat.

My only excuse is that I drifted away on the flow of Lorraine's conversation. Monologue, rather. My future mother-in-law has few soothing qualities, but one of them is her nonstop monologues that require only the occasional neutral comment to keep the flow running smoothly. Unfortunately, she also has a habit of asking a sudden sharp question—a tricky piece of submerged driftwood floating down the river of words.

In between making neutral comments, I was thinking about Saphi and Dad eating chili and wondering if they laughed more when I wasn't there, and I nearly placed one of Lorraine's prize bowls into the dishwasher, where it would melt and be ruined.

"I'm sorry," I say a third time.

She takes the bowl from me and places it beside the sink of soapy water.

"Don't you have a dishwasher at home?"

"No. We tend to take turns—"

"No! Amazing. How *do* you get along? I couldn't live without mine. I imagine you're eager to move into Colton's house, where you won't be without the necessary appliances."

I carefully scrape a china plate's contents into the disposal, then dip the plate into the soapy water to rinse it clean before placing it into the dishwasher. I can sense an underlying text to Lorraine's words, but I'm not sure if she is gauging the possibility that I am a gold digger or my unsuitability to be her son's wife; or if the subtext is merely a commentary on the foolishness of living a simple life without the proper accoutrements.

"I suppose the Methodist church couldn't be persuaded to buy a parsonage on the . . . south side?" Lorraine asks before I can form a suitable response. "Colton drove Howard and I past your house one day, you know. It's practically in the middle of a cornfield. And all those north-side houses are so old. Surely your father deserves better after all he's been through."

A knot tightens at the back of my neck. It has nothing to do with my quick effort to bite off my reflexive correction of the I/me grammar mistake I see nearly every time I see a student's paper. No, the knot comes from a different source. Colton never told me that he'd driven his parents past our house without even stopping to say hello. I wonder if he's ashamed of the house I love so much or if it has something to do with what I've learned seems to be an innate desire in human beings to avoid anyone disabled.

"You should have stopped by," I say. "We would have loved to have you in for a cup of tea or coffee."

"We didn't want to bother you and we hadn't called ahead. You might have been busy."

I don't mention Colton's cell phone or the cell phone Lorraine carries in her purse.

"Remind me to buy you a recipe box," Lorraine says, changing the subject. "You do cook, don't you?"

Rain patters against the kitchen window, and I stare out into the dark through the drop-spattered glass.

"Did Mom get to you tonight?" Colton asks as we drive home. "You're pretty quiet."

I briefly flash the headlights at an oncoming van whose driver has forgotten to dim his high beams. On the rolling two-lane county roads, forgetting to dim your headlights can be deadly, especially in a rainstorm like the one beating against the windshield and driver's-side window. Colton's breath smells of yeast and alcohol. Even though we take his BMW for the Tuesday-night dinner at his parents', I insist on driving home after Colton and Howard have spent the greater part of the evening sampling Howard's hobby—homemade wine and beer. At first Colton resisted—an old-fashioned male thing about being driven by a woman—but Lorraine surprised me by stepping in on my side and clinching the issue. It was one of the few times I've ever agreed with the woman.

I roll Colton's question around in my mind, searching for the right answer. Colton and his mother are close, and he tends to bristle at imagined slights, so my automatic response would be to say, "No, of course not. She's lovely," but I don't like the idea of starting out a lifelong relationship by lying. Still, what is a lie and what is just a kindness? My parents always placed a premium on telling the truth, yet in the last few years—

Cutting off the thought, I compromise by not telling Colton the whole truth, but not lying either.

"A little."

He shifts in his seat. The rain chatters on the roof while the wipers beat the seconds. My instincts tell me that he wishes I would have lied. Keeping one hand firmly on the wheel, I rub the knot at the base of my skull.

"Neckache?" he asks.

"Yes."

He reaches over and kneads my neck, not quite hitting the right spot, but doing some good. Several miles pass, and the rain has stopped when he says:

"You get used to it."

———

The accident happened the summer after I graduated from the University of Pennsylvania with an English lit degree. Before me, the future played out in simple elegance. First I would have a quiet summer at home, and then I was off to Johns Hopkins for graduate work, then more graduate work, then a professorship. A simple, elegant future until a rainy night, a slick road, and an oncoming pickup truck driven by a man in a hurry who didn't dim his lights or think about the possibility of hydroplaning. When he hit a patch of water, he slid across the dividing line just far enough to clip the bumper on Mom and Dad's Toyota. The truck spun away from the impact, went through a guardrail and into an overflowing drainage ditch. The lighter Toyota flipped and smashed sideways into an oak tree. Gail Gilbert Fletcher was pronounced dead at the scene. Warren Fletcher was left a paraplegic, crippled in mind as much as in body by the few minutes he tried to help his wife and could do no more than touch her still face before passing out from the pain. The driver of the truck had a cell phone and probably saved Dad's life by calling for help.

I was on the sixty-seventh page of Edith Wharton's *The House of Mirth* (*"I thought, after all, the air might do me good," she explained*) when someone knocked on the door. Saphira had used Mom and Dad's trip to a nearby town for a Singspiration service—where members of several churches get together to sing songs and eat desserts—as unasked permission for going off to who knows where. Probably with the guy I referred to as "the PGO," the press gang officer, because he looked like he enjoyed beating people senseless and kidnapping them into a life of service in the British navy. I'd locked the door to stop the creepy feeling when the lightning shadows made it look like someone was pushing it open.

"What? Back already from a night of illegal carousing?" I called jokingly to Saphi, who was, I knew, the person knocking on the door.

When I threw it open, I found a plastic-caped sheriff's deputy on the porch.

———

"You get used to it."

Colton stops rubbing my neck and leans back in his seat. A few more beats of the windshield wipers, and I can tell by his breathing that he's succumbed to an alcoholic drowsiness. I usually like times like this, when I'm driving in silence and he's sleeping. Once I kept driving on a star-bright summer night—passing Stoic and coming back into town from the far side—just so I could make the time last a little longer. When Colton looked at his watch, he asked if I'd been driving more slowly than usual.

"I must have been lost in thought," I said.

Usually I'm lost between one reality and another, my thoughts drifting free and stringing together in dreamlike sequences. It's peaceful and detoxifying. Not tonight.

"Did Mom get to you tonight?"

It wasn't the bowl or the dishwasher or driving by my house without stopping that got to me. It was dinner.

"You're so thin, I worry about you," Lorraine said at the dinner table.

The candles in the ornate centerpiece flickered wildly, almost as if ghosts of former conversations were hovering nearby and waiting to pounce. I swallowed a mouthful of mashed potatoes and opened my mouth to answer, but Lorraine beat me to the next sentence.

"Have you given any more thought to finding a real job?"

The ghosts of conversations past had settled in to stay. This is a topic Lorraine delights in pressing, as if tutoring were an undesirable activity, like dancing at a gentlemen's club on St. Louis' east side or posing for a Hot Chixxx calendar. I wasted precious seconds wondering if such a calendar exists and, if so, whether there's any money in it. I wasted precious seconds imagining pulling out the calendar at a future dinner. *"I took your advice and got a new job. What do you think? The nipple rouge was a nice touch, I think."*

"I like what I'm doing," I said.

"Yes, but it's so ephemeral. You never know how many students you'll have or how much you'll earn in a given semester. Doesn't that cause you a great deal of stress? It must. You're not eating properly."

"I've had to turn away students the last three semesters."

Lorraine watched me, but nodded to Howard when he leaned in and said, "More wine, dear?" Howard smiled at me and held up the bottle questioningly. I smiled back and shook my head.

"I'm driving."

Colton gave me a funny look, but held his glass out to Howard. I hadn't meant to imply anything, but Colton must have thought it was a subtle dig. He and Howard were a bit unsteady and a bit louder than usual, although they were both pretty quiet while Lorraine's keen eye appraised me.

"Then it must be all that responsibility you insist on carrying," she said. "I've read that caregivers often need a break in order to combat stress. Perhaps you should consider—"

"Dad isn't an invalid," I said.

I never interrupt Lorraine, as long as she sticks to running *my* life, but it pushes me over the edge when she starts in on Dad.

"He's not an invalid. He only needs help every once in a while."

"Well, there you are. Surely he wouldn't mind if you got a real job. Tutoring is unreliable. Whether or not students need tutoring all depends on the quality of early education, and with the recent changes in the legislature, they're sure to remove those wretched revisionist teachers and get back to the basics. Then what will happen to you?"

"I suppose I'll be out of a job," I said around a smile that was meant to remove any rancor from my earlier interruption.

"You young people. You insist on never thinking ahead."

A rumble of thunder reached us through the thick drapes covering Lorraine's windows.

Driving through the rain, Colton sleeping beside me, I try to come up with a response to the Lorraine in my memory, but I can't find the words that would prove to her that I could think ahead if I wanted to. I know that if I could just find the right cut-and-parry response, I could show her that I am not just living in that world outside of time that waits for the unbaptized dead—that I'm not in limbo. Lightning strikes the horizon, and I drive into another band of rain and hear the raindrops beating on the car's roof as if they want to be let inside.

———

"Hi," I said to Dad.

Thunder rumbled outside the hospital and rain splattered against the window over the nurses' station of the ICU. I sat down next to the bed and took his hand. He squeezed it, then let his hand go limp, but I kept it in mine, holding on while the machinery around us clicked and whirred.

I hadn't been able to locate Saphi. Unless she found my note, she probably thought I'd locked her out of the house deliberately and gone to bed, leaving her out with the press gang officer so Mom and Dad would catch her. She did that to me once when she was twelve or so. I had slipped out with Grady when I was supposed to be upstairs studying. Saphi locked me out, so I had to knock on the door to get back in. Mom answered the door. If Dad had answered the door, I could have asked what jazz tune he was playing and diverted him long enough to sneak away upstairs. Mom was undivertable.

"You're supposed to be upstairs."

"I know, but—"

"You're not."

"No, but—"

"And the explanation is?"

"I'm locked out?"

Mom had even liked Grady. She couldn't stand the PGO, and Saphi would have gotten it good, only I didn't think punishing Saphi was going to be high on anyone's list of priorities for a while.

"Shadows," Dad said through the painkillers that glazed his eyes.

At first I thought he was talking *to* me, asking me if I saw shadows; then I realized he meant there were shadows in the room and he was scared.

"No," I said. "I'll stay here until you go to sleep."

"Sing?"

So I held his hand and sang all the songs I could think of to charm the shadows away, trying to sing softer than the hum of the ICU equipment, softer than the rain on the window, until he fell asleep.

———

"You're home," Saphi says.

I shut and lock the front door. Outside, a new line of thunderstorms is moving in. Later the creeks and streams will run high as they surge into the Mississippi. It was sprinkling again when I pulled into Colton's garage and turned off the ignition.

"Do you want to come in?" he asked.

"It's late."

"No more than usual."

I tossed him the keys to the BMW and tried to find the right words to say.

"I guess I'm just tired."

He leaned over and kissed me.

"I told you Mom got to you tonight."

"Actually, you *asked* me if she got to me."

"A technicality."

He pulled back and looked down at my face. I tried hard to not look away, but the close scrutiny was painful after a night of being under the microscope.

"You do look tired. Maybe Mom is right and you're—"

"I'm just tired."

Shaking his head, he gave my shoulders a squeeze. I drove home with the imprint of that final pressure weighing down my mind.

You get used to it.

"You're home," Saphi says.

"You're still up," I say in reply.

She smiles and holds up a book. I'm too far away to see the cover.

"This is a real page-turner."

"That's good."

She's sitting in near darkness, much too dark for reading, even if the crescent moon could shine through the thunderstorm, but I don't comment on it.

"I'm sorry about this afternoon," she says. "About the tissues. I don't know what got into me."

I kick off my damp shoes and absorb the unfamiliar apology. Saphi and I got out of the habit of being polite to each other in the months after the accident.

"It's okay," I say. "No problem."

She flips through the pages of her book. The paper leaves rustle and rattle. Back and forth.

"I'd better get to bed," I say. "I tutor in St. Louis tomorrow."

The paper continues to rustle. I wait to see if she has something more to say, but she just flips the pages back and forth.

"Good night," I say, starting to climb the stairs.

Halfway to the second floor, her voice catches up with me.

"Good night, Gusti."

In my bedroom I open the window onto the rainy night. Lightning flashes among purple clouds just beyond the rolling, riverbank hills.

Six years ago, the lightning flashed outside the hospital windows as a doctor showed me an X-ray of my father's spine. Earlier I'd been asked to make a positive ID of my mother's body, and part of me had shut down. Somewhere under it all I knew Mom was dead, but I didn't really believe it. When I had asked to see Dad, I'd been shuffled into the doctor's office instead.

"The damage is here," the doctor said, tapping the X-ray. "T-one. We've relieved the pressure, but we won't know how successful we were or what the extent of the damage is for a bit. He's lucky to be alive."

Lucky. I thought of Mom's still face and the total lack of animation and wondered how, exactly, the doctor defined "lucky."

"What does T-one mean?"

"It means the SCI—the spinal cord injury—is in the first vertebra of the thoracic region. Your dad should be able to move his arms and hands without difficulty. With luck, he might even regain some of the feeling or even use of his legs."

Luck again.

"Can I see him now?"

"We've given him painkillers, so don't expect a response. And he's immobilized, so be ready for some unfamiliar equipment. We'll also have to talk about transferring him down to St. Louis, because we're just not equipped to give him the full range of care he needs." He glanced at my face. "But we can do that tomorrow."

It's funny how I can remember the words the doctor said but I have no actual memory of the unfamiliar equipment, just my father's limp hand and the lightning shadows on the floor as I later sang to him.

Outside the doctor's office, a man in his mid-twenties stood up as we walked out.

"Are you Augustina Fletcher?"

I nodded.

"I'm sorry."

I stared at him until I realized that standing before me, with nothing more than a plastered scratch on his forehead, was the driver of the pickup.

"Maybe the tires were bad. I don't know. Maybe I looked down. I'm so sorry."

Is guilt a heavier burden than grief? I walked up to the man and put my arms around him. Awkwardly, I admit, but I couldn't blame him for a mistake anyone could have made and most of us do, just without the deadly consequences.

In my bedroom, I lay my chin on my crossed arms and look out into the warm, wet darkness. Lorraine was right about one thing tonight: I don't think about the future. My story is caught in the past along with the life of its teller. I have no one to say, "And they lived happily ever after," so I'm in a state of perpetual waiting, just like the unbaptized souls waiting in limbo. Saphi, Dad, me . . . we're all waiting. But even if you are without a story, everyday life around you keeps on going. Eventually you get used to it.

Chapter 3

"*Feel the music in your toes!*" Dad said.

New Orleans jazz mingled with Saphira's gurgles and coos from her playpen as Dad danced me around the living room, my bare toes clinging to the tops of his shoes. Saphi stretched an arm through the bars and made "I wanna" noises that quickly began to escalate to a scream.

"Come on, baby girl," Mom said, swinging her up. "Let's dance."

The four of us twirled around the living room, Mom and Dad stopping to bump hips every turn or so until I was out of breath from giggling, and Saphi had drooled down the front of her shirt from having her mouth open in a two-tooth smile.

A door shuts and I'm shaken out of my half-dream memory. Outside my open bedroom window the rain has stopped, but a pre-dawn breeze bells out the curtains and brings in the scent of mud and wet oak leaves. Even though the stars are still bright, robins are already up and calling to one another as they hunt for worms forced by the rain to the dangerous surface. The toilet in the bathroom down the hall flushes, and the door that woke me squeaks as it opens. Five years of being the only person on the second floor of the house has made me sensitive to Saphi's movements. I wad the pillow under my head and turn to face the wall.

"Watch me leave!" Saphi screams at me out of my memory.

"You'll be back."

"Not in your lifetime."

"Thank God for small favors."

I threw the college materials the guidance counselor had given me onto the floor at Saphi's feet.

The counselor had called me in for a meeting the day before. During Dad's rehabilitation and therapy, I became the go-to person for the high school counselor's office. I'd been called when Saphi created finger-paint artwork on all the bathroom mirrors (including, gasp, the boys' bathrooms) and when she tricked the school into virtually shutting down for a drug search by keeping a small Ziploc bag of catnip in a prominent position in her locker. My sibling desire to applaud my sister's evil genius had begun to die a slow death in the face of continual frustration and a dread of the telephone's ring.

"I know Saphira has had a terrible time this semester, what with . . ."

The counselor had let her words trail off after I'd sat down in the chair opposite her desk.

For a few uncomfortable seconds, she'd waited for me to save the conversation. Understanding that silence was the best ploy until I knew exactly why I'd been called to her office, I hadn't offered to help the poor woman out of the rut she'd driven into. She had cleared her throat and tried a new route.

"Yes, well, I've been encouraging her to fill out these college applications, but she says she's going to beauty school."

I'd raised my eyebrows at that.

"One week she says that," the counselor had amended. "The next she says she's going to major in being a humanitarian-vegan beach bum, the next it's a U.S. senator, and yesterday she said she was going to work as a stripper for the Hard Times club. I don't think there even is such a place."

She'd shaken her head slowly and sadly, and I had known the time had come for the dreaded question.

"I'm concerned by Saphira's attitude. How are things at home?"

I'd been forced to fake blowing my nose to cover a grin at Saphi's responses to what I knew were the counselor's well-meaning but damned annoying—even to me—attempts to pry into her personal life.

"I'm sure she was just kidding," I had said, once I could control my expression.

"She's smart. She shouldn't waste her brain on silly jokes."

What the counselor didn't seem to understand was that silly jokes were what kept Saphi connected to the world around her. I had smiled again, taken the college application materials, and said I would talk to my sister.

Sitting at the kitchen table, I wasn't smiling.

Saphi looked down at the college applications where they lay at her feet.

"You think you're going to get me into one of those schools?"

"Up to you, I guess."

"Sure it is. I have all the say in the world in this house."

"Don't start that again."

"No, you don't start. You're not Mom. You can't tell me what to do."

I surged up out of the chair.

"You think I want to be your mom? You're fucking crazy."

"I'm gone."

She picked up her book bag and swung it over her shoulder. The kitchen's screen door banged behind her. I knew she would be back; I just didn't know she would be gone five years instead of five hours.

I wad the pillow under my head and turn to face the wall, but sleep refuses to give me a few more hours of rest. Guilt, as I said before, wears sharp spurs, even sharper when accompanied by its favorite friend: failure. Ignoring the cold sweat, I throw off the cotton blanket and sit up. I might as well go over the sections of Milton that one of my students is trying to wrestle into submission for a paper.

Sitting at the kitchen table, surrounded by fallen angels, I look up when Saphi comes into the room.

"You were up early," she says. "I heard you in the bathroom before it was light."

She pours a cup of coffee and leans back against the counter. We look at each other across the space of time.

Saphira came home two weeks ago. She arrived on foot, carrying a single soft-sided, brown-tweed suitcase. She arrived without warning, exactly as she had left, only quieter. I was throwing some salad greens and tomatoes into a bowl when she knocked on the kitchen door.

"Where's Dad?" she asked when I opened the door and we stood there looking at each other over the bowl of vegetables.

"In the study."

I didn't hear what she said to Dad, but they both came out crying—

"Didn't you sleep okay?" Dad asks me as he comes into the kitchen in Saphi's wake.

Saphi and I keep looking at each other across time and memories. We're both remembering the morning of that last fight, the last in a long string of fights that make the little refusal to carry the tissues and tampons upstairs look as dangerous as a marshmallow pie. We're both remembering the evening she came home. Looking away, I force a smile for Dad and grab the first excuse that comes to mind.

"Lorraine made gourmet potatoes. Unsalted butter, goat's milk—"

"Yuck," Saphi interrupts, her voice sounding relieved at the break in the tension. "Goat's milk is great in soap, but that's about it."

"Rich food," Dad says, nodding. "Someday you'll probably have chronic indigestion or acid reflux. The only things you'll be able to stand will be bread and water."

"That's comforting."

For a moment I catch a flash of the old Warren Fletcher as he holds up the bag of bread and grins mischievously.

"How about some plain, dry toast?"

————

The dying leaves in the very tops of the trees are blushed red in the slanting October sunshine. Soaring above the trees, the stone towers and gables of the university buildings push up into a new-washed sky that is deep blue, so blue you could dive into the color and swim forever through the warmth. Every Wednesday and Friday I work as an independent English tutor for college students in St. Louis. This means a lot of driving—from community college to four-year institution to coffee shop—but I always schedule my St. Louis University students for the end of my day, when I don't have to rush off to the next campus. There's really no explanation for it, except that I feel at home here.

I'm sitting on a cement planter that helps outline one of the many garden spaces. The sunshine called to me, and I decided to hold the tutoring sessions outdoors. That may have been a mistake. Jennifer stared off all dreamy into space and waved to her friends rather than concentrating on dissecting Milton's *Paradise Lost*. Taylor showed up with a Frisbee and his dog—a Lab mix that reminded me of Beaver when Beaver was younger and thinner. I was guilty of paying more attention to the dog than Taylor's halfhearted attempts to put together a paper for his expository writing class.

"Can you have spring fever in the fall?" he asked.

I said I didn't know, but sitting here with my feet tucked under me and the afternoon sunshine on my face, I have to admit that my heart cries out with the anonymous student voice in the *Carmina Burana*, *"Sol serenat omnia. Iamiam cedant tristia!"* The sun calms everything. Let all cares depart!

I call this sitting back in one of the campus gardens resting before the drive home, but I'm forced to admit that it's something more. Avoidance, perhaps. Living in Stoic is living in a fishbowl. After a lifetime of being a pastor's daughter on constant display for the church members and the town, I should be used to the glass walls, but four years of freedom at Penn gave me a taste of life where the only way to distinguish myself from the anonymous crowd was academic achievement. My own achievement. I could choose the level of transparentness of my walls.

Taking a sip from a paper cup filled with coffee, I watch sparrows argue over crumbs dropped from someone's lunch. One sparrow grabs something that looks like a bean sprout and flies away from the other members of the gang. They follow, chirring noisy indignation at his unwillingness to share the prize. On the road in front of me, a cyclist whizzes past, his book bag slung around behind him where it won't get in the way. I watch him turn the corner, still pedaling full tilt, and my stomach clenches with something I can only call longing. Not for the cyclist, since I don't even know him, but for his life. I long for the energy and passion that come only from the interaction of one mind with another. For the arguments with long-held beliefs and theories. For the feeling of your brain stretching as it works to wrap itself around a concept and wring out the last drop of meaning.

My stomach clenches. The sunshine isn't calming anymore, but burns through the thin shell of dignity and responsibility I've covered myself with since my decision six years ago to call Johns Hopkins and tell them I wouldn't be coming for the fall semester.

"You're not my mom," Saphi said to me, and I really and truly didn't want the responsibility of Mom's place, but someone had to explain Saphi's absences to the school, someone had to plead with her to not drop out, someone had to show up when the counselor called to say Saphi and a police officer were in her office. Someone had to, and the only someone who could was me. Everyone whispered that Saphi was behaving this way because the Fletcher family had dissolved in one rainy night, but Saphi had always pushed the limits. I guess the only thing that really surprises me is that she came home.

I shift my feet, and the group of sparrows flies up into the low branches before looking down at me to see if I pose any threat. Maybe Saphi felt a need to chastise herself by coming back and . . . not facing the music, exactly, but performing public self-flagellation and thereby expunging the guilty writing on the wall. Self-flagellation would explain her behavior when she stood up in front of the church and gave what amounted to a public confession.

"I haven't been a very good daughter," she said after going to the front of the church at the end of the Sunday service nearly two weeks ago.

I grew up thinking "the call" at the end of each Sunday service was something everyone knew about until I went to Penn and made some comment that going up to dance with our favorite bar band was like "going forward for rededication." My roommate and best friend, Tallulah, being raised Baptist, got the joke and laughed, but our friend Kameron was totally confused.

"It's like public confession," Tallulah said over the beat of the drums and the wail of the singer. "It's all about saying you want to be a Christian in front of everybody."

"Or that you've been a bad Christian and you want to be a better one," I added, yelling to be heard. "Or maybe you just want to join the church."

Kam shook his head. "Sounds bizarre."

On the Sunday nearly two weeks ago, Saphi chose that final hymn to go to the front, where Dad sat in his wheelchair, and whisper in his ear. As the notes of the hymn died away, she cleared her throat.

"I haven't been a very good daughter," she said. "I ran away when I should have been a better help to Dad and to . . . my sister. I'm asking their forgiveness and yours, too."

The church members sat in total silence while a baby down the hall in the nursery started to cry. Then June Winthrop, the organist and Saphi's and my piano teacher during our respective childhoods, stood up and hugged my sister. That started a wave of church members coming forward to encircle and touch the lamb returning to the fold.

Sitting in the sunshine, looking up past old buildings to the blue depths above me, I wonder if the unhappiness I've seen in my sister's eyes since she came home was any less over Sunday dinner that noon. I don't think it was. Perhaps the writing on the wall is harder to sponge away than the words on Ebenezer Scrooge's tombstone. Perhaps the feeling of past failure is harder to erase than that of future lost.

Standing up, I crush the paper cup and walk the half mile or so to my car, mastering the gnawing in my stomach as I walk.

———

"Once upon a time, Augustina and Saphira decided to sail away to China."

Mom stopped to smile, and Saphi and I looked up from the Valentine's Day cards we were making. Actually, I was the one making cards; Saphi was about four years old and mostly covered in glue and glitter. When Mom had left the room to answer the phone, I'd shown Saphi how to draw stars and hearts on her hands in glue and then dip them into the glitter. She had giggled, and I'd gone back to cutting hearts when she interrupted me, saying, "Look, Gusti!"

She had squirted nearly the entire bottle of glue into her hair. Speechless, I'd looked on in horror and fascination as she dipped her head into the glitter and instantaneously turned something cute and harmless into something I was sure I would get in trouble for, but Mom had just laughed and said it was a good thing glue was nontoxic and washable.

"Augustina and Saphira had been reading about China in school." Mom looked at me. "Wait, that's not right. Augustina—"

"I can read," Saphi said, blatantly lying.

Mom bit her lip and looked to me for help.

"She meant she didn't know which of us read about China," I said to Saphi. "It could have been you."

"Oh."

"Augustina took a map of the world and two sandwiches," Mom continued.

"I took my doll," Saphi said. She didn't actually remember the events in the story, as she'd been only two, but she carried Binky with her wherever she went, so it was a safe bet, even though I didn't remember whether or not Binky made the trip to China or not.

"And Saphi took her doll. And you both set off in a pea green boat."

"On the river?"

"In the sandbox," I said, answering my sister's question.

"How can you sail away in a sandbox?"

"Good question," I muttered.

"You sailed away in a sandbox because your sister loves you," Mom said.

I looked up, a little ashamed of my muttering and complaining. Saphi had wanted an adventure, and I'd tried to supply one, complete with buried treasure on some far-off, imaginary Asian coast. Saphi was too young for a real adventure, so I'd made one in the sandbox and felt a little silly sitting in a green cardboard box on an ocean of sand the neighbor's cat sometimes used for a litter box.

"Love doesn't have any boundaries," Mom said. "No fences can keep it out or in. It doesn't care about the past or the future, either."

Saphi was dipping her hair into the glitter again, but Mom was looking at me as she spoke.

———

My car's tires hum on the highway between St. Louis and Stoic. I like to take the back roads as much as possible, ostensibly for the scenery, slower pace, and fresh air coming through the window, but today I take the back roads to give myself time to wonder when Mom's childhood stories started coming back to me. And whether or not it has anything to do with Saphi's homecoming.

Chapter 4

I open my dresser drawer and stare down at the severely wrinkled shirts it contains. I'm not a stickler for clothing perfection, and if it had been Dad or me who took the shirts out of the dryer, dropped them into a basket, and left them in a not-quite-dry wad, I would take the wrinkles philosophically, if I even noticed them at all. It's the memory of Saphi walking past me with her load of freshly washed, dried, and folded laundry, Saphi refusing to take the tissues upstairs, that makes the wrinkled shirt into a red flag in front of a bull. I know she apologized for the tissues, but she either didn't remember leaving Dad's and my laundry behind in a clump or it was deliberate. Choosing a T-shirt at random, I shake it out and pull it on before going back to the window.

It's Saturday morning and the one day a week when I don't actually sleep late, but pretend that I do. I like to sit at my window and take the time to watch the sun come up over the lines of maples and oaks that rim Jackson's fields. As Lorraine pointed out, our house is near the edge of town and practically sitting in a cornfield. Behind us is a typical neighborhood from the early days of the previous century—narrow streets, trees, and Craftsman bungalows—but just across the narrow road that runs past the front of our house is the rolling river land. Looking out my window, I can see fields bordered by trees and the deep, untillable wrinkles lying in blue shadows.

The sun begins its journey by poking narrow fingers through the trees in the far hollow—a hollow that hides a small creek. As it pulls itself up into the sky, hand over hand, through the pink and orange and gold, the sun gathers strength. A pair of crows circle down on the almost-tangible light and join their relatives in picking over the cornfield. An autumn haze of humidity softens the air, and in the field's low spots, gray mist clings to the warm earth, but above the mist the crows' wings and the stubble of recently harvested corn glow red in the morning light.

Leaning my chin on my folded arms, I dream about falling right out of the world, flying up into the sun until my wings melt and I plunge back down into the sea. I wonder if Icarus thought losing his life was worth a chance to touch the heat of the sun. If I could make wings strong enough to climb ninety-three million miles, I would.

I close my eyes and feel the sun sink into my brain, lighting up the shadowy places I've spent the last few years trying to ignore. I wish I understood my sister, but pawing through the shadows only brings to mind the fights in our final months together, fights that slowly escalated from mild disagreement to that last screaming match over the pile of college applications. And yet there is something more in these shadows than the fights, something more that I picked up from a few comments Mom made about Saphi's "incidents" when I would call on Sunday afternoons while I was at Penn. I chalked those comments up to teen rebellion, leather, tattoos, and body piercing with the blithe chuckle of an elder sibling who's been there. I felt sorry for my little sister and understood her desire to kick the glass walls of the fishbowl extra hard now and again.

But somehow, in the months of shuffling back and forth between the counselor's office with Saphi and the rehabilitation facility in St. Louis where Dad was learning how to cope, I lost my sense of humor and my sympathy. Saphi began to seem more like a spoiled brat who needed a spanking, and rather than banding together, we drew battle lines on the scuffed hardwood floor of the house. It wasn't a continual war, just flare-ups over boundaries and who had the final say about something as simple as sweeping the kitchen or as complex as throwing away the mail, bills and all.

I open my eyes and blink away sun tears in the stinging light. I still don't know if Saphi is exacting revenge for the months I ruled the house with an ever-hardening fist or if she's just gotten so used to taking care of herself, she's forgotten how to live in company with other humans. Neither answer seems to fit. I can sense an underlying unhappiness and fury that I don't think are directed toward me, but are still incomprehensible.

I tiptoe downstairs and start the coffee. Saphira stayed up late last night, and I trip over a half-empty can of Diet Pepsi on the way to the kitchen. It rolls in a half circle, spewing liquid onto the hardwood floor, down through the cracks. I stare at the rolling can, following its back-and-forth progress, then go to the kitchen to make coffee. I'm on my knees by the spill, mopping it up with a damp paper towel, when Dad comes out of his bedroom. The wheelchair stops dead on a pile of books topped by a half-eaten candy bar.

Saphira left before Dad and I discovered life's new dynamics. When he first came home from the hospital, I carefully followed all the instructions given to us by the daily nurse who dropped by, the doctors, the experts. I was always on hand to help Dad out, smothering him with the overwhelming relief I felt that he was still alive. Smothering him with love to hide the uncertainties that I'd kept bottled up during the months he was in rehabilitation and we discovered for sure that he'd never be able to walk again. Smothering him in an attempt to make up for what I knew was my failure with Saphi. Three weeks after he came home, Dad rebelled.

"I have never followed the rules and I'm not going to start now."

I opened my mouth to argue that I didn't see how he was going to get around without constant help.

"Don't say anything, Gusti," he warned.

I glared at him.

"I'm crippled, not an invalid."

The first thing Dad bought was a used weight set. We were driving home from church when he saw the set sitting at the edge of a garage sale. Buying and selling on Sunday had the odor of crass commercialism in our house, but Dad bought the weight set, and the jolly fat man who'd had no use for strengthened muscles helped me load it into the back of the minivan.

"I don't get it," I said to Dad as we drove home.

"You will."

Dad lifted weights to strengthen his upper body so it could take over for his useless legs, and I did discreet things like rearrange the furniture and roll up all the rugs and store them in the tiny attic out of sight. We spent hours on the Internet and at the library researching various ideas for ways we could remodel the downstairs bathroom, the kitchen, and the porch to make our house disabled-friendly. Although church members pitched in when they could, we did most of the work ourselves when we discovered how much money remodeling cost. As I wielded power tools and crawled around under sinks replacing pipes, I was grateful to my childhood self for being so eager to help Dad with his home-improvement projects and to Dad for having the patience to show me how to help. Before the church held a secret (to us) fund drive and surprised Dad with a hand-controlled car he could get into and out of by himself, we built a ramp for the minivan and removed the backseats so I could drive Dad to visit hospitals and church members' homes as he slowly picked up his pastoral responsibilities where he'd left off over a year ago. We were both absurdly proud of the ramp the Sunday we left church without any help.

And because she left, Saphira missed all of that. Paper towels in hand, I kneel down beside the spilled cola and feel a slow burn begin in my stomach that has nothing to do with the sunlight coming through my bedroom window. Missing it is no excuse. No one over the age of six could be so self-absorbed that they would fail to notice that certain changes had taken place in their childhood home, which means that Saphi is scattering her belongings on purpose. The burn works its way up from my stomach to my face.

Dad looks down at the obstacles in the chair's path, reaches over, and gently pushes the books out of the way.

"Saphi must have stayed up late again," he says.

I stand up with the dripping paper towels and soda can. Saphira trips la-di-da, as Mom would have put it, down the stairs and gives Dad a big kiss on the cheek.

"Good morning, good morning," she trills.

Dad laughs in that easygoing way that usually brings a smile to my face, but today I go into the kitchen to throw away the trash and make bitter oatmeal. Nothing I make right now could possibly be anything but bitter.

"Isn't it a beautiful morning?" Saphi asks, leaning on the sink and looking out over Jackson's field and the slowly disappearing mists.

"Scoot over, will you?"

I measure water into the pan and put it on the stove to boil. Saphi leans a hip on the edge of the sink.

"Gee, what's eating you today?"

I bat my eyelashes over a childish, silly-sweet smile.

"Why don't you go watch cartoons, dear? I'll do the work."

Her eyes narrow and she stands up straight. I expect an explosion, hope for it even, but nothing happens, so I turn my back on her as I stir in the oatmeal. When I turn around again, she's gone.

A few hours later, when Saphi is lying on the couch reading and I'm sure Dad is deeply immersed in going over tomorrow's sermon, I give frustration its head.

"There's this thing in the house," I say. "It has wheels."

Saphi drops the book she is reading onto her stomach and looks up at me. The annoyance from this morning is still visible in her eyes. When she was seventeen, that annoyance would have already expressed itself. It surprises me to find how much I wish she would scream and throw down the book and tell me where I am free to go if I feel like it. I used to want her to keep her mouth shut, but now I want something out in the open so I can scream back. Maybe she's figured that out. During the months we spent on our own, she was very good at figuring out what to do to make me want to kill her.

I make little wheeling motions with my hands.

"This thing has wheels, and it travels happily along until *thud*, it hits a pile of books. Or a bag. Or some shoes. And then it stops. It doesn't go over the object, it just stops. So the person using this wheeled thing has to back up and go around the object or in some other way remove said object from under the wheels."

The annoyance in Saphi's face begins to fade to a ghastly green hue.

"I didn't know."

Part of my indignation falters at the evidence of her honest confusion, but I'm letting loose something I didn't even know was hiding in the shadows of my mind and it will not be denied its freedom.

"Try thinking," I say nastily. "It's a process of electrical impulses in the brain that we evolved years ago."

Saphi's green hue turns reddish. She tosses her book to the foot of the couch and stands up. *Be careful what you wish for,* a voice says out of the shadows. I don't remember her being taller than me, but she's got several inches of advantage in this toe-to-toe.

"When did you get as nasty as old man Fitzel?"

"Fitzel doesn't believe in evolution."

We're hissing at each other, having a fight without volume in order to avoid alerting Dad to the war going on in his living room. It's the only adult thing about this fight.

"Looking at you," she says, three inches from my nose, "I'm not sure I do either. You're all Ms. This Is My Territory, aren't you?"

"Only when someone is fouling the nest."

"So it's your nest now, is it? What genetic advantage makes it your nest?"

"If it's so precious to you, maybe you shouldn't have skipped out."

Ah. *A hit, a very palpable hit,* as Osric would have judged it.

Saphi falls back.

"Bitch."

Dad's office door squeaks. I collapse hurriedly into a nearby armchair. Saphi sits down on the couch. Her face is a mixed-up study of red and patchy white. I probably look equally distasteful. No one in their right mind would believe we were having a pleasant conversation about tulip bulbs.

"I think red tulips are the best," I say out loud. "They're loud, but loud colors are good after it's been gray all winter."

She stares at me. I'm almost sure she's missed her cue when she says, "Yellow. I like yellow."

"I like them both," Dad says. "You girls want some tea?"

"No, thank you."

"I just had some, thanks."

We speak at the same time. In the kitchen water runs into the sink, then into the teakettle. The gas stove clicks until the spark lights the burner.

"Let me know when that boils," Dad says as he goes back into his office. "We wouldn't want it to run dry and *burn the house down.*"

He says the last with a curious emphasis that tells me that he knows we're having a hot discussion rather than chatting about the garden. I look over at Saphi and see that she's come to the same realization, and I feel ashamed at being nearly thirty years old and fighting with my sister as if I were thirteen. Looking down at the floor, I ask myself why I'm fighting at all.

"Why don't you just say it out loud?" she says.

I look up from a contemplation of my motivations and the pattern in the wood floor to find her leaning back into the couch. Her face is lined from an exhaustion that runs too deep to be healed by simple bodily rest.

"Say what?"

"That you don't want me here, messing things up for you."

We're talking in normal tones, pitched below what could be understood in the office, but more normal than goose-style hissing.

"Picking up after someone has never been high on my list of aspirations."

I mean it to come out as a joke to relieve the tension, but it sounds waspish, even to me. The exhaustion on Saphi's face disappears.

"So now the picking up is all about you, not Dad's wheelchair?"

I know she's right. Dad hasn't expressed any annoyance at having to go around fallen objects or scoot them out of the way. The knowledge throws guilt onto my self-righteous fire, and guilt is as good as gasoline.

"Use the brains God gave a gnat and figure it out for yourself," I say.

"Oh, I have."

The water in the kitchen is boiling. I start to get up, but Saphi beats me to it.

"Don't bother," she says. "You're not the only useful person with a right to exist."

I glare at her retreating back. She wiggles her butt and slaps it with an open palm to let me know that she knows I'm watching and that I'm pissed off and she couldn't care less. I wonder what kind of people put up with her during the five years she was gone. If any people put up with her at all. "Try to be nice to your sister," Dad said. Does "nice" include buying her a one-way ticket to perdition? Right now I'd spring the money for that.

Standing up, I kick her shoes out of the way and head outside to mow the lawn and yank up a few weeds in the brick patio out back. One shoe rolls under the chair, and I have the childish hope that she never finds it.

———

Saphira has delighted in torturing me since she was born. She was a high-maintenance baby who never bothered to learn to sleep through the night, but howled displeasure every few hours. Both Mom and Dad had red-rimmed eyes and short tempers. The only joy I got from this period was the one time I overheard Dad say to Mom, "I don't remember Augustina screaming all night." And Mom saying, "That's because she didn't." I skipped off with Beaver, happy in the knowledge that I was superior to this interloper who took up so much of Mom and Dad's time.

Before long the baby was trying to walk, and I started to enjoy having a little sister. I would hold her hands and she would stumble along, not quite sure how to distribute her weight on the sausage links that passed for legs. No one could have guessed that she would grow up to have the strut and thighs of a model. But no one thinks about things like that when the child in question has drool running down her shirt from the gap between her baby teeth and her legs look like someone inflated them with a bicycle pump.

About the time she started walking on her own well enough to toddle after me, I began to realize my days of freedom were numbered. "Take your sister with you," became a common chant I dreaded. Seven years old and planning to cross Jackson's field to play on the creek banks and look at fish while Beaver sniffed out rabbits, I would ease the screen door open in an effort to steal away like a loaded-down thief. Beaver, in dog fashion, would barrel past me in an effort to be outside *first*, an all-important concept for a dog, and the screen door would squeak. One little squeak.

" 'Gustina, if you're going outside to play, take your sister with you," Mom would say from the kitchen.

"I'm going to the creek."

"Well, that's too far to take her. Why don't you stay in the yard and keep her company?"

My going to the creek alone was never an option, and a rabbit-deprived Beaver would mope on the porch, his nose resting between his front paws, while I rolled the plastic red-and-white-striped ball for Saphira to chase.

Saphira must have sensed my resentment at this curtailment of my independence. When walking became almost second nature, her revenge was to find me while I was reading or playing with my plastic horses, sneak up, grab huge fistfuls of my hair, and do her best to rip my scalp from my head. I was eight years old and she was three when she first adopted this tactic.

I ran to Mom.

"Deal with it," she said. "You're too old to be a tattletale."

I went back to Saphira and I slapped her.

Her eyes went round and wide. Her mouth went round and wide, and she began to emit loud howls of distress. Looking at her, I realized I definitely had *not* dealt with the problem in the right way. At eight, I was practically an adult, and I'd never seen one adult slap another.

Mom came running.

"What on earth . . . ?"

"I slapped her," I said glumly, owning up to the deed.

Later, sitting next to me on my bed while Beaver whined outside the closed door, Mom put her arms around my sullen shoulders.

"There's a difference between 'dealing' with something and exercising brute force," she said. "But I'll be the first to admit that I probably didn't make that clear."

"No," I said.

My sense of justice was outraged. Saphi ripped out *my* hair and yet *I* was the one getting in trouble. Mom cleared her throat.

"You're eight years old," she said. "Saphira is only three. You're bigger, stronger—"

"I know."

"Don't interrupt. You're bigger, stronger, and smarter. If she bothers you, figure out a way to outsmart her."

"You won't let me go anywhere without her!" I said. "How can I get away from her?"

"Is running away from your sister the only solution you can think of?" Mom asked. "I'm surprised at you."

Chapter 5

Listening to the confusion in my brain would make it sound like I'm a product of devolution. A person is supposed to grow up and leave the childish things behind, as the apostle Paul would have put it. I haven't heard the childhood stories my mother told me since I became a teenager and too grown-up to snuggle in under her arm for a porch-swing story. It's not that the stories weren't present in my mind, forming a solid and familiar past, just that I didn't recall them in detail until the evening Saphi showed up at the kitchen door. As for fighting . . . I stopped fighting with Saphi before I turned ten. Well, that's not quite true, but the fights didn't involve slapping or hair pulling, at least. Now I'm devolving, because not only am I remembering the stories, but I'm running away from my sister, and I came within a few inches of slapping her, too.

I turn the car onto the highway that will take me to Mark Twain Lake. It isn't really a lake; it's actually a reservoir—a U.S. Army Corps of Engineers marvel that makes sure the area has enough water and recreation besides. Twenty-five minutes later, the car is parked on the edge of the road, and I'm sliding down to a rocky bank overhung with willows and spreading oak branches. Disturbed in his midafternoon fishing, a great blue heron takes wing, throwing a few angry *gawk, gawks* in my direction. I watch as he flaps with deceptive slowness to the far side of the marshy inlet; then I drop down onto the rocky shelf above the water and open the bottle of water I bought at the gas station.

I can't really call this *my* special place, because Grady and I found it together on a day not all that different from today. I haven't been back since I went away to college and the high school romance dissolved. We used to lie on the rocks and watch the sunset and the bass flipping up out of the water, and talk for hours about people and things and what God might be like.

"Hasn't it ever bothered you," I asked one purple dusk, "that if you think about the mechanics of Protestantism—you know, the idea of a man dying on a cross and then coming back to life in order to forgive a thing called 'sin'—it all seems kind of strange?"

I was very proud of the phrase "mechanics of Protestantism." It sounded very adult and intellectual as it came out of my mouth.

"No," Grady said.

Come to think of it, maybe it wasn't so much Grady talking as me talking. I tip the bottle of water back and let the liquid trickle down my throat. In the angle of early-autumn sunlight, I can see a cloud of mosquitoes swarming together. They are as blind as sinners to their fate. A fate that dives on them in the form of rough-winged swallows taking advantage of the bug buffet before their migration south.

Although they never said anything, I suppose Mom and Dad worried about Grady and me drifting off to lonely places for hours at a time. They didn't need to. The most we ever did was kiss. I would never have done anything in private with Grady that I wouldn't have been comfortable doing in front of the church. Maybe that was a mistake. A little sexual sin and public confession might have made me the lost-lamb toast of the church, if not the town.

I wipe the crook of my arm across my eyes and sigh in disgust. I've become a bundle of childish emotion, and childish emotions are the strongest kind. The most hateful, the most hurtful, because they are reduced to their purest form. A child—a very small child—can experience an emotion without guilt or regret. If a child feels wronged, nothing stands in her way of pointing out the wrongdoing.

I'm not a child anymore, which means I need to start acting like the adult I was, or thought I was, before Saphira knocked on the kitchen door.

———————

"It's your sister's first day in elementary school," Mom said to me. "I want you to walk with her to school and make sure she goes to the right room."

Outside, the August sunshine burned away the river mists. Crickets, cicadas, and katydids competed in a late-summer chorus, singing down from the tops of the tallest oaks, elms, and cottonwoods in their last-ditch efforts to find love before winter.

I imagined myself—a cocky, on-the-verge-of-junior-high sixth-grade student—walking hand in hand with the lowest of the low: a first grader. I'd taken a lot in stride already. Thrift-store clothes, for example. A pastor makes next to nothing, unless he wants to become a veritable demigod, possibly a demagogue, in one of those big-city churches with three Sunday services. Given that Dad had no aspirations toward godhood, Mom and I had made a special trip up to St. Louis to go thrift-store shopping. Being twelve, and adult enough to understand poverty, I decided to make this a fun event and find clothes that would create a statement rather than follow someone else's dialogue. Mom's face had gone

from worried frown to outright laughter. We'd tried on outland-
ish Easter hats, appliquéd jeans, flowered shirts, and even a pair of
platform disco boots.

"I used to have a pair of those," Mom had said. "White, like
Nancy Sinatra's."

"Who?" I'd asked.

And Mom had dived into her own version of "These Boots
Are Made for Walkin' " right in the middle of the aisle. Everyone
in the store applauded.

I had made something that could have been totally miserable if
I'd acted like Shelley Wright—class drama queen without a stage—
into something fun. It had been a moment of adulthood, and I had
understood what it meant to put other people's feelings first. But
on this first morning of school, I had butterflies from what I imagined Shelley Wright and her friends saying when I walked into
school in the white, platform disco boots, and imagining myself
having to walk into the building holding Saphira's hand, too, made
my tower of adulthood crumble to its foundations.

"Do I have to?" I asked Mom, hearing my whine and hating
it, knowing it was wrong as much as my slapping Saphi for pulling
my hair all those years ago.

Mom turned from the sink and looked at me. I tried hard to
not flush and betray that I knew I was disappointing her.

"Yes," she said.

She dried her hands on a tea towel hanging from the refrigerator door, then sat down in the chair across the table from me. I
wasn't hungry for my Cheerios anymore, so I pushed them away.

"I had an older sister," Mom said. "Your aunt Margaret."

"Yeah."

"Once upon a time, when I was in first grade, there was this
horrible fourth-grade girl named Lisa Snyder. Every day she pushed

me off the swing. Margaret was only in third grade, but she played baseball with the neighborhood boys, so they were all friends with her. One recess she put me as decoy on the swings; then, when Lisa came to push me off the swing, Margaret sneaked up behind Lisa and pulled down her Polly Pocket underwear. All the boys had been instructed to point and yell, which they did. Lisa left me alone after that." Mom laughed. "As long as I didn't use the slide."

This all sounded very nice in theory, but a corner of my brain remembered being pushed off the swing countless times with no one there to pull down anyone's underwear.

"Younger sisters have it pretty good," I said.

Mom raised her eyebrows. I pushed back from the table.

"No one took care of me when I was in first grade. I lived."

"I took care of you," Mom said. "I'll always be here to take care of you."

————

The breeze dies down, and the mosquitoes catch my scent. After capping the bottle of water, I stand up and skip a rock off the glass surface of the lake. The rings of its passing flicker gold, and a lake gull pauses in midflight to watch for a surfacing fish.

I don't need someone to expose the bully's underwear anymore, but I would give anything to sit across the table from Mom and ask her what happened to me and why I feel like such a failure. I want to ask her if it's possible that running away from me was the only solution Saphi could find.

The sun is low in the sky when I scramble back up the bank to the rutted road and my car.

————

Saphi spends the next four days avoiding me. I regret all the things that I said to her about keeping the house clean. The living room and kitchen are spotless, but rather than feeling happy, I feel despondent. I want to put my arms around my sister and cry out an apology in an attempt to erase my bitter words, but she slips away whenever I enter a room, and when I knock on her bedroom door, no one answers. The trash can by my desk has a few torn-up drafts of mea culpas that I nearly taped to the upstairs bathroom's mirror before I realized I could never take the easy way out.

Saphi has been avoiding me, so I'm surprised when she appears at my elbow on Thursday evening as I'm putting on my shoes and getting ready to walk down to the church for choir practice.

"May I come with you?"

I take extra time putting my foot into the right half of the pair of fake Birkenstocks I bought at a discount store early in the summer. The cork is already separating from the rubber sole. I take time putting my foot into my shoe and try to figure out how not to put it into my mouth. This is the moment to apologize, but the words I've been oh-so-carefully stringing together since last Saturday drift beyond my reach and I can mutter only, "Okay."

The autumn evening is warm and damp from an afternoon rain. We pass a chinquapin oak, and the dark, earthy smell of its leaves mixes with the smoke from someone's burning brush pile. Rags of evaporation mist rise from the sidewalk and catch at our legs as we walk in unison. Saphi kicks at a rock with the toe of her shoe, and we both watch it skip along ahead of us until it skips off into the gutter.

"So you've been keeping the choir together all this time?" she asks.

"Since Mom ..." I fumble over the memories. "Since Mom."

A church is a machine. It takes lots of oil and lots of maintenance to keep things running smoothly. When Mom died and Dad spent months in rehabilitation, the church slipped a cog. Suddenly nothing ran right, things began to squeak, and breakdowns happened. Being a naive twenty-two years old when my mother died and my father lay in the hospital, I thought the church would run itself, that some person somewhere would take care of the details and install all the right parts. Instead the church ran itself into the ground. The organist came within inches of doing physical damage to the pianist when he suggested she might have the volume up a bit too high. The interim pastor sent to carry the church through the time Dad was "incapacitated" was very nearly burned at the stake for a heretic. I tried to step into my mother's place and keep the church's home fires burning, but not roaring out of control. I thought the best way to do this was by encouraging Sunday pot-luck dinners or making sure the choir didn't falter and disappear without Mom's enthusiasm and organization. I soon learned that I was not my mother, but somehow just having one member of the pastor's family remain interested seemed to calm the congregation down. Even if the organist managed to simulate a stack of ampli-fiers at a live concert in response to the pianist's insinuation that the previous volume level was still above average.

Stoic's Methodist church is small. The choir is nothing official. There are no robes, no fancy music folders, nobody to stand in front and wave their hands in meaningless gestures, and no disci-pline of any kind. That means whoever happens to show up at the one weekly practice will move up to the front on Sunday, shuffle together in some semblance of harmonic order, and sing a simple song or hymn. Out in the congregation, older men will use the time to take a quick nap before the sermon, teenagers will fidget and poke one another, and someone, Emily Spalding usually, will listen intently and inform me where everyone should have held a note a beat longer.

"Since Mom," I say as I fumble over the memories.

We're at the front door of the church when I reach out a hand and catch Saphi's elbow.

"I'm sorry," I say.

She looks through my words, through me, and says nothing.

"For what I said on Saturday. You were right. It *was* about me, not Dad. I was just using him to get at you."

Her eyes flicker and focus on my face.

"I'm glad you could apologize," she says.

Opening the door, she walks in ahead of me. It's not like I expected her to fall into my arms so we could kiss and make up, but I'm not sure what to make of her words. They were spoken in a flat, neutral tone, no hint of sarcasm or dislike; no hint of warmth, either. I catch the door before it closes and follow her into the church.

My favorite movies are those late-night horror shows, where a scene is shot in a towering Gothic cathedral filled with candles and flowers and rows of hard wooden benches. The heroine lights a candle, then kneels while ghostly airs ruffle the candle flames. Just imagining the weight of years and stone, the mingled scent of incense and candles, gives me a thrill. When I was in Philadelphia, I slipped into, appropriately, St. Augustine's church during the devotions to Santo Niño. Around me was the quiet whispering of prayers and responses and above me the dust motes swam in colored light from the windows. Somehow it felt like I always believed a church *should* feel. When I said as much to Tallulah on our weekly dessert splurges, she laughed and practically choked on a bite of tiramisu.

"Hon"—Tallulah calls everyone *hon*—"you like it because you were raised a Methodist. There are certain disadvantages to being raised Methodist or Baptist, and one of those is that they'll never film a horror movie in your church. It's the law."

I blink away memories of Philadelphia and Tallulah and tiramisu, and I'm standing in the church I grew up with. Smooth wooden pews, prized cushions on the seats, thick red carpet, and not a whiff of incense to be found.

Saphira sits down at the piano and begins to pound out Joplin's "The Entertainer."

"Well, isn't this lively?" June Winthrop says to me as she closes the door behind her.

"Hi, June."

June is the organist, and we usually go over what the choir should attempt this week based on my insider knowledge of Dad's upcoming sermon topic, but tonight June nudges Saphi's shoulder and asks her something. I can't hear what she says, but soon they are sitting on the same piano bench and playing an improvised duet that is some kind of distant relation to "Chopsticks," and they're giggling like two naughty little girls.

Saphi was always better at music than I was. I was a hopeless failure at all but the most simple four-part harmonies. Saphi played like a virtuoso within a few years. She acted like a prima donna within a few weeks.

"That," she informed me one torturous practice session, "is incorrect. It's played like this."

"Go away."

"You're doing it wrong again." Said with a deeply wounded sigh.

I pinched her.

She shrieked.

"Oh," says one of the women who just walked in the door, "is that 'I'll Be Seeing You'?"

More people are showing up for practice. Instead of the usual mundane chatter about jobs and children, the four women and three men crowd around the piano and sing the post-WWII-era song that June and Saphi both seem to know by heart in duet form.

I shake my head and smile, give in to everyone's pleasure, and slip in behind them. I do my best, but I'm the only person who doesn't know the words or even most of the tune. June must have been bored to death when she had to teach my piano lessons, but I didn't ask to be assigned all the dark classical pieces by morose composers. It always seemed like Saphi had the fun boogie-woogie music. I'm trying to make out the words on some sheet music June has pulled out of her bag, but in my mind I'm sitting in the Winthrop living room and June is saying to me, after I've tried yet again to convince her to let me try some lively tune, "Music is best tailored to personality."

We're nearly thirty minutes into the hour for practice, so I call a halt to the impromptu concert, receiving several moans of, "But this is so much fun." Everyone dutifully locates a hymnal, and I feel like an ogre who ate all the Christmas presents.

"What are you planning this week, Augustina?" one of the men asks.

"I was thinking of singing 'Be Still My Soul,' " I say. "It goes with—"

"Why don't we try something a little more fun, more complicated than a hymn?"

Everyone's heads turn toward the piano, where Saphi is still sitting. She's leaning forward, palms flat on the bench, toe rubbing back and forth across the wooden floor.

"Something that will really 'wow' everybody."

The choir members look at one another, glance at me; then Mrs. Watson chirps like a baby bird, "Well, why not? Do you have something in mind, dear?"

"I found this in the piano bench."

Saphi holds up some sheet music. Squinting, I can just make out that it's the piece by Bach. The choir members are gathering around the piano, and everyone seems willing to learn, even if they have to stay an extra hour or two. In the small, excited group clustering around Saphi are the same people who complained four years and nine months ago when I suggested we try the very same piece.

"Oh, this is just too much."

"We have to work tomorrow, Augustina. Let's just stick to doing hymns."

"Your mama never tried anything this difficult."

Looking at the earnest faces around the piano, I know they would have said the same words if I'd suggested the Bach piece tonight, and I feel a curious deflation.

Even more curious is the fact that Saphi won't look me in the eye.

———

On the warm August morning, on the first day of sixth grade when the katydids and cicadas sang from the tops of the trees, I walked to school with Saphi. She was dressed in an absurd frilly thing that made her look like a scoop of tutti-frutti ice cream on fat legs as she skipped and twirled ahead of me. I wasn't paying much attention to her, because I was rolling what Mom had said around in my mind. I still wasn't sure if it was fair that I had to be the eldest and look out for my little sister. I hadn't asked for this birth arrangement. It was just an act of fate. Scuffing along, avoiding the cracks in the sidewalk, I looked up in time to see Saphi walking into a strange yard inhabited by the meanest-looking dog on earth. His bared teeth were on a level with her face.

"Nice doggy," Saphi said.

Fido the man-killer lunged.

I screamed and swung Saphi up out of reach. Fido's teeth sank into my right thigh, just above the thick fake leather of the disco boot.

"Zeus! Come here now!" yelled the shirtless man on the killer dog's porch. "What the hell are you kids doing in my yard?"

Saphi screamed in my ear, her tears soaking the lace on her collar. I turned around and ran home, twisting my ankle only once.

The dog was in the neighborhood and had all the appropriate shots, so the doctor gave me only a tetanus booster. It hurt, but I pretended it didn't because Saphi had my hand squeezed in a death grip the whole time.

"I'll take care of you, Gusti," she said.

That night Mom sat on the side of my bed.

"Once upon at time—" she began, but I cut her off.

"I should have been watching her better."

"You protected her."

"It was my fault she got into the yard with the dog."

"You took care of her when it counted. You should be glad that you saved her from getting hurt."

Lying awake after Mom left, watching the shadows flicker over the wall, I crossed some indefinable line. I won't say it was the line between childhood and adulthood. Nor can I say that Saphi and I stopped competing with each other or stopped trying to cause misery and embarrassment on occasion, but from that point on, something changed. She became my sister rather than "the baby." We were sisters until the night of Mom's death, when something changed again.

———

Walking home from choir practice, Saphira skips and twirls ahead of me like a wraith in the moonlight and the rustling, leaf-laden wind.

"Wasn't that fun?" she asks me.

She hugs herself, then bursts into the final chorus. It took the choir ninety minutes of monotonous memorization in order to come anywhere close to approximating what Bach had intended when he wrote the piece. I don't mind if we sing with errors or if Mrs. Watson adds enough vibrato to each high note to sound like she's yodeling from a Swiss mountaintop, but something *is* nagging me, and I don't like what it says.

Saphi twirls to a stop in front of me.

"What's eating you now?" she asks.

I can see the smile on her face. It lacks warmth, and the coolness isn't due to the blue wash of the moonlight. I can see the cartoon-cat satisfaction.

"Why don't we try something a little more fun?"

"Nothing at all," I say out loud.

Tit for tat. The smile says it all. I understand why Saphi refused to accept my apology outside the church's front door. She planned this. Tonight's choir practice was payment for my making her feel unwelcome in her own house.

She reaches out and pushes up the corners of my mouth with her index fingers.

"You're always so glum."

"I'm actually not," I say, pushing her fingers away from my mouth.

"Just give in a little. Try not to be so horribly, desperately dull. You're not the piece that holds everything together. You're not as important as you think."

She hops up the porch steps and darts into the house. The final notes of Bach's chorus float out the lighted window to taunt me. I turn around and walk back into the darkness.

Chapter 6

Turning back into the darkness, I stop at the edge of the drive-way. If I go right, I'll end up walking on a gravel road under the stars; left, and I'll be walking back into Stoic. I turn right, pausing every once in a while to kick a piece of gravel from inside my shoes. I don't know who invented the Birkenstock style, but it's no good for walking on the side of a gravel road.

"You were pretty quiet tonight."

It was a night a lot like this one, only in spring. Between jobs and needing some pampering after a nasty breakup with the first serious guy in my life since Grady, I had come home for spring break my sophomore year at Penn. The internal movie of myself had me taking long, sorrowful walks in the moonlight, so I took long, sorrowful walks in the moonlight. One night, after another trip down self-pity lane, I came home and noticed Saphi sitting in the porch swing. It squeaked horribly, and I decided it was safer to choose the porch steps.

"You were pretty quiet tonight," I said to her. I almost added a droll comment about her new tongue stud being the proverbial cat, but the atmosphere was all wrong for teasing.

"I broke it off with Chris today," she said.

Saphi had a habit of collecting and tossing hearts without ever losing her own. Thanks to the absurdity of human nature, the contrary desire to have what cannot be had, her "love 'em and leave 'em" attitude made her the most sought-after prize in the school.

"I'm sorry."

"For what?"

"It's something to say when you think the other person feels bad."

"Oh. Well, it's dumb. 'Sorry' is an apology."

I tucked my knees up to my chest. From the creek just past Jackson's field, the peep frogs were piping their spring chorus of love. "Me, me, me, choose me."

"You're right," I said. "What happened?"

"Grady's still with that girl at the car shop," she said, instead of answering.

"I know."

"Doesn't it bug you?"

"No. Not anymore."

"You're better-looking than she is."

"Thanks."

The swing creaked ominously as Saphi set it in motion by pushing her toe into the floor.

"I liked Chris," she said. "I think I might have loved him."

Never having broken up with someone, I wasn't sure how to respond. I was always the girl in love, the last one to know, the one left in the dust as the hero walked into the sunset with someone else. I knew what love felt like—euphoria followed by heartache—and had never wondered if I "might have loved" someone.

"Why'd you break up with him?"

"I heard him telling a couple of friends that he'd do me before summer."

"You're kidding!"

"No."

"What a prick."

Saphi gurgled a laugh. "Well, from what Shan tells me, it's actually a very *small* prick."

"Ah. It must be a prick to his pride."

We both laughed at our childish humor; then the darkness and peeps took over again.

"Gusti?"

"Yeah?"

"I'm glad you're here. I miss you."

"I miss you, too."

Walking on the side of the gravel road, under the starlight, I shake another pesky piece of rock out of my shoe. Under my bare toes, the road is damp from the rain. Mist weaves through the fields, and the crickets are singing last-chance-for-love music. Here I am again, taking a trip down self-pity lane. It's not like I didn't deserve what I got tonight. If I'd been truly determined to apologize this past week, I would have broken down Saphi's door or grabbed her and pinned her to the floor and forced her to listen to me.

I'm angry at her. Furious. It's the only explanation for the pressure I feel inside that threatens to explode outward whenever I picture her screaming at me over the college applications just before she left.

"You're not my mom."

I needed a sister, not a child. I needed someone to help out, understand that changes had happened and we had to roll with them to survive, but Saphi acted like a toddler out of control. I had been *forced* to act like a parent, even though I didn't know how to be one and didn't have the energy to learn.

I drop the shoe down onto the road. Fine. We've both acted like spoiled brats since Saphira came home, but no more. The past needs to stay in the past. Looking out at the mists, I breathe deeply and feel the damp air travel through my lungs and out again. The past needs to stay in the past. If it can.

————

"Your mother bought me a recipe box."

Colton and I are sitting at a table just outside the sandwich shop, waiting for our number to be called. Despite being a Monday, it's one of those perfect October days when the world seems festive because the dog days of summer are long gone and the winter chill hasn't arrived. Colton and I met on a Monday, and ever since, it has become our day to take a little extra time for lunch so we can do those silly things people in love tend to do, like ride the Octopus at the county fair and get sticky with funnel cakes or walk hand in hand through the park. He's a paralegal with an attorney's office in Stoic, and since his attention to detail has made him indispensable, he doesn't need permission to take two hours for lunch on a Monday. I once asked him if things weren't actually busier after the weekend than during the week and he said, "No, everyone stayed home and watched football on Sunday instead of getting into trouble, so Mondays are pretty slow."

"Let's get takeout and have a picnic," I said when I picked him up. So now we're waiting for our food at Stoic's favorite sandwich shop.

"Why would she buy you a recipe box?" he asks.

"She thinks you'll starve on my cooking."

"You don't cook."

"I do too cook."

"You make sandwiches, soy smoothies, and pizza," he says. "And you buy the ready-to-go crusts."

"That's cooking."

"Technically, it's baking. And you're turning on the stove with only one of those items."

"Grilled cheese sandwiches!" I raise my chin in a triumphant gesture.

"Point made. Why did Mom buy you a recipe box?"

This is a question I don't have an answer for. On the surface, it is deceptively simple. Lorraine wants me to cook tasty treats for her boy, just as she has cooked tasty treats for her boy. No more and no less than any typical mother-in-law gauging the acceptability of the woman in her son's life. But somehow, this gift from Lorraine has taken on a strange literary symbolism. Despite my teasing, I want to talk seriously about it with Colton because of something Lorraine said when she stopped by the house to hand me the striped shopping bag from one of the expensive kitchen supply shops run for tourists and elites. I asked her inside for a cup of coffee, but, still looking down at the porch floor with its peeling paint, she refused. I thanked her for the present. And she said:

"It's no problem, you know. You'll soon be starting a whole different life."

After waving to her departing car, I looked down at the box. The label claimed it was a revolutionary design made of stainless steel and fully waterproof, dust-proof, and flour-proof. The label said nothing about symbolism, but after years of analyzing the world's literature, I would identify the box as being a stainless-steel trap or at least an evil omen of some kind. In a fit of superstition, I hid the box on the top shelf of my closet, behind the protective custody of a basket filled with the letters Mom sent me while I was at Penn.

I want to ask Colton what Lorraine meant by a "whole different life." It sounded so final and decided, as if people have been having discussions about my future without my knowing. Looking down at the plastic table surface in front of me, I frown at the thought.

"Maybe I should ask what you *did* with the box," Colton says in response to my frown.

"I hid it behind a bushel," I say absently, misquoting the Sunday-school song about little lights and bushel baskets.

His eyebrows go up; then he laughs.

"Isn't that '*under* a bushel'?"

At the sound of his laughter, two women eating at a nearby table stop talking and smile at us: the young couple in love.

"In the song, yes."

"That's a strange place to put it."

I smile back at the two women, and realize that he has no way of knowing about the basket filled with letters; nor do I want to explain.

"What kind of life do you see us having?" I ask him. "In the future?"

"Number nineteen?" someone inside the shop calls.

Colton slides back his chair and stands up.

"That's us."

He picks up our sandwiches and drops my question. I could bring it back up and force the issue, but what I really want is a return to the young couple in love. The good old days when Colton made me laugh and the future wasn't quite so near to the present.

"Where do you want to go?" he asks.

"The park by the river."

"That's quite a walk."

"Wherever you want then."

"Augustina!"

I turn at the sound of my name to find June Winthrop and another woman from the church.

"I didn't get a chance to talk to you yesterday after the service," June says, "but I wanted to let you know that yesterday's choir number was the most fun I've had in . . . oh, in a long time."

"It was beautiful," her friend adds.

"Thank you. I can't really take credit—"

"Your sister is such a blessing," June says, interrupting me. "You must be so happy that she's finally come home."

"Yes."

"And so gifted at the piano," the friend says.

"She should be," June says, snorting a little. "I taught her how to play, after all." She turns to me again. "Does Saphira have any other ideas for choral music? I was thinking we might be able to encourage more members to participate if they thought there was something exciting going on, something different."

"I'll have to ask."

"We're interrupting your lunch with Colton," the friend says.

"No problem."

Colton leads us to a park bench under trees whose leaves are starting to show yellows, browns, and a tinge of red. No one has ever come up to me and said, "You are such a blessing. We're so glad you stayed home. Thank you for keeping the choir going." I realize that familiarity breeds contempt, or at least boredom, and a philosophical shrug is the reaction I should have to their enthusiastic response to Saphira's suggestion and their short memory over the opposite response when I proposed the same piece. They're happy. Isn't that what is important? Isn't that why I stepped in to try to keep the choir going in the first place?

What is wrong with me?

"So Saphira is taking an interest in the church?"

I pick up my sandwich and take a bite, not sure I want to discuss this with Colton.

"Yes."

"It's about time she did something, I guess," he continues. He's already halfway through his sandwich. "She's been home for what? Three weeks? I'm surprised she doesn't have a job already."

His tone is condescending, bordering on outright rudeness to Saphi. I can feel the hair on the back of my neck rise up in a primitive protective response.

———

"Make her go home. She's a pain in the butt."

Denise and I were on our way to the Dairy Queen. It was the summer after my seventh-grade year, and Denise was my best friend. We'd bonded in opposition to Shelley Wright and her plans for domination of all the junior high girls. It was the middle of July, and so hot you ran across asphalt parking lots even if you were wearing shoes, and tar oozed out of repaired cracks in the sidewalks.

"Let's go to the DQ for ice cream," Denise had said.

Sporting a pair of hats I'd found during the thrift-store trip last year, we'd set off for the DQ. But before we'd reached the end of the driveway, Saphi had come running after us.

"Can I go, too?"

"Make her go home," Denise said. "She's a pain in the butt."

If Denise had slapped Saphi, my sister would have looked less hurt than she did right then. The hair on the back of my neck tingled in response to that look.

"She can come if she wants," I said.

"She's a baby."

"She's not the one acting like a baby."

"What's that supposed to mean?"

"It means you just want to go to the DQ and strut around for the cute guy behind the counter."

"So what if I do?"

"Unless Saphi comes with us, you can do it by yourself."

"Oh, all right. Let the little baby come with us."

Saphi's head had been turning back and forth between us during this exchange. I could feel my lips bared over my teeth, a little like the picture in one of my history books of the she-wolf standing over Romulus and Remus.

"It's okay, Gusti," Saphi said to me. "I can stay home."

"See?" Denise said. "She can stay home."

"She and I are going to the Dairy Queen," I said. "But *you* can come with us."

Denise threw the hat she'd borrowed from me into my face.

"I wouldn't go with you if you begged me."

Denise and I patched things up within a week, but that hot afternoon, Saphi and I ate chocolate-dipped soft-serve cones at the DQ, and the cute guy working there leaned over the counter and said to Saphi, "Hey, I have a sister about your age." Then he smiled at me.

————

"It's about time she did something," Colton says.

"You know what?" I say, my hackles rising. "A person who doesn't like to have his family critiqued should probably not offer critiques of other people's families."

His potato-chip bag crinkles and rattles as he opens it.

"Who's offering a critique?"

"You."

"I just said it was good for her to be doing something."

"You said 'it's about time she did something.' That has a completely different meaning."

"You're splitting hairs."

"Am I?"

He chews and swallows, then smiles at me in a placating gesture that only adds fuel to the fire.

"I've never told you that I don't want you to say anything negative about my family," he says.

"This isn't about your family—it's about you criticizing Saphira."

"You're the one who brought it up. And I don't think this is about me at all. I think you're upset about something."

If I were a bull in the ring under the hot sun of Hemingway's Pamplona, there would be no need for any extra prodding to get me to try to gore the matador.

"No. This is about you feeling like you have complete freedom to say something bad about Saphi, but putting your fingers in your ears and going, 'La, la, la,' when it comes to Lorraine or Howard."

"This is about the recipe box, isn't it? My mom hurt your feelings."

I rub my temples with my fingers. The words in my head are flying around like birds trapped inside a glass house. I can feel them slam into the sides of my skull, but I can't catch them and force them to make sense.

"No."

"That's what it looks like to me."

The entire topic has changed. I wanted to defend Saphi, but we're on completely different ground now, on a completely different topic. This is about honesty and lying and how we're going to communicate in the future. I push the rest of my sandwich into my empty drink cup and throw it away in the trash can. Then I pick up Colton's trash and throw that away, too. Colton is looking up at the leaves overhead. He reminds me of a Renaissance painting, perhaps one by Titian, as the light is similar to the kind loved by the master painter. Titian would have entitled this painting, *Man Seeking the Patience of God in the Face of Adversity from Woman*.

"Look," I say, sitting down beside him. "I'm sorry I said that about you putting your fingers in your ears."

"Really?"

"Yes."

The leaves rattle and a few fall down onto us. I pick one out of my hair and twirl it by the stem, searching for the right words.

"I shouldn't have said it like that. I get frustrated sometimes, though. When you say something I don't like about my family, I get mad and tell you, and that gives you the opportunity to argue back. When I say something you don't like, you wait until it all blows over and the little woman is calm again. Don't you understand why that would make me mad?"

"You want me to get angry."

He says it like it's the stupidest damn thing he's ever heard, and maybe in his opinion it is.

"I want you to be honest. Treat me like an equal."

"I treat you like an equal."

"Most of the time."

"You're really being unfair, Augustina." He sighs and rubs the palms of his hands on his knees. His fingers leave faint dark spots on the material. "Damn potato chips. Do you have a napkin?"

"No."

"Look, I'd better get back to work."

I don't look at my watch, but I know we have at least an hour left of the time we usually take for our Monday lunches together.

"Okay."

"For God's sake. Don't be angry about it."

Chapter 7

"Where did it go?"

" 'The foolish man built his house upon the sand,' " Dad quoted to me.

It was one of the golden springs of my childhood. The year Saphira was one year old. She'd learned that a few screams tended to get everyone's attention, so screams had become a daily part of my existence. Especially when I didn't want her to have or touch something I cared about.

"Augustina," Mom would say, "let her see your book. She won't hurt it."

Sulkily, I would hand over the favorite book. Saphi usually managed to rip something or mark it up with crayons, but it was never her fault because she was a baby. Life seemed cruelly unfair to me, and I think Dad could tell I needed some special attention.

On the morning of my seventh birthday, he took me on an exploratory walk along the river. The spring had been unusually dry, and we found a large exposed sandbar near the bank. A fallen log made a bridge wide enough for even my unsteady, childish sense of balance.

"Careful now," Dad said as I negotiated the final tricky part. Then he swung me up into the air and set my feet onto the firm sand.

"What are those marks?" I asked.

"Those are the tracks of a heron," he said. "See the three long toes? He stands in the water, very still, and when fish or frogs come along, they think his legs are sticks. Then *pow!* He snags them with his beak."

"Yuck!"

"Just think how a wet, wiggly frog would feel going down your throat."

He made little gulping noises while I provided appropriate howls of disgust. We explored other tracks. The swishy S-track of a water snake, the almost-human handprints of opossums and raccoons, the delicately rounded tracks of a skunk, and the deep twin curves of deer hooves, all mixed in with the fluttering tracks of kildeer. I skipped over the hard sand until I found the most beautiful thing I had ever seen: the shell of a river mussel as big as my hand, with swirls of blue and purple and pink and opal inside. The sun changed the colors as I turned the mussel shell in the light.

For days after the magical trip to the sandbar, I begged Dad to go back again, but an outbreak of the flu kept him busy visiting church members in the hospital. Weddings and funerals went on as normal, and there wasn't time for a trip to the sandbar. If I had been older, I would have been able to slip off by myself, but I wasn't allowed to go beyond the banks of the river without an adult. Mom was lenient about my wandering the countryside, but the mental image of her daughter being washed away by Old Man

River kept me within certain boundaries. Not that I didn't consider climbing the imaginary fence and escaping the boundaries, but I knew someone would see me and mention it to Mom, and then I'd be quite thoroughly grounded.

Finally Dad said he thought he'd have time to take me the next day. That night it rained. Buckets of water dumped out of the sky, ending the drought. "Gabriel and Michael are having a water fight," Mom said at supper.

I prayed for sunshine, and I got it. The dawn of the long-awaited river trip was blue and fresh. Robins sang from every corner of the town as Dad and I walked to the river. But the night rain had brought the river level high as flooded creeks and streams filled its banks. The log to the sandbar was gone, and the only sign that the sandbar still existed was a small twist of scrub bent by the catch of weeds, trash, and the force of the water. I gripped Dad's hand and stared.

"Where did it go? Where did the log and sand go?"

" 'A wise man built his house upon the rock,' " Dad said, paraphrasing the Bible verse slightly. " 'But a foolish man built his house upon the sand. And when the rains and wind came, it fell. And what a terrible crash it was.' "

He squatted down beside me and swept the area where the sandbar had been with a gesture of his hand.

"The river washes the sand into a different shape whenever the water runs fast. And the water has carried the log on down the river, where it will catch on another sandbar and provide a bridge for little animals somewhere else."

"But what about us?"

"I think you and I are going to have to stick with ice-cream cones today."

After Colton leaves to go back to work, I walk to the park along the edge of the river and follow the bank until I find an accessible sandbar near the edge. An old log, smaller than the one from my childhood, keeps my feet dry as I walk, arms outstretched, along its length and to the firm sand. The familiar tracks are all there— friends smiling from across a room of strangers.

The wise man built his house upon the rock, but the foolish man built his house upon the sand.

Looking up at the blue sky, standing on the edge of the water with the muddy wavelets lapping my feet, I feel the sand slipping and shifting under my toes. It's an interesting verse. It equates wise and foolish with building sites, yet building sites are controlled by money. Where a man (or woman) chooses to build is not determined by wisdom or folly, but by whether or not they can afford to live on the rocky area. Rocky areas are usually higher than the surrounding land. They are hills and the sides of mountains—the expensive sites that come with a view. The sandy low site might have been all the "foolish man" could afford, yet no one ever mentions that. When I asked Dad about it a few years ago he laughed and said, "You think too much. Besides, it's an allegory for building your life on the teachings of Jesus."

I pick up a mussel shell and turn it so the sunlight gleams pink and purple inside the concave space. It's difficult for me to explain why I had the fight with Colton at lunch. I think anyone looking at it from the outside would be as puzzled as I was by the disappearance of the sandbar on that sunny spring day. Can the river explain what it feels like to be in full flood? My emotions shift as easily as the sand under my toes, and yet . . . and yet I have a deep suspicion that my emotions are not just built on sand, but on a solid foundation. A foundation I don't quite understand but that I keep reaching toward with arms that aren't long enough.

"Why so glum, chum?"

I turn around and see Saphira. She's standing about ten feet away, barefoot like me, with her hands shoved into the pockets of her jeans.

"I didn't hear you."

"I was up there." She gestures vaguely to the area where the park overlooks the river. "And I saw you walk out on the log. Did you have a fight with Colton?"

"Kind of."

I don't want to talk about it because I don't want to have to tell her what Colton said—she doesn't need to hear his disparagement—but if I try to explain the situation without telling her, I may have to listen to a lecture. A lecture on how I've been deficient in my treatment of a kind, good-hearted fiancé.

She walks up to stand beside me.

"What's that?"

"A shell."

I hand her the mussel shell, and she holds it into the light, rotating it to see the colors.

"It's pretty, isn't it?" she asks.

"Yes."

"Colton is kind of proper and formal."

I sigh. "I guess."

"I didn't expect you—" She breaks off and quickly smiles at me. "He's nice, though."

She's trying to not sound critical. Looking at the shell in her hand, watching her turn it, I realize that I'm not the only one who made a vow to try to recapture our past, repair our relationship.

"Mom used to have a little box made out of mother-of-pearl," she says. "I liked to hold it up to the light to see the colors turn."

"It's still on their dresser. In the upstairs room."

"But it isn't the same."

About ten feet past my toes, the river ripples around the arm of a nearly submerged log, an arm raised in supplication to be pulled back onto dry land where the log can decompose in peace on the forest floor instead of rolling down the river until bits of it are scattered from here to the shipping lanes of New Orleans. Saphi means that certain things lose their magic when they are removed from their rightful place. The mother-of-pearl box was magic when Mom touched it daily, when it smelled like her lily-of-the-valley moisturizer, when it contained pretty, secret pirate things like rings and a lucky penny. Now the box is out of its element. It's nothing more than a dusty keepsake with a faint hint of floral lotion if you open it in a still room on a windless morning and if you forgot to put any furniture wax on the dust rag.

"No. It isn't."

Saphi leans back and neatly skips the mussel shell across the river's surface. We automatically count the skips.

"Seven," she says.

"Six."

"Seven. Beat that."

She grins at me. I look around until I find another shell, then carefully wipe off the damp sand from the ribbed, convex outer surface before sending it skipping over the water. Six skips and it hits a waterlogged tree limb, bounces off, and sinks.

"I win," Saphi says.

"No fair. It would have kept going."

"Don't aim for driftwood next time."

She sticks her tongue out at me just in time to receive a mussel shell on the head.

"Ack! Yuck."

We both laugh and I help her dust the sand out of her hair. Her head is bent over and I'm picking out grains from the white line of her part when I hear her whispered words.

"I'm married."

"What?"

"I was married, I mean."

She straightens up and smiles at me before skipping the mussel shell I put on her head out across the river.

"Married?"

It shouldn't be a surprise. She's twenty-three years old, after all. She was an adult when she left. I know, because the police refused to call her a runaway and try to help me find her. "Eighteen. Sorry, ma'am. She's an adult and can do what she wants." Yet somehow she is still my baby sister, and having my baby sister be married requires a paradigm shift in my head.

"Six skips," she says.

"What happened?"

She shrugs. Her face is turned away from me and all I can see is her profile. I never realized before how much she looks like Mom. My hair is dark brown, and I have some throwback genes to an ancestor with olive skin, because I tend to look like I've been out in the sun even when I haven't. Saphi is all gold honey and cream. Mom's hair was darker, but Saphi's skin is the same, and her nose has the same perfect straight bridge. I look away and across the river to the autumn yellow trees on the far shore.

"Are you divorced?"

"Yes."

"Did you tell Dad?"

"Just you."

I skip another shell, but forget to count the skips.

"Eight," she says. "Beat me by two."

"Why haven't you said anything? To Dad."

"I'm always the disappointment. I guess I'm not ready to be even more disappointing."

"But lots of people get divorced."

Still looking out over the water, she smiles a little. I realize that lots of people do get divorced, but neither of Dad's daughters has gotten a divorce—until now—and I can't honestly say how he will react to the news.

"Bad grades," she says. "Bad boys. Running away from home. Not going to college. Very disappointing."

"Dad loves you."

"Of course he does. He can't do anything else, can he?"

I open my mouth to argue that Dad's love is genuine and without conditions, but it's not the kind of argument a person can make. Love is a feeling between two people—a feeling of acceptance, communication, and empathy. No third party can step in and determine whether those feelings really do exist.

"I'm sorry," I say.

She looks at me for the first time. Her eyebrows are perfect arches over dusky blue eyes.

"That you feel that way," I add.

" 'Sorry' is an apology, remember?"

She turns and retraces her footsteps to the log bridge between the sandbar and the bank. I've said the wrong thing, but I can't call her back because I don't know what else to say.

———

"Once upon a time, before you were born, your dad woke me up in the middle of the night."

"It was only ten o'clock," Dad said from where he sat at the foot of my bed. "You went to bed early."

We hadn't moved to Stoic yet, and all I can remember of our apartment in Iowa are the glow-in-the-dark stars Mom had placed all over the ceiling of my room. That night I was looking up at the stars that glowed fluorescent yellow beyond the circle of lamplight cast onto the ceiling. Outside the window, rain splattered against the glass. We were in the middle of a bedtime-story ritual, Mom sitting beside me on the bed, Dad at the foot.

"It was pouring down rain," Mom continued, ignoring Dad's interruption. "And your father said, 'Let's fly a kite.'"

"At night?" I asked.

"At night. In the rain."

Mom paused for dramatic emphasis. I pulled the covers up around my neck and looked down at Dad.

"Why?"

"I wanted to know what it would be like to fly at night," he said.

"But you weren't flying. The kite was."

"I wasn't, but the geese overhead were."

With a child's wisdom, I accepted this as an adequate explanation.

"Did you?" I asked Mom.

"We got very cold and very wet, and the kite ended up in a tree."

She smiled down at Dad and something adult passed between them.

"Can we go fly a kite now?" I asked.

"No," Mom said. "Now you're going to go to sleep and dream about flying in the rain, just like a silly goose."

———

I watch Saphira walk away until she crosses the log and begins the climb up the bank and back into the park. A green heron, disturbed by her passing, lifts off and flies over my head. He crosses in front of the sun, and my eyes water and sting from the bright light and heat. Given how badly I want to follow the heron, given the number of stories about humans who wanted or tried to fly, you would think Jean-Baptiste Lamarck would have laughed himself silly when he came up with his theory about need and desire causing evolution. Like millions of children before me, I ran along the sandbar flapping my arms and hoping for liftoff, but giraffes didn't stretch their way to long necks, and the only mammal to flap itself into flying is the bat. I still have dreams about soaring over the world, lifting free of the ground until I'm nothing but a speck and the ground below is a patchwork of green trees, silvery rivers, and new-cut fields. If simple desire and arm flapping could lift me into the skies, I would be there.

I watch the green heron skim low over the water and land on the far bank. Flying is a human dream. Or perhaps, to be more specific, flying *away* from everything—flying *above* everything—is a human dream. A dream of soaring high above the difficulties the world creates for us or that we create for ourselves. Walking back to where I left my shoes, I dream about flying.

Chapter 8

On Monday evenings I hold a tutoring class at a small local college. For three hours, in the lounge area of the library, the students work on their papers or creative-writing assignments and I go around the room offering suggestions or answering questions. It's not technically a class, just a way to combine a group of students who can't afford one-on-one tutoring into a single room and offer them a cut rate. One semester I even worked on the barter system with a former mechanic going back for his college degree. He graduated with honors, and my car misses him.

I told Lorraine that I like tutoring, but like some singer said about reggae, I don't just like it; I love it. Tutoring is teaching without the hassle of preparing for classes. It's the joy of watching the light of understanding grow brighter in a student's eyes. It's part pain, part joy, because there are always difficult students who drive you to homicidal mania, but with tutoring, at least I have the option of suggesting the Difficulty and I part ways. Profs are stuck with the little beasts. But for every pain in the butt, there are ten students who make my life better than it was before I knew them. For three hours I sit in the lounge area of the library, surrounded by the smell of old paper bound into books and fresh paper bound into notebooks, and I forget the outside world exists.

After tonight's session, the distant rumbles of thunder have become a downpour that was silenced by the thick walls and windows of the library. One of my students offers half an umbrella and we arrive at the parking lot laughing and only partially damp. She honks as she drives away, and I wave back in the glow of her headlights. As her lights fade, my current life comes into focus.

Despite the heavy rain, I know that I need to stop and see Colton and try to explain the confrontation during lunch, if I can explain it, but when I pull up in front of his house, the deserted look tells me that he isn't home. I should have called first, but I didn't want to, and calling now would smack of checking up on him to see where he is late at night. I don't think that would help the situation. So I start the car again, and leave Colton's dark house behind while trying to shake off the gloom that the blank windows have settled over my shoulders. After parking the car and letting myself into the house, I make two cups of herbal tea, because Dad's study light is still on, and if he is awake when I get home on Mondays, I make tea and we talk. He looks up from the Bible commentary he's reading and smiles when he sees me in the study door.

"Back already?"

"Good students."

He stretches and thanks me for the tea.

"Does your back hurt?" I ask.

"A little."

I go around behind him and rub his shoulders. He sighs and rolls his head forward.

"Last night I dreamed I was running," he says. "I just stood up, walked out the door, and ran down the road. It felt good."

His words remind me of the green heron on the sandbar and my childish dreams of flapping away into the blue.

"I dream of flying, you dream of running."

"I used to dream I could fly. Now I'd be happy to walk. Even if I had to use crutches."

"But you dream about running."

"Of course."

I ruffle his hair and walk back around to the front of the desk before picking up my teacup again.

"Saphi seems sad tonight," he says, thumbing the edge of the commentary and making the thin paper rustle in the silence.

"Is that why you're still awake?"

"Your mom would have known what to do and say."

I've never thought of my father as a man lacking the right words to say, since saying the right thing goes with the pastoral territory. Maybe it's more difficult to connect with your own family than with church members. I think about what Saphira said to me on the sandbar. I don't for a second consider telling Dad what she told me—that's not my place—but just as I do when a student writes a crazy, convoluted sentence, I try to nudge Dad in what I hope might be the right direction.

"Maybe you should just talk to her. Maybe she's waiting for that."

He smiles into his tea and shakes his head.

"She's always been secretive. Not like you. I wouldn't know if she was talking with me because she really wanted to or if she was just going through the motions to make me happy. She likes a bit of mystery, I guess. Just like your mother."

His assessment is so far off the mark I'm not sure what to say in reply. Yes, Saphira is secretive, but she keeps her secrets when she thinks keeping her secrets will be good for Saphi, not because she likes "a bit of mystery." And Mom? The only mysterious thing about Mom was that she ditched her fine arts degree program to marry a financially strapped seminary student, and I call that "leaving it all for love" rather than a mystery.

"Saphi looks like Mom, but I don't think she's wired the same way," I say out loud. "Just talk to her."

"I don't want to look like I don't respect her privacy. I'll wait."

I'm being gently told that I am a daughter and sibling, and that Dad will handle this in his own way. He wanted to tell someone how much he missed Mom, but he wasn't looking for advice. I push away the momentary frustration that comes whenever I'm confronted by Dad's passive behavior and firm belief that "all things work together for good for those who love the Lord," even if all things would work together for good a lot faster with a little extra communication. I recognize that a large part of my frustration has less to do with Dad and more to do with the fact that I'm guilty of the same passivity. Nothing is more annoying than seeing someone do the same nutty thing you dislike in your own personality. Stretching my arms over my head, I feign a yawn.

"I need to call Colton before I go to bed."

" 'The tiniest birds, with softest downy breasts, have passion in them and are brave with love,' " Dad says, quoting George Eliot.

"Thank you. I feel so birdlike."

"Fly, little bird. Fly away."

He waves his fingers at me and I laugh. Just as I reach the door, I remember his monthly therapy appointment.

"We have to drive up to St. Louis tomorrow," I remind him.

"I was hoping you'd forget."

"Forgetting isn't in the genes. Neither you nor Mom ever forgot about those childhood shots I kept hoping you wouldn't remember."

"Shoo," Dad says, waving me out and going back to the commentary. I wish I could fool myself into thinking that he's actually getting a sermon rather than going back to worrying about Saphi. Shutting the office door behind me, I look up at the shade covering the hall light. The bodies of summer moths and bugs fill the glass oval. Mad moths attracted to the light and their death.

If Mom were still alive, would Dad tell her he was worried about the choices I am making? Does he sit hunched over a sermon, pretending to work while wishing Mom were here to talk to me? I wonder how much he doesn't say and if it would balance the scales when weighed against the myriad things I store in my mind, but don't express to him.

"I'm making some cocoa. Do you want a cup?"

It was Mom's standard midnight invitation when she and I were the only people left awake in the house.

"What's it like to be in college?" she would ask.

"Probably it's no different than it was when you were in school."

"I don't see you taking those white disco boots with you."

Wrapped in the ratty maroon robe she refused to give up, she would sit across the kitchen table from me, sipping cocoa and making small talk until my present gnawing worry would unexpectedly slip from between my lips.

Dad and I were always close, but it was Mom who bound us together emotionally. I've never even considered telling him about the strange feelings I'm having these days, about my doubts over the direction my life has taken, about how the future frightens me.

A tardy moth, forgetful of the proper season for his kind, flutters against the hall light, beating himself senseless against the glass shade. The hallway would be brighter without the dim cloud of lifeless wings. I toy with the idea of getting out the stepladder from the kitchen and cleaning the shade, then shrug and dig my cell phone out of my bag.

Colton answers on the fifth ring, just as I am about to hang up.

"Hi, it's me," I say, even though I know he has caller ID.

"Hi there. It's late. Is everything all right?"

I glance at the clock. It is late. Eleven thirty.

"I'm sorry. I should have looked at the time. I just got home and didn't know how late it was."

"It's okay."

I hold my breath. Perhaps I'm waiting to see if he will tell me where he was this evening.

"You didn't stop by after your class," he says.

"I did. You weren't home."

"No."

"It looked like you were gone."

"I was here all evening. Did you stop by the wrong house?"

The last is said teasingly, but somehow I know he's lying. I look up at the moth-infested light shade and wonder if I should call him on the lie or accept it as . . . something. Perhaps a small punishment, perhaps nothing more than a bit of turnabout-is-fair-play. Perhaps both, since Colton is adept at using small conversational reversals to his advantage. It's not something I've had directed toward me during our relationship, but I've seen him employ the reversals with his mother or a particularly obnoxious client when it suits his mood.

"Perhaps you had the wrong phone number?"

"Is it possible you had the time incorrect?"

"I believe you said seven o'clock."

Little reversals that shift the weight of proof to the other person and change the foundation under her feet from solid rock to sand. I wonder if I should call him on it, then close my eyes and blank out the crowded light shade.

"I . . . Are we having dinner with your parents tomorrow?"

"It's Tuesday."

"I know it's Tuesday tomorrow."

"Do you not want to go?"

"No, that's not what I meant. I was just asking."

"We always have dinner at their place on Tuesday."

"I know."

"If you don't want to go—"

"No, no. I want to go. I just . . . I want to go."

I hear him breathing through the phone.

"I'd better get back to bed," he says.

"I'm sorry I woke you up."

It comes out with just the smallest twinge of sarcasm, since I know he wasn't asleep.

"No problem."

He says it with the smallest hint of acknowledgment of my sarcasm.

"I'll see you tomorrow."

"Okay."

After he hangs up, the silence hums in my ear like a discontented buzzing of a bee kept from a perfect flower. The clock in the hallway, which spends most of its mechanical life being ignored, looms large in the silence as it loudly ticks off the seconds. Dropping the phone into my bag, I go to the kitchen for the stepladder. I'm tightening the screws around the clean lamp shade when from behind the closed door of his office, I hear Dad clear his throat.

"Your mom would have known what to say."

I remember the white line of Saphi's part when she was dusting river sand from her hair. I'm not Mom and I don't know what to say to bring Saphi to the kitchen table to talk over cocoa, but after climbing the stairs, I tap on Saphi's closed door. No one answers, and an experimental twist of the knob tells me the door is locked.

———

Tuesday morning is hazy as humid air collects in the wrinkles and hollows of the fields, lying still with the quietness that captures the river valley before a cold front moves in. The haze reminds me of summer days when I would walk to work with Dad and spend the morning lying on the teeter-totter in the little playground behind the church, looking up through the oak leaves.

By the time Dad and I get home from St. Louis, I can feel the first breath of wind coming in from the north. As I pull the minivan into the driveway, I see Saphira kneeling in the dirt of the flower bed that disguises the crawl-space lattice of the front porch. I glance at Dad. The therapy session and checkup went well, but he is usually exhausted and a little frayed around the edges after the trip to St. Louis. Although he says he "feels like a boiled noodle" after the therapy session, I think the fraying comes more from whatever memories must be called up by being forced to physically grapple with the life he has lived since he first woke to a world without Mom.

"Saphi seems to have taken up gardening," he says.

Saphira looks up and waves at us. She has dirt on her nose.

"She looks like your mother, doesn't she?"

I'm busy hooking up the ramp, so I don't look over at Saphi.

"I guess," I say, pretending I didn't notice the resemblance myself yesterday afternoon.

After helping me slide the ramp back into the van, Dad wheels himself up the sidewalk. I shut the van door and rest my forehead against the cool glass before following him. Standing beside Dad's chair, I look down and see a small variegated daphne shrub that has been hacked at and then yanked up by the roots. Its leaves are already wilting.

"Look what I bought!" Saphi calls from where she is digging.

Surrounding her are loads of bright chrysanthemums. Gold, orange, purple, and sunshine yellow—the colors of fall. She's dug up the entire bed of flowering shrubs and grasses that Mom planted over the years. Even the butterfly drinking stone has been removed and sits among the pathetic remnants of the garden.

"I thought it was time for a change, and these were so pretty down at the grocery store. I borrowed your car, Augustina. Hope you don't mind."

I shake my head and she goes back to digging. I look down at Dad's face. The lines radiating outward from the edges of his eyes are deeper than usual. He swallows, and I know he's remembering an afternoon spent chiseling the shallow drinking pool out of the flat rock and the way Mom laughed when she said, "I'll put this in the sunshine among the thyme." The thyme that lies in clumps three feet away from Saphi's vigorous shovel.

She stops digging and a worried frown begins to pull her forehead down over her eyes.

"Is—?"

"It's beautiful, Saphi," Dad says. "What a great idea to plant autumn flowers. Let me get changed and I'll help you. Well, I'll try, anyway."

He slaps the wheel of his chair and laughs a little. Saphi laughs back and starts to lay her shovel down.

"Great! I'll help you get up the ramp."

"No, I'm fine. Keep working. I'll be out in a minute. Just a minute. I'll be back."

"I'll be here."

She lunges back into shoveling the garden bed and begins to sing the Bach chorus. I look away from Dad's retreating figure and back down at the destroyed daphne. Can't she hear the tears in his voice? How selfish and thoughtless does a person have to be in order to make the rest of the world constantly dance the hornpipe of going along to get along?

"It's like the mother-of-pearl box," Saphi says.

"Why?"

"It's not the same without Mom. I think maybe it's better to change everything. Better than keeping her things around as a kind of shrine."

I nudge the daphne with a toe and feel a deep sadness flood my chest. I swallow the flood to keep it inside.

"Maybe it's better to not make those kinds of decisions for other people. Maybe they'd like to be allowed an opinion or two first."

She throws the shovel onto the ground, just missing a flat of dark burgundy mums. Something about her immediate anger over my quiet words tells me that she has been having doubts about what she is doing since she started digging. She's been worrying about my reaction—no, about *Dad's* reaction—with every shovelful of dirt and ripped-out plant. She tears off her dirty gloves and drops them onto the shovel.

"Things have to move on. Why does nothing ever change around here?"

"Everything has changed. You have to be willing to see the changes."

"Nothing has changed. No one has changed."

Jamming my hands deep into the pockets of my jeans, I try to find something that will argue my point, but nothing swims to the surface.

"It's only a garden," she says.

I lift a wilted branch of daphne with my foot.

"I bought this for Mom as an early Mother's Day present before she died, during spring break my senior year of college. We planted it together. It has memories for me that I care about. I'll always have those memories in my head, but I would have chosen to keep the physical reminder if someone had asked me what I wanted."

Saphi bends down and grabs the shovel.

"Fine. I'll replant it."

"Do you see that thyme?" I ask, ignoring the fact that the daphne can't be replanted.

"What?"

"The herb lying all over the grass in front of you. Mom planted that for the butterflies, and that rock over there was a butterfly pool."

"I was going to put it back."

"Dad made that butterfly pool for Mom. She set it there in the thyme because the butterflies like the thyme flowers and she thought they should have something to drink with their food."

"So I'll put the plants back, too."

The flood breaks the dam I threw up to hold it back.

"The funny thing about mums is that they flower only once a year. The rest of the time they look like shit."

"Augustina."

Dad's voice hits me like a slap in the face. He's wheeled out of the house and is at the top of the wheelchair ramp.

"Watch what you're saying," he says.

"It's all about appearances, isn't it?"

Like the wind and driving rain that accompany a summer thunderstorm and send the Mississippi over its banks, my childish emotions of anger, petulance, and unfairness threaten to overwhelm me. This isn't just about Saphi coming home and changing everything; this is about six years of living with a smile on my face while watching all the little thoughts and ideas that come into my head. Making sure that all the little thoughts and ideas are sanitized before they are expressed.

"It's all about appearances," I say again.

Chapter 9

Silence follows my words. Dad picks at a thread on the hem of his shirt, and I know he isn't going to respond. I feel small and silly in the silence. Old habits of smoothing things over die hard.

"I—" I begin, words of apology on my lips.

"Why don't you go change and help us with this truckload of mums," Dad says.

Saphira has turned away from me and is pulling on her gloves. I force a smile for Dad.

"I have to go to the Morleys' tonight."

"But not for several hours."

"We're going early."

Saphi laughs. It's a rude little sarcastic laugh, and my desire to wipe out what just happened dies.

"Is something funny?" Dad asks her.

"Just something ticklish in my glove."

"Watch out for centipedes," I say. "Sometimes, when you

leave your gloves on the ground, they crawl inside. Then when you put your gloves on, they bite you."

She looks down at the gloves still in her hand.

"Centipedes?" Dad asks.

"Maybe they're just millipedes. Millipedes don't bite, but I can't tell the difference between the two. I'd better go."

He frowns at me, and I can see the frustration he let shine through the other day in the kitchen when Saphi and I were acting like spoiled children. We tried to hide our behavior that day. I'm sick of hiding.

"Are you going to the Morleys' like that?" he asks.

I look down at my faded jeans and the favorite sweater with the small raveling hole near the hem.

"It's casual night," I say.

"Smile," Mrs. Watson said to me. *"Smile and you'll bring happiness to others and to yourself."*

I was eleven and we'd just buried Beaver under the redbud tree in the backyard. Mrs. Watson didn't know that—she would never have been deliberately cruel to a child who had just lost her best friend—but I desperately wanted to lash out at her smiling face and scream about the hurt inside of me. Good manners, instilled in me by years of training to be polite and respectful to adults, kept me from saying anything. I just ran away.

Walking home from church with Dad, I pulled myself together enough to ask, "Is it good to hide when you're unhappy so that other people won't be unhappy, too?"

Dad walked a few steps farther along the cracked sidewalk. He always avoided stepping on the cracks. It was a game to him, one that he had taught me at an early age when we would walk downtown for a dish of ice cream, and I think he played it unconsciously every time he walked from the house to the church and back.

"Not in our family. You don't have to hide when you're un-happy or sad or even angry. You don't want to say angry things you don't mean, but you don't hide your emotions with your family."

––––––––

I grip the steering wheel of my car. I've been driving aimlessly along the county roads for the last few hours. My unconscious mind notices the reds and browns of the oak leaves, the deep, clear blue of the October sky, the red, yellow, and orange leaves still clinging to the maples and lighting up the tree lines with fire. Virginia creeper and poison ivy add their touches of scarlet and orange to the tree trunks and peep out from among the cedars clinging to the rocky ledges beside the road. My unconscious mind registers the beauty of the tree lines and fields and rocky ledges, but my conscious mind plays the image of Dad picking at the thread in his shirt over and over; it listens to the silence of his refusal to talk about the garden or Saphi's behavior since she came home. If we paste on a happy face, then Saphira will be happy, and maybe this time she won't pack up and leave without bothering to say good-bye. Turn the other cheek and get slapped again, and maybe after your enemy slaps you twice he will recognize the error of his bullying ways and not bother to hit you in the stomach. Never mind the fact that you're squished flat in front of the door and have "welcome" stamped on your face.

So much for honesty in the family.

After driving aimlessly in mind and body, I arrive at Colton's front door about five minutes past our usual departure time. I leave the car running and knock on his door.

"—here now," Colton is saying into the phone as he opens the door.

Hi, I mouth.

He gives me a big smile and kisses me, holding the phone away from his ear.

Mom, he mouths back, pointing at the phone and rolling his eyes.

I grin and some of my anger slips away in the wake of his smile.

———

Colton and I met for the first time during the insurance dispute after the wreck. The pickup driver's insurance company was arguing that it didn't have to pay damages because of old tires on the pickup—it hadn't been properly maintained, the driver must have known it might hydroplane in heavy rain, thus the company wasn't liable. Twenty-two years old, overwhelmed by continual trips to St. Louis to be with Dad and by Saphira's hostility, I grabbed the first attorney's name from the phone book. When I walked into the office, Colton stood up from behind his desk and he smiled. His smile made me feel calm for the first time in weeks. He could have told me his boss didn't know insurance from Ensure, and I still wouldn't have shopped around just because of that smile. Colton said nothing of the kind. Instead he handled everything with calm efficiency. I was happy to turn the whole mess over to him. Well, ostensibly to his boss, but Colton was the one who called me to say the insurance company had caved in to pressure. No insurance company wants to be known as withholding money from a grieving pastor's family. It's not good press.

Three years later, Colton and I literally bumped into each other in the grocery store.

"I'm sorry," he said.

"Excuse me," I said.

We smiled over the tangled carts, and I recognized the smile immediately by the warm, calm feeling that came over me. The man behind the smile had put on a little weight and the hair over his ears was threaded with early gray, so I might not have recognized him in passing, but his smile was unforgettable.

He leaned on his shopping cart.

"Augustina, right?"

"Yes."

"Would you have dinner with me, Augustina?"

And I said yes again.

———————

"She wanted to know why we hadn't left yet," Colton says as he ends the call with his mother. Reaching out, he pokes a finger through the frayed hole in my sweater. "Slumming tonight?"

A twinge of guilty conscience over my appearance causes me to lie.

"I didn't have a chance to change."

He shrugs.

"What?"

"I didn't say anything."

"Is it really that important?"

"No," he says.

"The car's running."

"Let's go then."

I slide into the driver's seat and click the seat belt home, but I don't put the car in gear. He rubs his fingers in the dust on the dashboard.

"You need to clean your car."

"I've been driving on a lot of gravel roads lately."

"Out to the lake?"

"That's one place."

He smudges out a little face he drew in the dust, then sighs.

I wait for him to say more, but he just runs his finger across the dashboard.

"Do you want me to go home and change?"

"We'd be late."

"Do you want me to go home and change anyway?"

"No. I just wish you'd changed before you came."

"So it matters."

"You matter, too. I don't want to be critical."

He rubs his fingers together until the dust coating them is gone.

"All we seem to do lately is fight," he says.

"You call this fighting?"

"In a way. Ever since your sister—"

"Let's not talk about her."

"Why is she so taboo?"

I search for something light and teasing to say.

"Because the topic of my sister sends me into a blind rage and I need to see in order to drive."

He laughs. The laugh is equal parts humor and relief and something I'm not sure I want to define. It smacks of superiority and the self-satisfaction that can be found only in hearing about someone else's problems.

"I really can go home and change."

"Mom would be upset if we were late."

I put the car into gear and wonder if Lorraine always calls around the time we should be leaving to make sure that we've left.

———

My relationship with Colton was nothing like the roller-coaster rides of emotion I experienced after moving in with Tallulah and Kameron my sophomore year at Penn. Part of the emotional ride came from adjusting to living with best friends. That was the fun loop-the-loop part of the ride. The other part came from falling in love with all the wrong people. That was the sickening part that happens when the ride jerks to a halt.

The state of my love life was practically a joke with Tallulah, Kam, and me. "Augustina falls in love and five minutes later he calls to say he can't see her anymore because he was hit by a truck and died last night." It was practically a joke, but not quite, because more often than not, it was true. After one of these "let's be friends" calls, my roommates would take me to the bar and Tallulah would come up with ways to ensure the fickle lover was hit by a genuine truck, while Kam would pat my shoulder as I cried into my beer about the state of love in the world. Thanks to Tallulah's sense of humor and Kam's sympathetic nature, I survived the lurching halts of love's roller coaster.

About a year ago, Tallulah called from Atlanta to tell me she was getting married. I'd just put the phone down when Kam called from New York to cry and say it was the end.

"We'll never be the Three Musketeers again," he said.

"You and Raj have been partners for two years," I said. "You didn't cry about leaving Tallulah and me behind when you made it official with him."

He laughed. "Oh, yeah, I didn't."

Seeing Kam and Tallulah after almost six years was a shock to my system. They were adults. Not that we acted like adults when we snorted at our own jokes while helping Tallulah into her wedding dress, but there was a division between us that felt like three runners on a track who have run neck and neck for miles until one begins to tire and fall behind. Somehow I had fallen behind.

The feeling stayed with me on the lonely flight from Tallulah's hometown of Birmingham, where the wedding had taken place. It stayed with me during the drive from the airport in St. Louis back to Stoic, even though Colton kept up a reasonable amount of small talk about his boss' clients and the gossip from the insular world of a small town seated beside one of the world's largest rivers.

"Did you have a good time?" he asked.

I wasn't sure how to explain what it felt like to be back on the now-unfamiliar roller coaster of emotion. I didn't know how to explain the joy I felt at being free to say the words flowing through my head without having to censor my speech; at being together again with two friends who accepted me as I was and liked me because of, or in spite of, it. Nor could I explain the pain I felt at leaving them and that life behind. It was a gnawing pain in my stomach that I couldn't put a name to but that increased exponentially the closer the car came to Stoic.

"Yes," I said out loud.

"I was thinking," he said. He stopped and wiped one hand down the leg of his jeans before gripping the wheel again. "Maybe we should think about getting married."

I looked over at his profile and I saw a future. Marriage, in-laws, shared problems, cohabitation, possible children, old age, and secret smiles across the table when someone said something that sparked a memory. Secret smiles like I'd seen pass between Tallulah and her new husband; between Kam and Raj. Smiles that signaled the kind of harmony the Three Musketeers had shared and that I hadn't experienced in six agonizingly long years. When Colton asked me to marry him, I didn't feel like I'd just gone around the loop-the-loop. Instead, I came to the rational conclusion that this was the next step for us. The next logical step for my life.

"Is that a proposal?"

"Yes."

"Then I accept."

———

"What do you think I should do about it?" Colton asks.

I'm ripped from my memories and dropped back into the driver's seat of my car, listening about one of his boss's difficult clients as we travel over the river and through the woods to Lorraine's house.

"About the client?"

"Isn't that what we've been talking about?"

He sounds a little petulant.

"I was listening. I'm just thinking it over."

I defend myself quickly to stave off his annoyance and soothe the fevered brow of the beast of contention.

"So what do you think?"

"I don't think it sounds like he wants to sue her. Not really."

Colton shakes his head.

"You're wrong. Dead wrong. Let me explain it again."

I bite my lip and censor the sharp, gouging retort begging to come out. I know by now that when Colton talks about work, he is looking for a kind of mental bolster pillow from me. He knows what he wants to do; he just needs confirmation that he is right before he can proceed. I wonder if Howard shows all his architectural drawings to Lorraine for a similar confirmation. I don't remember Dad looking to Mom for a seal of approval to every action, but maybe Mom's death has skewed my memories until I no longer have an accurate picture of what made up their relationship.

"Do you see now?" Colton asks as I turn into the Morley drive.

"Yes. You're right."

I wish I weren't just saying that.

"I think I'm on the right track," Colton says, nodding to himself.

"Yes."

I pull up the parking brake and shut off the motor. Lorraine's gardens are filled with a variety of fall bloomers and colorful shrubs. The garden was originally planted by a landscaping company, but Lorraine maintains the look while wearing trim garden gloves, rubber boots, and a wide-brimmed hat. When I first saw the garden, I felt awe. I'd never stood in a magazine spread before, and a sudden longing for the rigid order of the perfect garden surrounding the perfect house overwhelmed me. I wanted to be in control for a change, rather than just responding to life.

Shutting the car door, I lean my elbows on the roof. After having driven down the wild county roads earlier today, I find Lorraine's garden oddly sterile in the evening glow of the October sun.

Chapter 10

"A garden is like a government," Mom said as we planted the little plugs of thyme into the cracks between the rock border of her garden. "It should experience a revolution every ten years or so."

"What if the garden is fine the way it is?"

I was thirteen or fourteen and had been roped into a Saturday morning spent gardening rather than lying in Memorial Day splendor down at the newly opened swimming pool. Denise and I were fighting again, so gardening with Mom wasn't much of a sacrifice, even for teenage dignity. I figured Denise would just be prancing around showing off her new belly-button ring to all the boys. While shopping for bikinis, she'd called me pasty and I'd called her pudgy, and we hadn't quite made up yet. Mom had taken one look at my sullen, curled-up form in front of kiddie cartoons and the next thing I knew, I was hauling mulch and fertilizer out of the garden shed out back.

"Nothing stays the same. But you can decide to create the change or enjoy the change, or you can just fight the natural order of things."

I scratched a handful of bonemeal into the soil. The sound of the shifting dirt mixed with the soft *two-whoo-hoo-hoo* of the mourning doves sunning themselves on the power line across the road to create the yearly ritual of an almost too-warm May afternoon. I liked knowing the seasons would come again. I liked knowing I could rely on a too-warm Memorial Day heavy with the scent of peonies and iris. I liked looking across the same fields to the same line of trees every morning.

"I don't like change," I said.

I leaned back on my heels and said the words almost defiantly. Mom pressed the dirt down around a thyme plant that was already showing a bit of purple flower.

"Someday, someone will come along and pull this little plant up," she said. "And that someone will put something new in its place."

"I won't pull it up. It was too much work to plant it."

Mom laughed.

"The first garden I had was a window box of pansies," she said. "And once upon a time, this horrible little toddler decided to pick every pansy I'd planted, roots and all. She gave me a very nice bouquet, even if it was a bit dirty."

She raised her eyebrows at me.

"Who, me?"

"You've got dirt on your nose."

———

Standing in Lorraine's garden digesting a painful dinner in the waning light of October, I reach up and rub my nose. Dad said that Saphira looks like Mom, but I've never considered that the similarity goes deeper than appearances. Despite my desire to cling to memories and keep things the way Mom always kept them, necessity has dictated changes to things, like the height of the kitchen sink and the loss of a favorite rug. I've always regretted those changes and felt they were a small piece of my past that was lost forever, but Gail Fletcher would have embraced those changes as a brand-new adventure. The garden was Mom's garden, and although I'm still angry that Saphi charged forth with shovel in hand without bothering to ask the rest of us, I have to admit that Mom would have been down on her knees digging up the thyme right along with Saphi. She might not have dug up the daphne, but that would have been out of love for me and my gift to her rather than a desire to keep things the same.

I hear footsteps behind me and tense as I recognize Colton's tread. I'm not ready to talk to him yet.

Dinner this evening was an abysmal, painful affair from the moment Lorraine opened the door and said simply, "You're late and the food is ruined." And that promising beginning was the highlight of the evening.

"I'm sorry, Mom," Colton said to Lorraine. "Augustina had something come up."

"Well . . ."

Trailing off, Lorraine looked down at my sweater and missed the frustrated look I gave Colton. While the blame was definitely mine, a white lie would have been appreciated.

"You must have caught your sweater on something."

Lorraine said it in a tone of voice that implied self-destruction might be the proper path for my sweater to pursue unless it was determined to be a continued source of offense to the world in general.

"Yes. A while back."

Turning away from me, I could hear her *tsk* a bit through her teeth as she returned to the kitchen. Glancing down at the old sweater, faded jeans, and ancient Led Zeppelin concert T-shirt I'd rescued from Dad's ragbag, I realized exactly how I must look to the Morleys. To Colton. A profound sense of embarrassment rose up from my stomach to my cheeks. My behavior wasn't so far off from my sister's. By not dressing for dinner, I trampled a sacred garden of tradition and asked Colton and his parents to accept me and love me for who I am rather than what I look like or how I behave. In fairy tales, the hero is loved for himself or herself, despite appearances. In real life, fairy tales don't exist.

Howard gave me a glass of ginger ale and brushed my cheek with his.

"Just keep your head down and the shields up," he whispered in my ear. Perhaps I imagined it, but his retreating smile seemed commiserating, one poor soul to another.

"This beef burgundy is perfect for a chilly evening," Lorraine said after we had sat down to the table. "I've printed up the recipe for you so you can perfect it on your own."

A breath of air, stirred by the heater or dissatisfied ghosts, played with the candles and twisted their bright flames to one side and then the other.

"Augustina doesn't cook," Colton said.

My fork paused halfway to my mouth as my world halted in midspin, and I waited for Colton to spill out the story about the recipe box's current location in my closet. He sipped Howard's latest vintage and smiled at me. The smile didn't calm me or make me happy in any way. While his comment about my being late could have been simple honesty, this was unnecessary cruelty served up with a twist of revenge. I had a sudden sympathy with Saphira as she tossed down the shovel. *"Things have to move on. Why does nothing ever change around here?"*

"You don't cook?" Lorraine asked. "What do you feed your father?"

I looked away from Colton's smile and into Lorraine's puzzled face.

"Dad does a lot of the cooking."

"That poor man."

Her look of infinite sadness confused me. Something about its quality wasn't right, and it clashed so horribly with my memory of the day Dad declared that food was his new province. *"Gusti, from now on, I'm doing the cooking."*

"Mine is that bad, eh?" I had teased.

"I feel useless. You're doing everything, but even sitting down I can stir a pot and light the stove."

"He said—" I began, trying to explain the true situation to Lorraine.

"We all—everyone—sympathizes with you and your difficulties," she interrupted. "But I think someone needs to point out that you have a responsibility."

"For?"

"For your father, of course. And yourself. Howard and I have talked about this quite a bit."

I glanced down the table in Howard's direction. He refused to look at me, instead tilting the bottle of wine up to the candlelight before pushing his chair back from the table.

"It looks to me as though we're going to need another bottle of wine."

"You'll be starting a new life with Colton," Lorraine continued, dragging my attention back to her. "Your responsibility and duty will be to him after you're married."

Almost before my eyes, it seemed as though Colton the adult became Colton the pampered golden child, the cosseted darling of his proud mama. A cosseted darling who was studiously avoiding looking at me and pretending that his mother wasn't talking about him or me or our future in any way.

"I think you should consider moving your father out of that house. Perhaps into an assisted-living facility or at least a ground-floor condo, where he'll be able to care for himself more easily. Living in that two-story house just isn't practical. It's almost—and I hesitate to say this, you understand—but it's almost as though you were clinging to the past."

If I could have formulated an answer, I wouldn't have had the chance to voice it before Howard bounded back up the basement stairs.

"How about some more wine?" he asked.

Colton stood up and reached for the corkscrew with pathetic eagerness.

"Here, Dad, let me help you."

For the first time in history, I drank a large glass of Howard's hobby. He has a future as a professional vintner if he ever decides to abandon architecture.

Colton helped Lorraine and me with the dishes, almost as if he were afraid to leave us alone together. He didn't need to worry. I didn't have any words left to give—for good or ill.

"I'm sorry," Lorraine said, when Colton deemed it safe to retreat to the basement for a brew and sports on Howard's wide-screen television. "I'm sorry to have brought up your family during dinner, but . . ."

There is always a "but" contained in Lorraine's apologies. I've learned to expect it. For Lorraine, an apology is a chance to restate her grievance with you, and the best thing to do is grit your teeth and prepare yourself to hear about your shortcomings a second time.

"... you have to admit that it would be best for you and Colton if your father were in the care of professionals."

This was not the rehashing of my faults I had been expecting. I leaned back against the counter and gripped the demitasse of espresso in both hands.

"Have you and Colton talked about this?" I asked.

Lorraine's lips thinned a fraction, but nothing in her manner confirmed my fears or alleviated them.

"Colton would never force you to make a choice, but if you love him ..."

Her voice still echoing in my head, I escaped to the great outdoors.

Now, standing in Lorraine's garden in the fading light of an October Tuesday, I contemplate the perfect borders outlined in French curlicues of wrought iron. The riot of flowers contrasts harshly with the immaculately conceived lawn where a dandelion would never dare to plant a seed. My mind seeks a pattern, a bit of literary symbolism between the garden and its owner, and the result strikes me as almost amusing.

The world sees only the pristine side of Lorraine, never the riot of hurtful words. Her coffee klatch would never understand why I would feel reserved around her, even angry. Her hairstylist, the recipient of countless hefty tips, would judge me a complete lunatic if I were to say Lorraine carried a streak of cruelty in her breast that grew as wildly as the late-blooming roses. My smile fades as I think about Mom on her knees among the thyme.

"A garden needs a revolution every ten years or so."

Despite the riot and the green lawns, Lorraine's garden never changes. Why did I ever want the perfect security of unchanging serenity?

I hear footsteps behind me and tense as I recognize Colton's tread. The tension is replaced by surprise when it's Howard who clears his throat and lays a hand on my shoulder. I've never noticed much similarity—physical similarity—between Howard and Colton, but I've never relied on hearing alone to tell the difference between them.

"It's a nice garden," he says.

I'm not willing to share my inner philosophical ramblings about gardens and their caretakers with anyone close enough to Lorraine to mention it, so I confine my reaction to a nod and a horticultural observation.

"I like the dwarf cypress in the corner. Do you know the variety?"

He shakes his head and smiles. Lifting his hand from my shoulder, he points toward a patch of goldenrod.

"I know that grows along the ditches, but other than that . . . I pretty much leave the garden up to Lorraine. You'll have to ask her."

"I'll do that."

"Tonight . . ."

Howard begins to say something; then he trails off and rubs his upper lip with an index finger while struggling for some deep well of wisdom. I can tell that the subject has changed from plants and that Howard is trying to find the words to express the reason he came out into the garden to stand beside me.

"Sometimes Colton's mother . . ."

This sentence is equally aborted. I consider stepping in and relieving him of his conscientious burden. After all, he isn't the one who told me that marriage to his son meant I should bundle my family into a closet where no one will have to be embarrassed by them.

"Lorraine is a dynamic woman," Howard says.

I focus on the little cypress. I think it might have bagworm.

"She wants to make sure everything is perfect, and some-times . . ."

The conversation is becoming painful for both of us.

"It's—" I begin.

"You get used to it," he interrupts. "You get used to it."

The words echo painfully in my mind. Colton's voice and Howard's voice blending together to tell me that I, too, will some-day know the rules and abide by them if I want to breathe the same air as Lorraine, if I want to be a part of this family.

"Thank you, Howard," I say, without a single trace of irony. "That clears some things up for me."

Chapter 11

"Do you agree with Lorraine about putting Dad into a nursing home?"

Beneath my chilled fingers, I can feel the vibration of the motor as it thrums through the steering wheel. We're sitting in Colton's driveway, the light from my car's low beams shining back onto us from the white door of his garage. The reflected glow turns Colton's face into a smooth marble sculpture with carved shadow features.

"Not a nursing home. An assisted-living facility."

"Is there a difference?"

Colton has been to my house. He has listened to Dad's jazz records and laughed over meals. I always knew that Colton wouldn't want to move into the same house with my father, but somehow, some way, I thought we would work something out. Perhaps by buying one of the bungalows nearby. A Craftsman-style house with my own garden and porch swing all within walking distance of my childhood home and Dad. As I said to Lorraine, Warren Fletcher isn't an invalid by any stretch of the imagination. Sure, sometimes he needs help, but he's not lying in bed babbling nonsense and being fed thickened gruel to keep him from choking. Nor am I as totally alone as Lorraine likes to make it sound. Church members drop in "to visit" when they know I'll be gone for a day, and Jackson Dover actually *moved* in and slept on the sofa bed while I was in Alabama for Tallulah's wedding. Then there's a weekly visit from a nurse and a quick-response button on a strap around Dad's neck that he can press in an emergency and bring fire trucks and an ambulance to our door in a matter of minutes. I know: We hit it by mistake once.

Warren Fletcher is part of a small community of caregivers, and he probably would be slightly relieved to have more time to himself. So I don't think it's surprising that I thought I could keep a foot in both worlds: one world that would allow my father the dignity of his independence and another that would allow me a future.

Looking at Colton's marble face, I feel betrayed.

Colton has been to my house, and never once did I imagine that he was quietly plotting ways to remove my father from the picture. I'm not sure I believe it even now. Things are not always a case of like mother, like son.

"Is there a difference?" I ask again. "Between a nursing home and an assisted-living facility?"

"Of course there's a difference," Colton says.

"So you agree with your mother that Dad should be moved to an assisted-living facility?"

His eyes are dark in the reflected light. I wet my lips with my tongue. The lower one has cracked, thanks to the dry, warm air from the defroster I used all the way home to keep the windshield from fogging in the humid autumn night. I pull my lower lip into my mouth and taste blood. Colton sighs.

"Everything is fine right now," he says.

"Right now?"

"Well, we have a future to consider. I know you want to go back for your master's degree. Then there's the possibility of kids. It just starts to look complicated after a while."

Children seem more an improbability than a possibility simply by virtue of my not ever taking future images of myself far enough into the future where I might see myself dandling some infant on my knees. But going back to school is different. Isn't that what I dream about every Wednesday and Friday as I sit in the middle of those old buildings on the St. Louis University campus and look at them stretching up to the sky?

"I can go back to school without moving Dad into an assisted-living facility."

"Then why don't you?"

I open my mouth to make an argument, but the argument doesn't appear.

"Have you ever talked to your father about what he wants?" Colton asks in the silence of my confusion.

Have I asked? I've been so busy just trying to keep everything afloat that it never even occurred to me to ask Dad what he wanted. He never said he had a different plan for himself, but would he? The fingers gripped around my steering wheel seem to belong to someone else as my mind whirls away on a wind of threatening—frightening—possibility. Colton lays his cool, dry hand over mine where it's clenched around the wheel in an effort to keep me from blowing away.

"Do you want to come inside? For a cup of coffee or something?" he asks.

"I . . . I have to go to St. Louis tomorrow. It's late. I probably should get some sleep. It's a long drive."

The words come out in a flood of excuses. Going inside with Colton might mean spending the night, and right now I can't imagine lying next to and holding the man who has spent the last few hours overseeing the destruction of my little world.

"Okay, then." He gives me a quick kiss that I return automatically. "You need some lip balm," he says as he opens the car door.

I weave through Stoic's deserted streets and the flashing yellow traffic lights that advise a late-night caution I'm incapable of giving. My frayed sweater feels uncomfortably warm, yet I'm shivering with a cold lodged deep inside my chest. Pulling my car into the driveway, I turn off the headlights, but continue sitting in the darkness as the warm motor pops and pings in the night air. The light of the nearly full moon catches the bronze and gold chrysanthemums that surround the porch.

"How do you know what flowers you want to plant?" I asked Mom as we finished putting all the little plugs of thyme into the ground that sunny Memorial Day weekend.

"I go to the store and I pick out the prettiest things they have."

I looked down at the wilted, scrubby bits of thyme.

"Beauty is definitely in the eye of the beholder."

"Smart aleck. Go turn on the water, will you?"

Mom had nearly finished watering the new-planted thyme when I finally worked up the courage to talk about what had been keeping me awake during the long nights since my eighth-grade graduation.

"Things are going to change a lot next year. When I go to high school. Aren't they?"

"Is that a hopeful question or a dread-filled one?"

I shrugged, too embarrassed to express the combination of fear and excitement.

"You'll go to classes and that will feel pretty much the same, but a lot of things will be different and scary," Mom said. "Your grandma swears I cried in my sleep for a week before my freshman year of high school."

"Not when you were awake?"

"Do you cry when you're awake?"

"You weren't really asleep, were you?"

"I'll never tell."

I turned off the water, then watched as Mom nestled the new butterfly drinking pool Dad had made for her in among the little plants.

"You don't like change either, do you?"

She smiled up at me, and for the first time I caught a glimpse of what it was like to be an adult.

"It's not about whether or not you *like* change—it's about how you respond to it."

––––––––

Standing on the front porch, my keys in my hand, I look down on the moonlit mums that have replaced the thyme. The thyme is gone, but the butterfly pool rests in a corner where the sunshine will warm the stone and attract the "flying flowers." Saphira's attack on the garden is no different from my accepting Colton's proposal on the road home from the airport. Both actions were little more than desperate attempts to scale the walls of limbo built by Mom's death; built by a change too big for us to handle.

I miss you, Mom. I'm sorry I yelled at Dad and Saphi.

I unlock the door and step inside, inhaling the familiar smells of mint and chamomile tea mixed with the smell of shelves and shelves of old books that really should be aired and cleaned before they mildew. Underscoring it all, I also recognize the scent of Saphi's shampoo.

"Hi," I say as I nudge my discarded shoes into a straight line.

"Hi."

She's sitting on the couch with her feet tucked up under her. Sitting in the dark and drinking tea.

"Is the water still hot?"

"Probably."

I go into the kitchen and find the tea bags and a mug by the glow of the moon. Somehow the darkness feels safe and warm, not like the harsh glare of an overhead light. I'm not in the mood for shining light on anything, including the kitchen. The water isn't quite hot enough, but it will do. I sit down on the far end of the couch from Saphi and stretch my legs out under the coffee table.

"I tried to replant that shrub, but it didn't work," she says.

"No. It was a goner."

I dip my tea bag a few times, then squeeze it out and set it on this morning's paper, which is still lying neglected on the lamp table.

"I'm sorry," I say. "I'm really sorry that I acted like a shrew this afternoon and said all those things."

"It wasn't fair of me to just dig things up without talking it over."

Warm, silent darkness blends with the sounds of our breathing.

"But when it comes to taming shrews? Petruchio wouldn't have stood a chance with you," she says, a smile in her voice.

"And you needed a good spanking."

In the warm, silent darkness that smells of mint, chamomile, and shampoo, we both grin, our teeth white smears in the pale light streaming in through the window.

"So why are you sitting in the dark?"

"I'm pondering the unponderables."

"Imponderables."

"Whatever. Why did you sit in the car for so long?"

"I don't know. I was tired."

"Have a fight with lover boy?"

I shrug and finish off my tea.

"It was a strange evening," I say. "And I didn't feel like spending the night with him."

"Strange because of . . ." She waves a hand in the direction of the garden. "Or because of something else?"

"I haven't really thought it through yet."

I pull my legs back out from under the coffee table and start to stand up.

"Do you want some more tea, little sister?"

"Do you know, I thought you and Grady had been having sex for years?" she asks.

"I never did anything with Grady."

"I know. You told me. Was Colton the first?"

Sighing, I sit down again.

"No."

"Thank God. The man's an ass."

"Gee, what does that say about me?"

"That you've been trying to make yourself into somebody you're not. Someone solid and serious and predictable. That you've *made* yourself into that kind of person. I don't even think you know it. But you're not like that."

"No, I'm just a wild child."

"I'm serious, Gusti. You can't change who you are. You bottle it all up and then it explodes out in little bursts."

"Maybe I just think you're really, really annoying and the bursts are all your fault," I say, only half teasing.

"Okay, granted. I'm annoying. But for God's sake . . . you act like a dictator all the time."

"I do? I mean, yeah, when Mom . . . Yeah, I was awful, but good God . . . so were you."

"I know, but this is about you . . . I don't think you even know yourself or what you need or who you are anymore."

"I need to find myself?"

"I'm saying you need to start listening to the voice in your gut instead of the one in your head."

The pain in my stomach, the one that has been a constant, frightening companion since Saphi came home, tilts back its head and howls in the moonlight. I cringe. Saphira has interpreted my silence as anger and she's reached the foot of the stairs when I call her name and stop her.

"Do you ever get a gnawing feeling?" I ask.

She stands silent and still, a square of blue moonlight just touching her feet. The silence between us stretches for so long I begin to wonder if I actually spoke the question or if she's still waiting for me to say something. Then she walks back and sits down on the edge of the couch.

I lay my hand just under my breasts, between my heart and my stomach.

"A gnawing. Right here."

"Yes," she says.

"Like something inside of you is screaming to get out, but you aren't even sure what it is exactly so you have no idea what you want to scream?"

"Yes."

I flop my head onto the back of the couch and stare at the dappled shadows rippling like water on the ceiling.

"I feel like I've got the Big Bang inside of me, waiting to happen, but I don't know what it will do if I ever set it free."

"I'm not sure anyone close to you would notice the difference."

She says it with a smile in her voice, but it's just a response born of long years of teasing, long years of absence, and recent weeks of acrimonious behavior. Even recognizing the words for what they are, I want to lash out. I close my eyes and try to remember the frilly tutti-frutti dress and Mom's voice telling me that, yes, I am my sister's keeper.

"I'm sorry," Saphi says. "It's not something to joke about."

I nod, a forward and backward rolling of my head on the stuffed back of the couch.

"I ran away," she continues when I don't make any other acknowledgment. "And I can't say it did a damn thing."

"You still feel it?"

"Yes."

" 'Liberation is not deliverance,' " I say, quoting Hugo's *Les Miserables*. " 'One gets free from the galleys, but not from the sentence.' "

"Exactly."

"Shit."

I say it softly and regretfully, but she lets loose a small chirp of laughter.

"Did you really think it would be that easy? Just slip into a responsible activity like planning the future and, what do you know, I'm like everyone else and everything is just fine?"

I sit up straight and look at her. She's perched on the edge of the couch—a small bird on the point of flying if it senses danger—her hands in her lap, her face a round, pale reflection of the moon.

"Is that what you think I'm doing?" I ask.

"You think marriage is what a person does to prove they're moving forward in life."

"No, I don't," I lie.

"Yes, you do. You think that marriage has to be like Mom and Dad."

I lied about the moving-forward bit, but this last isn't true. I've never seen a marriage like Warren and Gail Fletcher's.

"They were romantics."

———

"Tell me about when you and Dad met."

Mom's laughter mingled with the sound of the peep frogs in the creek. We were sitting on the porch waiting for the distant thunderstorm and counting the beats between the flashes of lightning and the rumbles of thunder. Looking over at Dad, who sat in the rocking chair we'd pulled out of the living room, Mom laughed again.

"He was a mad marathon man," she said. "And he ran me down."

"I was walking," Dad protested.

"He ran me down. I was on my way to my painting class and I'd just bought this tube of genuine cerulean blue—"

"And it was expensive," I said, supplying the next part.

"Very expensive. Not a fake cerulean blue, but the real thing. He ran into me and stepped—"

"And it went everywhere."

"You're getting ahead of the story," Mom said.

"Somehow," Dad's voice said from the darkness, "I have the impression that history is going to be revised and not in my favor."

"I still have the shirt to prove it," Mom said, and some current of shared memory passed between them. She looked down at me. "There I sat on the sidewalk with my cerulean blue all over my new shoes. Your father pulled off his T-shirt and tried to wipe it off. I fell in love with the top of his head."

———

"They were romantics," I say. "Mom told me the story of how they met lots of times."

I scrunch my shoulders into the couch and let my head flop back again so I can see the shadows on the ceiling. The moon has risen higher since I came home, and the shadows are reaching for the opposite wall.

"I wasn't talking about how they met," she says. "I was talking about their marriage."

"They were happy. They loved each other."

"I'm sure they *did.*"

Something about her final emphasis bothers me. I roll my head toward her.

"What are you getting at?"

"Nothing. I just . . ."

"You just what?"

She stands up in a rush of white cotton and fakes a yawn too sudden for sleepiness.

"I'm going to bed."

A little confused, I watch her as she walks to the foot of the stairs. She pauses, then turns to me.

"I love you, Gusti. If you figure out how to make the gnawing go away . . ."

"I'll let you know how to banish it forever."

"I'm not sure what I'd do without the pain," she says, the words carrying a bitter tang across the space of hardwood floor that separates us. "I've gotten used to it."

The day Beaver died, I felt like someone had opened me up and scooped out all my insides, filled the hole with sawdust, and sewed me up again. Only the someone had left a needle inside that hurt whenever I moved or had a thought. I was a nearly grown-up (to my mind) eleven, but I stayed in the kitchen with Mom instead of going upstairs to do my homework at the little desk in front of the east window. I loved daydreaming while watching the crows and wild turkeys pick over Jackson's field, but today I didn't want to be alone.

"I feel so heavy," I said to Mom. "It hurts so much inside."

Her movements were slow and tired as she cut up the carrots for stew.

"I know. I feel like that, too."

I knew adults had emotions, but sometimes it seemed like all the emotions happened on the inside rather than the outside. Saphi had cried herself to sleep on the living room couch. I had seen Mom and Dad cry when we found Beaver curled up and cold in the bed we'd fixed for him when arthritis had made it impossible for him to climb the stairs. But both Mom and Dad had moved with swift efficiency from grief to the burial procedure, and I wasn't sure they really felt what I was feeling. Somehow, I wanted Mom both to feel as bad as me and, at the same time, to make me feel better. She'd made Saphi feel better by stroking her hair and sitting with her until she fell asleep. But I still felt the needle pain inside of me whenever I moved or thought about Beaver's happy face when I would bounce down the steps every morning.

Now Mom was saying that she felt pain, too. But if she felt like I did, she wouldn't be cutting carrots or making stew. I didn't want to eat ever again.

"Losing someone hurts," she said.

"Beaver wasn't just someone, he was my friend."

"It hurts," she said again, ignoring my interruption. "But eventually it will hurt less and you'll be able to think about Beaver without any pain."

I knew she was lying. I would never get used to the pain.

————

I watch Saphira climb the stairs. My cracked lip is bleeding. I release it from my teeth and grab a tissue to catch the blood before it lands on my sweater. Despite the hole that was the object of so much contention this evening, I still love this sweater.

I don't want to learn how to live with the gnawing in my stomach. I don't want to get used to living this way. Tissue pressed to my lip, I watch the shadows swirl and dance on the autumn wind.

Chapter 12

"I'm in love," Taylor announces.

We're sitting under the rustling, drying leaves of an oak tree just outside one of St. Louis University's cafeterias. Taylor's Lab mix has his damp lips spread over my bare feet. I brought him a dog biscuit and he responded with undying adoration.

" 'My creed is Love and you are its only tenet.' "

"What?" Taylor asks.

"John Keats."

"Keats? This guy?" He taps the cover of his British literature anthology.

"That guy. One of his letters to the love of his life, Fanny Brawne. It didn't work out."

Taylor looks slightly depressed at the news.

"I'll probably end up the same way," he says.

One of the joys—and I use the term loosely—of tutoring is that I am outside the usual circle of people my students interact with. This distance often means I am a kind of spiritual tutor as well as someone who just corrects grammar and aids comprehension with difficult texts. Life can be the same as a difficult text, but while I feel capable of analyzing and understanding the nuances of *The Grapes of Wrath*, the past few weeks I've felt out of my depth when it comes to real life. I don't have any words of wisdom, so I stick to questions.

"Why do you say that?"

"She won't have anything to do with me."

I try hard not to smile. Taylor is a flirt whose most enduring relationship seems to be with his dog. In the two years I've worked with Taylor, I've heard lots of feminine names bandied about, but no one has ever refused to have anything to do with him. The resulting . . . vulnerability is touching.

"Aren't you engaged?" he asks. "It's working out, right?"

I look down at the simple gold band ringed with carved swirls and roses. In the jewelry store, Colton asked to see the diamonds.

"No," I said to both him and the jeweler. "Just something plain. Anything that sticks up will catch on things and be annoying."

Colton asked to see the diamonds anyway, as if looking at them would change my mind. I picked out the carved band that made me think of wild roses along the fence lines, nodding heavy with white flowers in the June sunshine.

When Lorraine saw it, she shrieked. "No diamond? How could you, Colton?"

At the time I stepped into the breach and soothed everyone's ruffled feelings without giving it a lot of thought beyond the ring's being a crime against engagement etiquette. I didn't give a lot of thought to Colton's sulky look of defiance.

"Are you trying to figure out how to get out of it?" Taylor asks.

I realize I'm tapping my pencil against my notebook and that

Taylor's dog has felt my tension and lifted his mouth off my foot. The warm breeze feels cool on the damp spot his lips left behind.

"If you were getting married, would you ask this girl, the one you like, to put her father into a nursing home if she were taking care of him?"

Taylor pushes back slightly at the personal question. I watch the old habit of looking for something to say that will get a laugh war with his newfound vulnerability thanks to a girl not falling at his feet. The vulnerability wins.

"No," he says. "Wouldn't that be like . . . going out with a woman who has a kid, then telling her you won't marry her unless she gives up the kid?"

My pencil tapping slows.

"A little. Not quite, perhaps. What if you thought it was for her own good?"

"Did he say that?" Taylor asks, disgust in the lines around his mouth.

"No," I lie. "Let's take another look at your draft."

"Your lip is bleeding."

I'm dabbing my lip with a wad of paper napkins from the cafeteria when Jennifer shows up thirty-two minutes late.

"I got a D-minus," she announces.

A low throb of pain enters my head at a point just behind my eyes.

She slaps her paper on *Paradise Lost* down in front of me. Picking it up, I turn to the back page and the professor's comments. *Although the early part of this paper is good, you never wrapped up your points and you offered no proof for your claims, just a summary of Milton. In addition, you might consider a refresher course in the basic structure of the written English language.* The first part of the paper is what we worked on last week. I take a quick glance at the last half of the paper.

"You plagiarized CliffsNotes," I say.

"I'm getting a new tutor. This isn't working out."

"Okay."

"That's it? That's all you have to say?"

"I think this is a relationship that has reached its limit."

"I'm breaking up with *you!*"

"And I'm agreeing that it's a good idea."

She grabs up her paper.

"I'll tell all my friends to avoid you."

I look at her and think about the countless times she was late or never showed at all, the countless times she would say, "Can you write that down so I have an example?" and my words would appear verbatim in the paper, the countless thankless hours of listening to her talk about sorority functions and her sorority sisters—

"Please do. I'd appreciate it."

She stomps away and I realize Victor Hugo was wrong. A galley slave really can be freed from both the galley and the sentence by the simple act of someone releasing her from the chains. Ah, freedom. As beautiful as sunshine. I briefly flirt with an imagined conversation where I give Colton back the ring carved with June roses and say—

My conscience recoils from the imaginary scenario as if I were Saint Augustine confronted by the contemplation of sin. The sinful scenario is like . . . picking pears and throwing them to the pigs.

We took away an enormous quantity of pears. . . . Perhaps we ate some of them, but our real pleasure consisted in doing something that was forbidden. The famous pear theft in Saint Augustine's *Confessions.* Probably one of the most well remembered passages by students the world over who have been forced for one reason or another to read Augustine's long litany of the sins that made up his black depravity so wonderfully wiped clean by God. What surprised me when I finally read the *Confessions* in a college Western Civ class was that my father loved them enough to name me Augustina. It just didn't sound like Saint Augustine was all that interested in enjoying life to the fullest. Unlike Dad, Augustine was so caught up in himself and his crimes, he would never have had the mental room for appreciating the blue of the sky or the sight of a heron lifting itself out of the marshes on slow-beating wings. When my parents made their weekly Sunday-evening call to the pay phone in the dorm hallway, I told Dad what I was reading.

"Your namesake," he said, laughing. "It's about time."

"He's strange. Everything is some kind of sin."

"It is. That's what makes redemption so beautiful."

"So Jesus the boy never stole any of the neighbors' fruit? I find that hard to believe."

"Aha! Now you're getting into the whole humanity-of-Christ debate."

And Dad was off. Until Mom broke in and said, "Warren, can we discuss theology sometime when it doesn't cost fifteen cents a minute?"

I can't remember if Mom was laughing when she said that. The words in my memory are a little sharp, a little cutting, a little ... unhappy.

Standing up, I gather my papers into my bag and push the memory away. This morning the rising sun caught me curled up on the couch, where I must have fallen asleep while thinking about all the stories Mom told me as we sat on the porch swing in that long-ago time when my legs stuck straight out in front of me and Mom had to push her toe into the wooden floor to rock us both.

"What happened after Dad squished your paint?" I would ask.

"Well, the next day your father came running after me with a tube of paint he'd bought at the student union store."

"Was it the right paint?" I asked, already knowing the answer.

"No. It was a completely different color of blue, but I never said a word. Then he took me out for coffee and asked me to marry him."

"But you said no."

"I said no. So he bought me coffee every day until I said yes."

It was love at first sight. Mom said so. She just played hard to get for the free coffee. And every time she would say the words "free coffee," she'd look over at Dad (if he was in the room), and they'd smile a secret smile at each other.

Just beyond the top of the steps leading up out of the cafeteria, I stop and rub my aching forehead with chilly damp fingers.

"I fell in love with the top of his head."

"I wasn't talking about how they met. I was talking about their marriage."

"You think marriage is what a person does to prove they're moving forward in life."

"Everything is fine right now, but we have a future to consider."

I don't see the bicycle until it slams into me.

I have a vague impression that bike and rider are lying on the sidewalk next to me. The sky overhead is blue and clear without a single wisp of cloud. Burnished sugar maple leaves float down on the wind. It would be even more beautiful if I could just get some air into my lungs.

"Calm. Slow. Breathe just a little," says a voice beside me.

Milton's Lucifer in the flesh as Jennifer was never able to understand him, as even Milton wasn't able to understand him. Lucifer wasn't golden. He was more of a dark-haired, green-eyed anarchist. Someone who didn't like the totalitarian regime of heaven with all of those trumpets, armies, and daily bowing and scraping before God, the supremely jealous dictator. Here's Lucifer now, telling me to take shallow little breaths. Oxygen returns to my lungs, but the vision of the fallen angel remains. I sit up and groan.

A little crowd of people has gathered, and one of them asks if they should call an ambulance. I shake my head.

"I'm fine. Just winded."

"Are you sure?" Lucifer asks.

"Yes. You can go back to roaming the world looking for souls."

His hands probe my head.

"It was a joke, not a head injury."

He sits back and I notice that his cheek is bleeding.

"You're the mad cyclist."

"You're the pedestrian who stepped into the bike path without looking."

"Did I?"

The knot of people is untying, the strands strolling off to classes where they can blame their lateness on stopping to help an accident victim. My bruised ribs and nearly dislocated hip will become blood splattered on the sidewalk. *Honest, Professor Nelson, it was all over the place.*

"Can you stand up?"

"Yes. You should get your cheek looked at. It might need stitches."

He frowns, touches his face, and looks at the blood on his fingers. The gesture is oddly compelling. I look away and focus on getting to my feet. I can feel bruises, but my bag of books and papers saved me from a broken rib. It hurts to put weight on my left leg, but there's nothing seriously wrong. I'll probably have a mild case of whiplash. The bike is still lying on the curb, my bag lying on the front wheel. I tug at it, but the strap is woven into the spokes. I bend over and unwind the strap. The movement hurts enough to leave me a little dizzy.

"You should go to the health center. You might need X-rays."

I shake my head and hoist the bag's strap to my good shoulder.

"I'm not a student. Just a tutor. Should we exchange something? Insurance? Something?"

"It's up to you."

"I stepped into the bike path. I guess I'd call it even."

He holds out his hand. It's such an old-fashioned, person-to-person thing to do that I just stare at it for a bit before reaching out to shake on our agreement.

"Hang on."

I dig into my bag and hand him the spare paper napkin from the cafeteria that I picked up in case my lip started bleeding again.

"For your face," I say.

He takes it and lays it against his cheekbone.

"How is it?" he asks, taking the napkin away.

"Piratical. Or maybe a brand from God for misdeeds. A butterfly stitch would do it."

He grins, and I suddenly understand why Augustine spent so much time talking about his sins. Bending down, he picks up the bike and rolls it back and forth experimentally. The front wheel squeaks with each revolution.

"Is it broken?" I ask.

"A little bent."

"Will it be hard to fix?"

"It will be fixed before the bruises fade."

I have to extricate myself from this situation. All the thoughts I was having before I landed on the sidewalk are starting to come back, and instead of dealing with them, I want Lucifer to smile and take me to hell with him. Or at least out for coffee.

"Take care," I say.

I turn around and walk away like a good little student of the dull, pompous saint. I turn and walk away from the temptation of stealing some kind of forbidden fruit, even if the fruit is nothing more than waiting for another smile.

Beside me, I hear a squeaking wheel.

"I'm not incapacitated," I say. "I can make it to my car. You don't have to be all solicitous for my well-being."

"Meaning you'd rather I wasn't walking with you?"

"I'd rather you weren't walking with me."

The wheel squeaks once, twice, three times.

"But it's better than having you run me down," I say.

"What's your name?"

"My name is Augustina."

"What do you like to be called?"

Coming to a dead halt, I realize he's picked up on something that no one has ever noticed. I started saying, "My name is Augustina," when I was four, hoping that someone would ask me if I liked my name and give me the opportunity to say that I would really like to be called "George." Why George? Curious George, of course. He always got in trouble and he annoyed the man in the yellow hat.

"George," I say, on impulse.

He nods.

"Glad to meet you, George. I'm Alec."

"Like the guy in *The Black Stallion?*"

"I was a fan of the books, but not the movies. Mickey Rooney as Henry? Come on."

"The horse wasn't right either."

"I know."

I wonder if Alec is his real name or if it is the opposite side of the George equation and just a fictitious name he adopted for his childhood imagination.

Alec looks at me from across the bike and says, "Would you like a cup of coffee?"

I wonder if Alec is his real name, but I think he will always be Lucifer to me since he appeared during a moment of weakness and held out the hand of temptation.

Chapter 13

History repeats itself, or so they say. I read a book once that said family history told and retold as stories tends to breed repetition throughout the generations. An easier explanation might be the same as my using Lorraine's garden as a symbol for her public and private personas. The human mind seeks patterns; therefore a child who has listened to tales of familial foibles and special events is more likely to see those same foibles and events in her own life.

Alec locks his damaged bike to a rack and I insist on buying the coffee. Our steps gravitate toward the church. St. Francis Xavier or College Church, depending on whom you're talking to. We sit on the rim of the fountain just outside the front doors. I tilt my head back and look up at the Gothic spires I envy so much and that are so absent from a Methodist church.

"The church was haunted by the devil," Alec says.

"Like in *The Exorcist*?"

"To a T."

"It still is haunted, I suppose. If Milton had it right about Lucifer's regret."

"All rebellions that fail are characterized as being run by people with nothing on their minds but self-aggrandizement. The winners like to paint the rebels as ultimately realizing the error of their ways but first enduring punishment and regret."

I reach down and touch the surface of the water in the pool surrounding the fountain. A gust of wind scatters water drops onto us, making dark spots on my jeans and leaving diamonds in his hair. The church doors open and a bride and groom—looking impossibly young—step out into the fall sunshine and the flood of cameras and well-wishers.

"What about teen rebellion?" I ask, still watching the couple.

"Especially teen rebellion. Didn't your parents ever say, 'Someday you'll have children of your own, and I hope they're just like you'? First the punishment, then the regret."

"Actually, my parents never said that to me."

"You must not have rebelled."

"I don't think I did. I was a good girl."

He looks away from the couple escaping into their limo and down into my face.

"The good girl. The worst kind of rebel."

Somehow, sitting in the sunshine under the spires of a perhaps-still-bedeviled church, being the worst kind of rebel sounds like a good thing to be. I drink the last cold swallows of coffee in my paper cup.

"Can we go inside?"

"Sure."

As I look up high into the vaulted ceiling of the church's interior, my mind floats on the colored sunlight streaming down into the nave. Despite the remaining guests who have been roped into cleaning up after the wedding, the sheer volume of atmosphere creates an impression of silence and peace.

"If I were the devil, I would never leave this place," I whisper to Alec. "No exorcism could drive me out."

"If you were the devil, you would have run out the door screaming."

I tear my focus away from the crisscross beams overhead and look into his face. His eyes are dark, the pupils wide after the bright sunshine around the fountain.

"Why do you say that?"

He shrugs and looks up to where the dust motes dance on the light.

"Have you ever read Mark Twain?"

"I live on the Mississippi. It's required."

"In *Letters from the Earth*, he wrote about how strange it is that people endow God with emotions humans despise. Like jealousy and being unforgiving. If that's the case, and Satan rebelled against God, wouldn't that make the devil interested in people? Because they dislike the same qualities they attribute to God? And since humans tend to act . . . well, more *human* when they aren't in church, I'd guess that the devil wouldn't be very interested in haunting one."

Standing here in the stained-glass colored light, I can feel doors opening on cobwebbed recesses in my mind that have been unused for years. The doors might be small and insignificant, like the door Alice had to crawl through in order to get out of the shrinking Wonderland house, but I throw them wide open and dance in the light. All those long monologues about heaven and hell, human and divine, that I had with Grady beside the lake resurrect themselves, only this time I'm talking with someone who doesn't want to steer the conversation back to the latest football scores.

"Let me guess. You're getting an MA in psychology, right?" I ask as a way to cover up the excitement that is tinged with more than a little fear.

"Religion and philosophy."

"Steal a lot of pears in your youth?"

"None. I hate pears."

"Me, too."

"Have you seen enough of the church?"

"Eager to get back out into humanity?"

One corner of his mouth kicks up into a smile.

"You think *I'm* the devil?"

I can't stop the laughter that bubbles up in tune with the fountain in the courtyard, but I don't answer his question.

Outside, the angle of sunlight has sharpened, casting longer shadows onto the ground. I can feel every bruise, but I don't want the afternoon to end. Oddly, Alec makes no move to end it, and we walk until we find a grassy spot near a few trees which hasn't been claimed by anyone. Sitting down, he pulls a pipe and a small package of tobacco from his bag.

"Do you mind?" he asks.

"Not as long as you share."

I watch his fingers tamp the leaves.

"I think I'm in the middle of a revolt."

He raises his eyebrows and holds a lighted match to the bowl. Inhaling, he holds in the smoke and hands the pipe to me.

"This is tobacco, right?" I ask.

He laughs on an exhalation of smoke.

"Tobacco. Plain and simple. A pipe might look a little pretentious, but it's cheaper than cigarettes."

"And it's easier to carry around than a hookah."

The smoke, unfamiliar after years of abstinence, makes me cough. I hand Alec back the pipe.

"Will you be the winner or the loser in this revolt?" he asks.

"I don't know yet."

Lying back on the warm grass, looking up through the die-hard leaves and into the blue sky beyond, I feel free to be the win-ner. My cell phone rings, and the feeling of freedom disappears as if the sunshine were blotted out by a cloud.

"I have to take someone to the airport," a voice says in my ear. "I can't make it this afternoon."

Tony's words catch me by surprise. A glance at my watch shows that he and I should be in the middle of a tutoring session that I forgot more thoroughly than he did for a change.

"Leaving early for Thanksgiving break, I suppose," I say, teas-ing him.

"Yeah. *No!* I mean, no. They just have to go . . . somewhere. Home."

"Okay, Tony. See you next week."

"Thanksgiving?" Alec asks.

"Just a naughty boy playing hooky," I say.

"Goodness is overrated."

"Not goodness. Responsibility."

He hands me the pipe, and I attempt a smoke ring. It fails miserably.

"I take that back," I say. "It isn't responsibility that is the prob-lem. It's having someone tell me that what they would like me to do is in my own best interests. In the best interests of everyone. Everyone but them, of course."

"Their joy is your duty."

"Exactly. I also hate pretending to be happy when I'm not."

"The quintessential adult falsehood. Everything is okay. We don't have any problems in this house. If you want problems, you should go knock on the Joneses' front door."

I remember Colton's smugness when I told him that Saphi was driving me crazy. Does being an adult mean that I have to stop admitting that it hurts or face public humiliation? Does it mean I have to play along with the Lorraines of this world who make it impossible to stand up to them because they are adept at keeping a wrought-iron barrier between the public persona and the ugliness inside?

The bowl of the pipe is carved in the shape of a horse's head, with some of the smoke coming out of the horse's nostrils. I hold the bowl into the sunshine to better see the twin curls from the nose of a fiery steed reminiscent of a black horse stranded on a desert island with only a red-haired boy for company.

You don't have to get used to it, a voice deep inside whispers to me.

"If I end the relationship with my fiancé, will that mean I have to sell you my soul?" I ask the smoke as much as I ask Alec.

"No."

"Good."

———

"Once upon a time, there was a little girl who could fly," Mom said as she tucked me in for the night.

I rolled onto my side and tried not to cry. Every spring my elementary school competed with Stoic's other elementary schools in an all-day track-and-field event. I couldn't jump and I lost every sprint, so the PE coach had signed me up for relays.

"Just grab the baton, run as fast as you can, then pass it to the next person," he'd said, clearly hoping that my pathetic ability to run would be compensated for by three other people. In a stroke of inevitability, I dropped the baton.

"Pick it up! Pick it up!" the girl who had passed it to me screamed. "Come on, come on, come on!" said the girl I passed it off to. My relay team had finished last, and one of the girls had managed to whisper, "Fuckup," to me while we watched the other teams receive ribbons and faux medals.

"I can't fly," I said to Mom. "I can't even run."

"It doesn't matter what you do with your legs and arms. What matters is if you can fly up here." She tapped my forehead. "Someday you are going to soar above the world and see how small and how beautiful it can be. Then no one will be able to cage you or call you names."

———

Nothing lasts forever, and the afternoon inevitably ends with an unmystical, completely normal exchange of phone numbers in the parking lot. Driving home, I ache all over, but I know something broke free as I lay on the sidewalk and watched the yellow leaves drift down out of the clear blue sky. Something broke free and rose up on slow-beating wings to skim across the lake waters until no one could catch and cage it ever again.

Dad's car is in the shop, but the minivan is gone when I pull into the driveway. Dad has left a note on the table that says he and Saphi have gone out to "see a man about some new undershirts." Meaning they've gone to the discount store for the necessary bits.

Upstairs, lying on my bed, I put my feet up against the wall. My feet are high above me, up on top of my legs, which are stretched out straight in what I'm sure is some variation on a yoga position if I only knew enough about yoga to pinpoint it. My ankles are thin and bony, prone to twisting on uneven ground. I never could seem to run without hurting myself. Part of the problem might have been the heavy, hard-soled shoes that were all my parents could afford for the requisite PE footwear. Running the track was torture. Trying to fly over the high bar during PE classes covering track-and-field events was a little like running forward on eggshells—waiting for the inevitable twists and catches—then leaping into the air with lead weights tied to my feet.

I stretch one foot toward the window and slide it up. My love of open windows keeps it well-oiled, so it slides up without comment. Alec slipped the pipe and the last of the tobacco into my jacket pocket before I got into my car, almost as if he were making sure we kept a connection and wouldn't forget the afternoon.

I don't think forgetting is possible.

I fill the little horse-head pipe and light it. The vaunted effects of nicotine—the emotional calm, the increased sense of concentration— are lost on me, probably the reason why I never followed in Kameron's and Tallulah's footsteps down the path of nicotine addiction. Even now, I'm only smoking a bit of the remaining tobacco because I want to relive the afternoon and remember what it felt like to soar without the lead weights.

Chapter 14

My soaring slows as I hear the minivan pull into the driveway. The weight of responsibility begins to fill up my shoes and drag my feet back down to solid ground. I catch myself wishing the underwear shopping trip had lasted just a few minutes, a few hours more; then guilt floods in on top of the wish.

What if Lorraine is right about you?

The voice in my head is biting, sarcastic, and nearly audible. I close my eyes and reach for the blue sky and burnished leaves, but all I find in my mind are fear and questions floating down like so much confetti. I've spent so much time just getting through each day, each minute; so much time solving the immediate problems that the future has been nonexistent. Is this what Lorraine and Colton see? I think I'm showing them a person who is eminently capable and has things under her control. What if they see a nearly thirty-year-old woman mired deep in denial?

I reach over my head and set the still-smoldering pipe on the bedside table. The whole afternoon feels like a dream, and if it weren't for the pipe and the bruises, I would probably wonder if I slept the day away and missed going to St. Louis at all.

Saphi knocks on my door. Even if she weren't the only other member of the family who can climb the stairs, I'd know it was her by the distinctive Beethoven's Fifth knock that she adopted after learning to play the opening bit on the piano.

"Hi," she says after I tell her to come in.

I loll my head back over the edge of the bed and look at her upside down. She's wearing one of my sweaters.

"Been closet raiding, I see."

"I don't have any warm clothes."

"Mom's are still in her closet. In boxes. We could open—"

The upside-down Saphi shakes her head.

"No. Can I just borrow yours?"

"Sure."

She sniffs the air.

"I smell a substance known to be forbidden in this house. Didn't you ever learn to use incense?"

"Like that would have fooled Mom and Dad."

"Oh, it did."

"You think?"

I laugh at her surprised expression.

"Every child," I say, "believes that the adults could never guess what basic naughtiness lurks in their hearts."

"I'll be damned." She points to the pipe. "Share?"

Rolling sideways, I pull my knees to my chest and pat the bed with my foot.

"Enjoy. Have a seat."

She settles on the bed and relights the pipe.

"This is beautiful," she says around the smoke, holding the pipe up into the sunlight. "Where'd you get it?"

"The devil."

She looks over at me, then winces in shock.

"My God! What happened to you? You've got bruises all over—"

"The devil ran me down, too. I wasn't watching where I was going."

Pulling on the pipe, she's looking for hidden meanings. I don't enlighten her because I don't want to talk about it. Not yet. Maybe never. I'm afraid that if I talk about it, Saphi will melt my wings and drop me into the ocean, and I'm not ready for that.

"I never would have figured you for the type."

I point my chin toward the pipe in her hand and raise my eyebrows in a question.

"No. The type to consort with the devil."

"And you are?"

She smiles and shakes her head.

"Maybe. More than you anyway."

Autumn cricket song filters in through the window, slow and melodic, playing the harmony for the rhythmic hum of the grasshoppers rubbing their rough legs together.

"How did you meet?" I ask her. "Your husband. Exhusband."

"Flynn. Flynn Macy. I was bartending up in Alaska. He owned the gas station across the street."

"You were in Alaska?"

She nods.

"So why do you need to borrow sweaters?"

"I left everything behind."

"What about the suitcase?"

She smiles. It's tender and rough, like the insect melody.

"Have you seen what's in the suitcase?"

"No."

"Some things are more important than clothes."

The pipe gives up a last gasp of smoke, then goes out. She rolls it between her fingers, then reaches over me to set it on the side table.

"He was kind to me," she says. "And when he found out he had cancer, I married him and moved in. Call it guilt if you like."

"Why would I do that?"

"That's what he said at the last. That I married him out of guilt. After I told him what had happened here, with Mom, all our fighting, Dad crippled up, my leaving . . . After I told him all that, he refused to believe in me anymore."

"So he thought you were just trying to make it up to one invalid by caring for another?"

"Something like that. He just . . . pulled away and wouldn't come back."

"Did you love him?"

She leans her head back against the wall. In the strong light coming through my west window, she looks older. Lines radiate out from her mouth and eyes and blend together to create a face that has seen more life in five years than I have. No, that's not quite right either. She's seen different things than I've seen, done different things than I've done, but we've both seen and done more than we're willing to share.

"I'm not sure I know what being in love means," she says.

The words oddly echo my impression of her that long-ago night on the porch when we talked about her breakup with Chris "I'll do her by summer" What's-his-name. Her eyes are closed and I can't see into her memories and probably prefer not seeing into her memories.

"Me, either."

"You're engaged."

"You were married."

"That's different."

"Is it?"

"Colton doesn't need caring for."

I start to laugh. It isn't a pretty laugh, and it opens up the door to all the things I've shoved into my little internal closet until today.

"Everyone needs caring for. In some way or another. I thought Colton would take care of me."

"You've never needed anyone to take care of you."

At first I think she's joking, but she looks genuinely puzzled.

"How can you say that?" I ask.

"Because you're always there for everybody. Telling everybody what to do."

"Is that how you see me?"

She rolls her head on the wall and looks at me. I think she looks at me for the first time through the eyes of five years of seeing and doing things rather than the eyes of an angry teenage girl packing her things and leaving a sister tyrant and father who had become a visible reminder of a loss she wasn't prepared to deal with. Not just the loss of Mom, but the loss of a way of life.

"I'm not sure anymore."

I stretch my arms over my head and grip the metal bars of my bedstead in clenched fingers. Shadows flit across the ceiling and the last rays of the sun have turned everything to red-gold.

"Why did you leave Flynn?" I ask.

The metal under my fingers has turned warm before she answers.

"I didn't leave him. He asked me to go. But he'd already left me long before he asked."

"And you went?"

"Yes. He cried when he asked me to go. I'd never seen him cry."

I don't think she realizes that her cheeks are wet with her own tears.

"I tried everything, Gusti. To make him understand that I didn't just see him as a replacement for Dad. For my guilt. He wouldn't accept it."

Words are a useful form of communication, but I don't have any words to give my sister. She left in the throes of childish grief, but she's returned carrying a hurt that goes beyond childhood and stretches into forever. Children feel a fast, sharp pain. It hurts intensely, but then life goes on. A boxful of free puppies becomes an exciting prospect a month after the faithful dog is gone, after the mound under the redbud tree has flattened and weedy grasses are beginning to fill in the dirty spot. A child moves on, always sure of her own immortality and the immortality of the people around her. An adult is plagued by mortality and the rush of years that feel like weeks. The creeping calendar with the end of each year signaling another year lost that will never return. Signaling another wasted twelve months. Death is no longer a mere possibility. It is a certainty.

"Do you believe in eternity?" I ask Saphi.

"You mean like heaven?"

"If you like."

"Don't you believe in heaven?"

I squeeze the bars of the bedstead even tighter.

"No."

This is rank heresy. I've never said the word out loud before, but it's a certainty that has been growing inside of me until today, when I lay on my back and watched the leaves fall down and reached out to the pear tree and said, "I am alive. Right now I am alive."

"Shit," Saphi says.

A part of me already regrets the word I said and that I can no longer take back. Once spoken, twice regretted. I know the pain it would cause Dad if he heard it. I know the excuses he would make about faith needing to be tested. But this isn't a matter of faith. This isn't a matter of belief. It's the simple knowledge that this is life, and when it is over, it is over. All that's left is the fallout death leaves behind.

"In a way," Saphi says, "I'm glad he asked me to leave. I don't think I could have sat through another funeral."

"We've been sitting in a funeral for six years," I say, letting go of the metal bars above my head.

———

Everything after the accident was turned upside down. There wasn't any time to think about Mom's death until Saphi and I sat on the hard bench at the funeral home and stared straight ahead as a pastor we'd met in passing talked about Gail Fletcher as if he'd known her. Mom's parents were unable to travel up from Florida, where they were living in a retirement village along with other Michigan emigrants, but they called Saphi and me every night to ask us how we were doing. Grandma Fletcher stayed with us off and on until a few weeks after Dad came home. I remember Grandma Fletcher's drugstore perfume as she sat next to me on the bench and the vaguely familiar pastor droned. The scent had always been mixed with childhood memories of cookies and Thanksgiving turkeys, but now if I happen to catch a whiff of it at Walgreens, my stomach churns and I'm back on the bench sitting straight and still and unmoving between Saphi and Grandma Fletcher. It was at that moment, sitting between my sister and grandma, that I realized Gail

Fletcher was never coming back. I didn't feel any different inside; I just knew something about my world paradigm had shifted. I stopped making plans because plans seemed so futile when your entire life could blink out in a single moment.

After the funeral, the vaguely familiar pastor stopped by to "visit the family" several times. Usually at times that were horrifically inconvenient. I'm sure he heard me screaming, "For God's sake, grow up!" at Saphi once, and Saphi screaming back, "You goddamn self-righteous bitch," just before the doorbell rang and we both froze in place like two people who have just been caught in a photograph. He stopped by to console us and tell us that Gail Fletcher was in a better place, as if being separated from the people you loved could possibly be a better place. Saphi sat beside me on the couch, her arms folded across her chest as the pastor read us passages from the Bible that we could have quoted to him by heart.

"How do you know it's a better place?" Saphi asked him.

He stumbled for a moment, then started in on the Bible verses again.

While he talked and Saphi sulked, I watched a spider build a web among the dried, dead flowers of the lilac shrub outside the window. Her tiny legs caught and attached silk to silk as she worked, forming a spiral net to catch souls, dreams, and fluttering moths.

Gail Fletcher wasn't in a better place. She was gone and I was left behind. Saphi was left behind. Dad was left behind. And the only consoling words coming from the pastor's mouth were that we would be reunited in death in a hazy, far-off better place. Sitting and watching the spider, I thought it all seemed ludicrous and delusional. If the people being consoled in this way actually *believed* they would see their loves on the other side of death, then truly lonely people would stand up, walk into the kitchen, and slit their throats to speed reunion. The pastor was playing with death and banking on our own deep-seated sense of self-preservation to keep us from doing just that. I wanted to ask him what he would do if I took him seriously, but instead I offered him iced tea and stared at him while he talked. When Saphi stood up and said, "Thank you for stopping by, but I have work to do upstairs," and left, I didn't try to stop her.

"She really misses her mother," the pastor said.

I knew he was trying to help. I knew the drill—I even sympathized—but I wanted to scream at him to please leave and couldn't he see that the verb "miss" couldn't even begin to capture the open wound left in Gail Fletcher's place.

"We all miss her," was all I said out loud.

After the plastic-caped sheriff's deputy knocked on our door that rainy night with the news about the accident, a part of me couldn't help waiting for Gail Fletcher to put her key into the lock and open the front door. "I'm home! Did anyone miss me?" Nearly every night I dreamed about her walking through the door, and the resulting flood of relief and joy would be so strong I would wake up only to find a midnight darkness of shadows and reality. I started sleeping on the downstairs couch so I could roll over and check the front door without having to leave my bed to make sure that the sound of the key in the lock had been only a dream.

On the day of the funeral, sitting between Grandma Fletcher and Saphi on the bench and staring at a memorial of flowers and pictures—Mom had designated cremation in my parents' living will—I finally realized that the key was never going to turn in the lock. I didn't cry, but when I stood up, I left part of myself behind, sitting on the bench.

———

"We've been sitting in a funeral for six years," I say to Saphi. "Leaving everything behind."

My hands are sticky with sweat and my fingers are cramped from the death grip I had on the round bars. I clench and unclench my fists to relieve the cramping.

Saphira's silence causes me to look up at her face. The reddish glow from the waning day reflects off my bureau mirror and onto her cheeks, turning her tears to tracks of blood. She slides off the bed without saying a word, and the door clicks shut in her wake.

Chapter 15

The warm feeling of blue sky and golden leaves fades as quickly as the last of the smoke drifts away through my open window. For a few moments, sitting together on my bed, I had a communion with Saphi that I never thought I would have. The gulf between a young woman of twenty and an only-just-out-of-childhood girl of fifteen is immense. Twenty-eight and twenty-three are not so far off. Someday we'll probably forget any years separate us from each other as time compresses with age.

I put my bare feet down onto the chilly hardwood floor and feel my toes curl. The pleasant floating feeling sinks down into the wood and leaves me heavy and tired and knowing that it's long past time for me to call Colton. He should be home from work by now, and if I can catch him before he leaves for his evening run, I might be able to deal the deathblow to this relationship before I add any more guilt to my overflowing cup. Scripturally, cups overflow with blessings or burdens, but, like the crow in *Aesop's Fables*, the afternoon I spent with Alec added a lot of guilty stones to the cup of guilt, and the water level is high.

There's an extension line in Mom and Dad's old bedroom, and I decide to use this instead of the phone downstairs, where I will run the risk of being distracted or having to explain myself to someone who might overhear. The phone in the bedroom is dusty, because I take only an occasional swipe at it with the dust rag on Saturday afternoons. I slide the wooden chair from Mom's sewing desk over by the phone, blow dust off the receiver, then dial Colton's number. At first I think I've missed him; then he picks up.

"Augustina."

I'll never get used to caller ID and the way people on the other end know that it's you before you have a chance to say a word. I don't miss Colton's lack of salutation, either. Sitting in the car with the lights reflecting off his garage door seems like a million years ago to me. A million miles ago. Colton's brusque use of my name tells me that for him less than twenty-four hours have passed.

"I need to talk to you," I say.

I forgo any effort to make things comfortable or pleasant. Something in Colton's voice says that he couldn't care less how my day went, and telling me about his day would expend effort he doesn't wish to waste. Even if I were to say that I spent my afternoon being seduced by the devil, he'd probably shrug and say, "That's nice. Why are you calling?"

"Could it wait?" he asks.

"Not really."

I can see the frown line on his forehead as he thinks about what I've said. He may even be glancing at the clock and trying to work me into a busy schedule.

"I can't right now," he says after the silence has stretched a little thin. "And I'm having dinner with some clients of the agency, so I'll be out late."

I control the frustrated sigh and think of alternatives.

"Tomorrow? Lunch?"

"I'm sorry. And tomorrow night I'm taking my parents out for dinner."

Colton has gone out with his parents without me on a number of occasions since our engagement, but his voice sounds exclusionary rather than matter-of-fact when he mentions this particular dinner. I realize that Colton knows what I want to say to him. I could even say it over the phone right now and he would probably just tell me to drop the ring into an envelope and mail it to the office, care of Colton Morley. I could say it now, but I won't. A relationship of nearly three years deserves a proper bon voyage party, even if the people in the relationship will feel more relief than pain as the luxury liner leaves the dock in a cloud of balloons and confetti.

"Friday then," I say.

"I'll stop by your house on the way to work."

He hangs up, and I nod at the receiver a few times.

The first Christmas I came home from college, I thought everything would be just as I'd left it four months before. I remember the ride home from the airport, leaning forward and resting my elbows on the backs of the front bucket seats where Mom and Dad were sitting and talking nonstop about everything from Pennsylvania's colder weather to an annoying trig class. Mom told me to put my seat belt on, and Dad asked if I were studying any Greek history. It all felt very cross-purpose and similar to my senior year of high school. My first indication of change was the sparkly stud in Saphi's nose.

"You got pierced," I said.

"Yeah."

I stared at her.

"I always wanted one," I said, "but Mom always said no."

"I didn't ask."

"Forgiveness is easier than permission?"

Saphi flashed one of those melt-the-boys'-hearts smiles she had perfected.

"Yeah."

My little sister was baby going on bad girl. Mom and Dad both had threads of gray in their hair I didn't remember. The house felt smaller.

The next day I walked down to see Grady. He'd decided to take a year off from school and work at his father's car dealership rather than go straight on to university. I found him mowing the large expanse of golf course green that passed for a yard. The weather had been unusually warm, even for Missouri, and the grass had just kept growing. After becoming acclimatized to Pennsylvania, I didn't even need a jacket.

"Hey," he said when I waved.

He shut off the riding mower, but didn't climb out of the seat. The image of me leaping into his arms and being swung around into a long kiss that I'd nursed into a romantic fantasy over airplane pretzels and tomato juice died in a whiff of exhaust.

"Hi."

We looked at each other. After a few uncertain moments, I looked around at the grass and the last leaves holding on to the trees.

"I'm home," I added, as if he might need confirmation that I wasn't a vision but a reality.

"I see that."

He smiled and for a moment he was the Grady I remembered.

"How's the Pennsylvania winter?" he asked, as if we hadn't spoken on the phone barely a week ago.

"Cold."

"Do you like it?"

"Yeah." I nodded. "Yeah, I do."

He leaned forward on the wheel of the tractor-look-alike mower.

"That's good."

"Do you like selling cars?" I asked, taking my cue from his apparent denial of our having had anything to do with each other since I'd left.

"Most of the time."

I was beginning to suspect that some of the lackluster phone calls Grady and I had been having lately were not just because I was overworked and tired, which was the excuse I'd been giving myself throughout the month of November. He had . . . removed himself from me. Four years of knowing him inside out, or thinking I knew him inside out, and yet now he was a virtual stranger. His eyes, the dimple that appeared only on his right cheek, the scar over his eyebrow, even the way he swallowed when he was nervous were all familiar points on the map, but the destination had become a mystery.

"Do you want to go out to the lake?" I asked.

He swallowed. I noticed.

"It's kind of cold, don't you think?"

The sun warmed my shoulders, and the gentle springlike breeze lifted a strand of hair off my neck and up into my eyes. Pushing the strand behind my ear, I smiled at Grady.

"It's over, isn't it?"

"You mean you and me?"

"Yes."

He scratched the back of his head.

"There's this girl working in the service depart—"

"Who?"

"Linda. She was a year ahead of us."

"I know her."

"We kind of . . ."

He trailed off and scratched his head again.

"Why didn't you tell me? When I called you?"

"It didn't seem right. I thought I should tell you to your face."

I nodded, then stepped up to the lawn mower and kissed his cheek. He smelled exactly like he always did. The smell of skin, laundry soap, and shampoo. Nothing had changed, but everything was different. Just like Saphi was still my sister and Mom and Dad were still my parents and the old house was still my home. Things looked, felt, smelled, and sounded the same, but everything was different.

"Good-bye, Grady."

He caught my face between his hands and gave me a quick kiss on the lips.

"I'm sorry. If you start to feel bad, call me."

I knew he still cared and that he didn't want to hurt me. Absence doesn't make the heart grow fonder; it just opens the heart to new possibilities. I turned and walked home, but behind me I could hear Grady singing. Grady couldn't carry a tune in his own hand. He sang only when a problem had been solved and the world became a wide-open space of freedom and possibility.

———

The soul selects her own society, then shuts the door. Emily Dickinson. I set the phone back into the cradle and realize that I've just selected my own society. This afternoon, I had an imaginary conversation with Colton in which I ended our engagement. Although at the time it was little more than a sinful thought, now things have changed. Somehow, in the time between my collision with Alec and Saphi closing my door, I've discovered the wide-open space of freedom and possibility. My future is finally beginning to connect with my past.

I push away from the table beside what used to be Mom and Dad's bed. The bed still wears the old patchwork quilt that Mom inherited from her grandmother. Years ago I would sneak in with the dawn light and crawl into bed between them. Mom would grumble a little—she wasn't a morning person—and Dad would say, "Here's that lost puppy" or "Look what the cat dragged in," and I would giggle and go back to sleep, curled up at Mom's back.

I lie down on top of the patchwork and stare up at the ceiling, where the shadows are so different from the ones in my room. I wish I could curl up behind Mom and ask her how she felt when Dad ran into her that long-ago day and squished her tube of paint. How she really felt, I mean, not the story sanitized by years and convention and childish ears. Was Dad a kind of devil tempting her away from the art degree and into a life of motherhood and family?

Sleepless nights and emotional days catch up with me, and exhaustion pulls my eyelids down. I hear Mom laugh and feel her push a strand of my hair behind my ear as she wakes me up from where I've gone back to sleep in the warm space between her and Dad.

"Come on, critter, it's time to get up."

The voice is too real. I open my eyes and see Saphi standing beside the bed and looking down at me. She reaches out and pushes a bit of hair off my cheek.

"Why are you in here?"

"I came in to use the phone. To call Colton."

She nods, then sits down beside me on the bed and plucks at the quilt.

"Do you wash this?"

"Every once in a while. It's fragile, so I have to take it down to the Laundromat because they have those machines with no oscillator in the middle."

"Why don't you just pack it away?"

I shrug, my shoulders moving up and down against the quilt and the pillows.

"I wouldn't either," she says. "I'm thinking about spaghetti or some kind of pasta for supper."

"Sounds good. I'll help."

We decide on alfredo, since I bought a jar of the cream sauce the last time I went to the store. While making the salad, Saphi hums something under her breath that sounds a little like "Desperado," but is probably by some modern copycat band that can't come up with a tune on its own. I'm tossing the cooked pasta into the sauce when the phone rings.

"I'll get it," Saphi says.

She trills a "hello" into the receiver, then listens for a moment. "I'm her sister. Hang on."

She holds the phone out to me and says, "One of your students, I think."

"Hello?"

"Hi, George."

Alec's voice lends wings to my lead feet, and the room swirls beneath me.

"Aren't you supposed to wait a few days before using the girl's number?"

"That's so old-fashioned. Is there any chance you'll be in St. Louis again soon?"

"How soon?"

"Tomorrow?"

"Why?"

I hear the smile in the change of his voice.

"I thought you might want to haunt the church for complines."

"Don't forget my curry!" a voice says from the background.

"And my roommate is making curry," Alec adds. "He needs a new guinea pig. He says my gourmet tastes have been ruined by tobacco and philosophy."

"Hmm, tomorrow."

I pretend to think about it. The banter is easy, because I've already decided to go to St. Louis. Tomorrow, the day after, or the day after that. If Lucifer crooks his finger, I'll come running. But somewhere deep down, I know that Alec would come to me if I asked. It's a strange feeling to know what's in someone else's mind, to have someone's mind open like a book before you, and to already know the story of what's inside even if you've never read the words.

"Tomorrow night," he says. "Complines start at six. Phil says curry at five."

Tomorrow night is Thursday and choir practice. That traitorous group of people who prefer Bach when someone new suggests it. I look over at Saphi and realize that I'm *glad* the choir prefers her over me right now, because it means I can say the word I want to say.

"Yes."

"Great." He gives me directions to a house in a gracefully run-down area of the city; then he hangs up.

I take the phone away from my ear. The room swirls around my feet. Solidity is slow to return, but it settles around me as I put the phone back in its place.

"Who was that?" Saphi asks.

She is holding a cherry tomato up to the light over the sink, turning it over and over in her fingers before popping it into her mouth. I watch her jawbones move up and down under the skin of her cheeks.

"The devil who ran me down. He's a friend."

"More than."

"What makes you say that?"

"The tone of your voice. Are you sleeping with him?"

"No."

"You could have fooled me. You positively *lilted* when you realized who it was."

"It's not like that," I say, even though I know it could be like that if I wanted it to be. That someday I want it to be.

"Are you going to let Colton in on this? Or are you planning on forming a love triangle?"

I try to gauge Saphi's tone. I realize that she hasn't worn the amber-jeweled nose stud since she came back home. I remember seeing it when she stood at the back door holding the brown-tweed suitcase. She's holding another cherry tomato up to the light.

"A lot of these are rotten," she says. "The grocery store is getting away with robbery."

"That's disgusting."

"The rotten tomato or the triangle?"

"Both."

"Are you breaking it off with Colton?"

"If he ever finds the time to listen. What happened to your stud?"

She turns and looks at me, her eyebrows high. I tap the side of my nose.

"It fell out in the shower and went down the drain."

I touch her cheek to turn her head, and look at the little hole where the stud used to be.

"Oh, good. For a minute I thought you'd become a progressive pilgrim and followed Christian onto the straight and narrow."

"Not likely. I hated that book."

"Shh."

I hold a finger to my lips and tilt my head toward Dad's study. *Pilgrim's Progress* is one of his favorites. She rolls her eyes.

"Can you take over the choir for me tomorrow?"

"Why?"

"I have to cultivate a life of sin."

She sets down the tomatoes and leans her hip against the counter.

"Are you sure you're doing the right thing?"

"Wasn't it you who said the man was an ass?" I ask, feeling defensive. "Last night you practically told me to do exactly what I'm doing."

"Gusti . . ."

She trails off and chews on her lip. I pick up the little carton of tomatoes and dig through them.

"These two are okay."

"Since when did you start being unresponsible?"

"Irresponsible. And Colton's the one who says he doesn't have time to talk to me, so how am I being irresponsible?"

She shrugs.

I set the tomatoes back down on the counter. I almost hug her because she thinks I'm behaving irresponsibly, because the feeling of lightness and relief inside of my chest is strong enough to break walls, but I catch her hand instead.

"How old were you when I was in college?"

She frowns at me and pulls her hand away.

"I don't know. Twelve or thirteen when you left. I was eighteen when . . . when Mom died."

"I feel"—I tap my chest—"I feel like I did when I was at Penn. Like there's *possibility* in my life. Like for the last six years I've been *waiting* for the future. Just waiting. And now—"

"The future happens, Gusti. No matter what you do, it just happens. And then it's your present."

Chapter 16

"Here. Like this."

Dad wrapped my child's fingers around the smooth wooden handle of the handsaw.

"Now up and down on an angle, and be careful to follow the line. Let the saw do the work."

I carefully sawed the board in two while Dad held it steady. The line wasn't perfectly straight, but pride had me standing up straighter when Dad said, "Atta girl!" as he held up the separated board.

Mom was my confidante, but Dad and I shared a bond of books and interests. Mom taught me how to mix paints and stretch canvas, but my favorite painting project was slapping latex on the exterior of the house while the notes from Miles Davis' trumpet floated out the open windows on the summer breeze and Dad hummed beside me. Dad sang the shadows away and helped me understand that Saphira wasn't there to replace me in the family, but was a new and exciting addition to my life. Dad taught me basic plumbing, car care, and how to replace a wall outlet without

getting hit with a jolt of one hundred and ten volts. And somewhere along the line we made an almost spiritual connection that
happens to two people who work together and think alike. Which
explains why, when Dad sits down to a supper of alfredo and salad,
he looks over at me and says:

"Something happened to you today, Augustina."

My mouth is full of pasta, so I have to force myself to chew
and swallow. I borrowed some of Saphi's makeup to cover the
bruise on my cheekbone from where I connected with handlebars,
elbow, or cement, I'm not sure which, but maybe the bruise shows
through. I try to gauge what Dad is reacting to. Chewing and swal-
lowing gives me time to think, but thinking isn't necessary because
Saphi opens her big mouth first.

"She's breaking up with Colton."

Dad is in the act of spearing a tomato. His fork slides off the little red sphere and scratches across the plate and across my nerves.

"Thanks," I say to Saphi. "Thank you very much."

"You're welcome. You might as well get it out into the open."

"I haven't actually talked to Colton yet," I say to Dad. "He's
too busy."

He frowns and rolls the tomato around on his plate.

"This has something to do with me, doesn't it?"

"No," I say, lying only a little. "Why?"

His smile is lopsided.

"I hear things. Probably a lot of things I shouldn't hear. And
I've been thinking that your getting married . . . It might be difficult having me—"

I could talk for hours, explaining over and over that Colton
and I were on a collision path with disintegration, but Dad would
always have a doubt in the back of his mind. He would always
have a still, small voice telling him that it was his fault because he

stood in the way of our happiness. I don't bother with the hours of explaining.

"I ran into someone in St. Louis today," I say, interrupting him. "And I'm seeing him tomorrow night."

Dad looks up from the tomato, the surprise at this announcement freezing the worry lines on his face.

"His name is Alec. I don't know his last name. He's a graduate student in philosophy."

Saphi is stuffing salad into her mouth as fast as she can. The lines around Dad's eyes relax, and I can see a bit of a spark in the brown depths of his irises that I haven't seen in a long time.

"I assume that you literally ran into this philosophy major."

"He ran me down with his bicycle, actually."

"That would explain the bruises."

"Yes."

"Philosophy."

Dad looks across at me as he says it, and I feel the connection with him that I felt while painting the house exterior to trumpet music. The same connection I would feel on those trips to the river. The connection that has kept me here even as the inner child in me chafes at the facade of responsible, upright, spiritual daughter that I've maintained the last six years. The connection that keeps me here in the present without any acknowledgment of the future and what I want the future to be. I should thank Colton for pointing out to me that I've unwittingly denied myself a future because of this connection, but I don't need to remove Dad from my day-to-day life in order to have a future. And maybe, in a way, Colton pointed that out to me, too, by forcing me to make choices I have been putting off in favor of living solely in the present.

"Philosophy and religion," I say out loud.

"All that's missing is the tube of paint," Dad says.

His voice is part happy, part sad. Six years have dulled the pain and allowed the memories to be beautiful, but the memories heighten the sense of loss. Saphi pushes back from the table.

"I'm going to take a walk. Just leave the dishes for me, okay? I'll do them when I get back."

I'm a little surprised at her abrupt words and can see that Dad is, too. Something about my encounter with Alec bothers her, and it isn't the fact that I am essentially two-timing Colton, despite what she said earlier in the kitchen. The screen door in the kitchen slams and she's gone. Dad is resting his chin in his hand and he looks a little bemused, but he's always been bemused with Saphi. We both have. After a moment he returns to eating. I poke at the noodles congealing on my plate.

"Dad, I need to ask you a question. Do you want to live somewhere else? A different house, maybe, or Ashbrook Cottages?"

He sets his fork down. He's unprepared for my question, but not surprised. I can tell he's looking for the right thing to say, balancing my needs against his own, wanting to say what he hopes—

"Not what you think I want to hear," I say.

He nods, but it's an absent nod, and I know he didn't catch what I said, so I lean my elbows on the table and push forward.

"*Not* what you think I want to hear," I say again. "I want to know what you want. Honestly want."

"That's not a fair question to ask. I want what's best for you."

"You don't know what's best for me. I do."

"Do you?"

His smile takes the sting out of the question.

"I have no idea. But I need you to tell me what *you* want. Colton raised the possibility that I've been creating what you want to suit my needs rather than yours. Do you like living here? Do you want something else?"

He rubs his fingers along the edge of the table.

"Meredith Carlson cornered me in my office the other day. There are times when being in a wheelchair is a terrible disadvantage."

I picture the wolfish Mrs. Carlson trapping my grocery cart in a dead-end aisle, the better to torture gossip out of me, my dear.

"I can imagine."

"She hinted that I was being selfish keeping you here in this two-story house that is . . . 'beyond my abilities' is how she put it, if I remember correctly."

A mental nudge reminds me that Meredith Carlson and Lorraine belong to the same coffee klatch. I can picture the recent meeting perfectly.

"Yes, we're looking forward to the wedding, but I just don't know how Augustina is going to manage with her father still living in that rambling old house. I've tried to talk to her, but . . ."

"What do you want?" Dad asks me.

"I asked first. You can't pull a switcheroo like that. Nice try, though."

"Stubborn as Jackson's mules."

"I like Jackson's mules."

In the far distance, a cop turns on his siren to chase some male-factor bent on Wednesday-evening naughtiness. The siren has faded before Dad speaks again.

"Sometimes, when I come out in the morning, I see your mom standing in the sunlight and looking out the window. If I don't blink, she turns around and smiles at me."

I bite my lip. Dad has managed to not directly come out and say what he wants, but I understand what he's saying. He wants to stay in the house where the memories of Gail Fletcher are close enough to touch.

"I see her, too. In the shadows on the porch swing."

"I miss her."

"Me, too."

Although the impression of mutual sadness has always been there, I realize this is the first time we've ever vocalized the gaping depth of our grief.

———

Halloween weather has gripped the river basin. I wake up to a cold, foggy dawn. It's beautiful and spooky at the same time. Humps in Jackson's field stick up like ships on a sea of mist, and the tree line along the river is a dark blur alive with the calls of the crows. I drink my coffee outside on the porch steps where the steam from the cup and my breath can mingle with the fog. When the cup is empty, I tuck my hands into my armpits and hunker over my knees.

I want a dog again. A puppy that will chew furniture and shoes and bound along beside me on a walk. We had a furry mixed-breed named Bonzo after Beaver died, but I never felt quite the same about him. Bonzo was Mom's dog, and I think he died of a broken heart when she never came home. Neither Dad nor I have talked about getting another dog since I buried Bonzo, but the timing seems right.

Saphi doesn't come downstairs until after lunch. Dad's car is still in the shop. I've taken him to the church office for a series of marriage-counseling appointments and meetings, and I'm just about to go upstairs and knock on Saphi's door to remind her to pick him up after choir practice when she comes down the stairs in the flowered robe I gave her one Christmas. She yawns and makes another pot of coffee. I watch her movements from where I'm sitting at the kitchen table paying my part of the household bills.

"Good noon," I say.

And I wonder why I've started relying on her to take over

things I normally would do or ask someone at the church to do. The garden incident was only two days ago, but something has shifted inside of me, allowing me to trust her.

"I read until late."

"It was a cold morning, too."

She smiles over her shoulder.

"Hardly cold. Balmy, maybe. Cold is forty below."

"Death is forty below. Are you still willing to handle the choir?"

"So you can run off to repeat history in all its disaster with the philosophy-and-religion man?"

"Why do you keep saying that?"

She shrugs and pours a cup of coffee.

"I'll handle the choir. Something by Handel?"

I let out a frustrated huff at her change of topic, but let it stand.

"Handel's fine if you want to be there for a few hours. Dad's at the church, so you'll need to take the van to pick him up. The shop says the parts are on order from God knows where and his car won't be ready until early next week."

"What about supper?"

"I usually take him a sandwich and some decaf tea when he stays late. He's doing some premarital counseling."

"Ah, love. Yes, I'll take the food."

"Thanks. For both—choir and food."

She raises her eyebrows. The steam from her coffee makes her look like Madame Edberta, the county-fair psychic who wreaths herself in incense to create atmosphere.

"Somehow, I think my little stunt with the choir backfired on me," Saphi says around a rueful smile.

Leaning back in the chair, I push the bills I've been paying around on the table.

"Look, about that. Before that. I know I've been a bitch. I think I was angry because—"

"Forget it, love," she interrupts. "I need a shower."

"Wait."

She leans back against the counter and sips from her mug. The steam lifts the strands of flyaway hair around her face.

"I'm waiting."

"You keep hinting at something between Mom and Dad," I say at last. "Just tell me. Up front."

She sets the coffee mug down on the counter and rests her hands on either side of her.

"If you never figured it out, then you don't want to know and I don't want to tell you."

"I just said I do want to know. And if you don't want me to know, then why do you keep making all these not-so-veiled remarks?"

"I don't want to see you make a mistake."

"I agree."

"Yet you're running up to St. Louis this afternoon."

"That's different."

"In what way?"

I don't have an answer for her, so I hop off the detour she's trying to set up.

"This isn't about me. It's about Mom and Dad and your hints."

She shrugs and looks out the window.

"Didn't you realize Mom and Dad were having trouble?"

"Trouble?"

"Marital trouble. Fighting. Divorce. Falling out of love."

"I fell in love with the top of his head."

When I was seven, I saw *Invasion of the Body Snatchers* on afternoon television. I just knew my parents had been replaced by aliens. The certainty lasted for about a month; then, in typical childish fashion, it disappeared.

"Are you sure?" I ask. "Could it be you just imagined it? You were only a kid."

"Where were you the last four years Mom was alive?"

"College."

"I was here. Living with them. Mom was screaming—"

"Perimenopause?"

"I wish. She was tired of living in a fishbowl."

"That doesn't mean she would get a divorce."

"It kind of depends on what she was saying while she was screaming, doesn't it? And after Mom died, I read her journal."

I've read Mom's journal, too. It's filled with the usual things a journal contains: the frustrations, anxieties, and petty complaints of everyday living.

Saphira wants a tattoo. I wouldn't be surprised if she gets one on her forehead so every church member will be sure to mention it for the next fifty years.

Does Augustina even know what she wants? She acts like she does, but she's just fooling herself and thinks she's got me fooled, too.

If I hear one more discussion on theology before I die, it will be one too many.

Sometimes I wonder if I should start painting again, but I'm not sure I have the energy. What happened to my life?

"Did you read all of it?" I ask.

"Enough."

"Did you get to the part she wrote a few weeks before she died, where she says, 'Anyone reading this would think I was the unhappiest person in the world, but I'm not'?"

Saphi stares at me.

"Have you ever kept a journal?" I ask.

"Sure."

"I mean the kind where you let it all hang out and say whatever you want."

"In junior high." She smiles. "I burned them in the fireplace because I was afraid Mom and Dad would find them."

"Mom never snooped."

"It wasn't worth the risk. You don't know what was in them."

"They were probably a lot like mine when I was fourteen."

"I doubt it. You've always walked the straight and narrow."

"I was pretty good at sinning in mind only."

She laughs a little and I laugh along.

"I stopped writing things down when I married Flynn. I just didn't have any time." She pauses. "And I was worried he would find it. Like I found Mom's. Did you show it to Dad?"

I shake my head.

"So you think there's some truth in it, don't you?" she says. "Despite that little part you memorized. You don't think it was all just the annoyances that Mom wanted to get out."

She picks up her coffee cup and takes another sip. The liquid has cooled down and steam no longer teases her hair.

"No, it's just that I read it right after she died. And later I forgot to mention it."

"Please. Give me a break."

"Okay, I didn't want Dad to read it when he was all cut up inside. Now I'm embarrassed. He'll know I found it ages ago when I boxed up her clothes and stuff."

I push the bills around again while Saphi pours herself a second cup of coffee.

"Mom's not here to ask," I say. "So I'm accepting that sentence where she said she wasn't as unhappy as the journal made her sound."

Saphi sighs and sits down across from me.

"I guess I never thought of it like that."

Something in the way she says the words, the years-lost sound of them, pulls back the curtains on a window I should have noticed a long time ago. It pulls back the curtains that have covered a connection I've never made.

"All that rebellion, all that anger Mom told me about when I was at Penn . . . It was because of Mom and Dad, wasn't it?"

Dipping a finger into her coffee, she traces circles onto the table.

"At one point in her journal, Mom said she wished she lived all alone on a mountain so she could paint and daydream her day away rather than meet one more time with the school counselor about my deliberate bad grades. Where she wondered why she ever had kids in the first place."

"And you thought living alone on a mountainside might not be a bad thing?"

"No, I thought Mom didn't want me anymore."

She wipes the wet coffee circles off the table with the sleeve of her robe.

"Do you ever wonder if—" She breaks off to clear her throat. "If she died because she didn't think she could find the courage to leave us?"

"I think she died because a driver lost control and ran them off the road."

———

I sounded more confident with Saphira than I actually feel. My confidence is not a matter of truth; it's a matter of faith. My evidence for believing that things between Mom and Dad hadn't changed since the blue paint and free coffee comes from memories—even though I wasn't living at home the last four years, and I know the memories are older than the journal—and from that rare sentence in Mom's journal where she seemed to laugh at herself and her complaints. I told Saphi what I want to believe, but my doubts make true belief impossible.

Saphi touched a nerve when she mentioned that I have never shown the journal to Dad. Dad glosses over unpleasant things with laughter and a song. Mom's death knocked that out of him for a while, but his natural resilience kept him from sinking into despair. If he and Mom were beginning to fall apart as a couple, I'm not sure he would even remember, much less acknowledge, that such a thing was happening. Usually this character trait is the one that annoys me, but in this instance I think Dad and I are in tacit agreement. I'm not sure I want to know the truth. When it comes to undermining the world of my childhood, it's easier to ignore a possibility and blindly follow a path of faith.

I pull my car up near the sidewalk just beyond the front of the house Alec's directions have led me to. When I knock on the door, it opens and lets out the smell of curry.

"We don't want any," the man at the door says.

He's holding a spatula and has managed to splatter the flowered apron he's wearing with turmeric-colored curry sauce.

"You'll never get those spots out," I say. "Is Alec home?"

He looks down at his apron.

"Damn. This is one of my favorites. So you're not here to drop off tracts on salvation or sell me chocolate to keep you off the streets?"

I hold open the flaps of my coat and pretend to wait for inspection.

"No tracts. And it's too late to keep me off the streets because

I have a driver's license. I might have chocolate somewhere on my person, however."

"Good girl."

Holding the spatula behind his back, he makes a leg and bows like a character out of a Molière play.

"Welcome to our humble abode, gracious lady. I am Philippe. At your service."

"Charmed, I'm sure," I say, dropping a curtsy.

"Alec's upstairs. Tell him the curry will be done in fifteen minutes. No dawdling. You know the way?"

"No, but the steps are over there."

"Ah . . . she's observant, too. What a pleasure!"

I'm halfway up the stairs when he calls after me, "Fifteen minutes!" Looking down, I see him gesticulating with the spatula and splattering more curry over the apron as he walks back into the kitchen.

"Hi."

Alec is standing at the top of the stairs. The light is behind him, and I resist putting my hand up to shield my eyes—or my heart, which is pumping at full throttle. I can feel the same tug and pull I felt yesterday during our conversation over the squeaking bicycle.

"Hi. Curry in fifteen."

"I heard. Are you hungry?"

"Yes."

"Phil's a good cook."

"He makes a nice leg, too. Acting?"

"French lit."

I nod and feel stupid standing three steps down from him. He holds out a hand and I take it, letting him pull me three steps up and into the light.

Chapter 17

"Come and take a look at our upper patio," Alec says, still holding on to my hand. "It's kind of dull without the plants, but the view of the trees is good."

The upper patio is a flat section of roof just outside a door at the end of the hall. From the noises under my feet, I'd say we are standing right over Philippe and his spattered apron and bubbling curry. Someone—perhaps the original owner of the house back before it became part of a "student ghetto," as the more snobbish residents like to call it—has put up a knee-high railing, a kind of widow's walk, around the perimeter of the roof. Alec and his roommates have added plastic Adirondack chairs and a hibachi grill. Flower boxes still contain a few determined impatiens and petunias. The limbs of a giant burr oak spread out overhead, brown leaves clinging to the ends of the branches. Through the remaining leaves, we have a view of this part of the city. Trees and roofs and the gleam of upstairs windows. The sweet gums and red oaks are brilliant spots of color among the bare branches of trees that have already dropped their leaves. Through it all, the last fingers of morning mist tangle in the leaves and the hollows of streets.

"It's beautiful," I say.

"You should see it around Christmas when everyone has their lights up."

"I like this better. It's ... natural. Unpretentious. If you couldn't hear the cars and freeway, it might be a hundred years ago."

He picks up a pack of cigarettes from the plastic milk crate that serves as a table and shakes one out.

"You like things to be honest, I take it."

"What I like and what I do seem to have become mutually exclusive these days."

I watch him light the cigarette, and think about Colton and how I probably shouldn't be here right now. And yet I *am* here, which only goes to prove that I'm turning into someone I don't seem to recognize.

"I think I'm becoming dishonest. With myself and others."

"The fiancé?"

I open my mouth to say that I would have already talked with Colton if he could have managed to find the time, but I realize that I could have forced the issue. I could have broken it off over the phone. I could have driven over to his office or his house and handed him his ring. All my high-sounding excuses about breaking things off gently and in person were mere excuses. A little like the excuses I've used to pacify that nervous part of myself that wonders about Gail Fletcher and if she wanted to leave her family.

"There is no such thing as a completely honest relationship," Alec says. "You can have a fairly honest relationship, but there will always be aspects hidden from each other. Things that piss you off, but not enough to talk about. Or maybe they are enough to talk about. But you weigh the hurt to the other person versus the gain and make a decision to leave it alone or to act."

"You make it sound unselfish. Most of the time it's selfish. Fear of having the other person be angry. Fear of losing their love or respect. Fear of them leaving."

"That, too."

"Why?"

"Are you actually asking me to delve into several million years of emotional evolution or was it a rhetorical question?"

I reach out and take his cigarette from him, pull the smoke deep into my lungs, then let it out into a bit of drifting gray fog where the warmth of my breath doubles the cloud of smoke.

"Rhetorical."

"You're not a smoker."

"I was in high school. I hid it. For selfish and unselfish reasons."

He takes the cigarette back from me, inhales, then offers it to me filter first.

"Like what?"

"Fear of losing my parents', particularly my father's, respect. Fear of making them angry. Fear of making them sad. I always knew they would love me no matter what, but I didn't want them to think less of me."

"It's just smoking."

"Not for a pastor's daughter who is always on display."

"Here. Not like that."

He wraps chilled fingers around my hand, changes the angle of the cigarette, the attitude of my fingers.

"You don't want to look like you've got a nineteen forties–style holder and are really Bette Davis. Think negligent."

"Thanks for the cigarette-as-accessory tip."

He leans over and kisses my forehead.

"Why did you call me?" I ask after his lips leave my forehead.

"Selfish reasons. Why did you come?"

"My sister thinks I'm being influenced by the stories that create my family history."

"I said fifteen minutes, children," Phil says from below.

Looking down, we can see his head sticking out the kitchen window.

"If you're done being deep, maybe you could have the decency to come and eat before it's completely ruined."

————

Despite my love of cathedrals, I've never been to complines and I'm not sure what to expect. The interior of the church is as hushed as a symphony hall when the violinists settle down to tune their instruments. Except for a few knots of people, the benches are nearly empty.

"Why are there so few people?" I whisper.

Nothing has started, and a threesome about twenty feet away are laughing and talking in normal tones, but the pressure of years and height make me feel insignificant and whispery.

"It's not really a service. More like . . . a devotional. Bedtime prayers, if you like."

I nod. Something about the expectant atmosphere bothers me, tightening my stomach like a tuned string. Turning slightly, I catch Alec watching me.

"If you don't believe," I ask, "why do you study religion?"

"People create philosophy, and although I'd be burned as a heretic for saying this, people create religion, too. The two go together."

"It is you, O Lord, you alone who make us rest secure."

The spoken words sound loud in the silence as they interrupt our conversation, and in the music that follows, I forget what I was going to say to Alec about being burned at the stake. I always thought chant was a little like the responsive reading of scripture that gets printed into the Sunday bulletin or like the Episcopal church I went to once where a priest says words in a singsong chant and the congregation responds. Nothing could be farther from the truth.

The melody and harmony of unaccompanied voices rises and falls, notes chasing one another until the whole arrives at a single point of agreement. I rest my head on the back of the bench. The music creates colored patterns like birds flying in dives and swoops among the vaults above me. Each time the music stops for the reading, the birds rest, only to take flight again with the next song.

I realize, suddenly, that everyone is gone and that some poor soul is turning off the lights in the hope that we will get the hint and leave.

"Where did you go?" Alec asks as I turn my head on the back of the bench and blink at him.

"I flew."

Outside, the fountain is splashing against stone and the mists curl around the lamps lighting the sidewalks. We find a coffee shop and this time Alec buys.

"I dream about flying," I say.

We're walking in the general direction of my car, warm cups cradled in chilly hands.

"I dream about flying away to someplace where I'm happy."

"That would be a popular vacation spot," he says.

"It's hard to find. If you do find it, you have to grab on to it, hold on to it."

We walk silently for a bit and I notice that I'm avoiding the cracks in the sidewalk.

"Happiness isn't something that's just out there," he says. "It's like a plant. You cultivate happiness."

"Happiness is like homegrown? Is it illegal, too?"

The words come out a little sharper than I mean them to. He sounds like a greeting card or a motivational poster. I feel his hand on my arm, stopping me.

"I'm sorry. That was trite."

"A little."

"What I meant was that if happiness is dreams fulfilled, the path to happiness depends on your dream."

"That sounds like an advertisement for mediocre dreams."

"No, just that dreams are constantly changing forces. What you want so desperately to come true at six or sixteen or sixty isn't going to be the same dream. Dreams change, and happiness is knowing what your dream has become and what path you need to take."

"What wings I need to make in order to reach the sun," I say.

"I can think of better dreams than being fried to a crisp."

"But flying into the sun would be a magnificent way to go."

"Insignificant, too."

In the eastern sky, the moon peeks over the top of a building and through the gnarled branches of a tree. I sit down on a bench that floated in a summertime glory of flowers, but now floats on dried and wilted stems. Alec sits down beside me and it seems the most natural, most honest thing in the world for him to put his arm around my shoulders and for me to settle into his warmth.

"I've always wanted to take a picture of the moon looking just like that," I say.

I can feel his smile through the sleeve of his jacket under my cheek.

"Some things should be seen and stored in your mind. Taking

pictures either distorts the beauty, diminishes it, or lets you forget what you saw because you can rely on the camera to see it for you."

"Or everyone looks happy when actually they were all screaming at one another five minutes before."

"Yes."

The moon climbs higher, but I can still see the stars and a faint hint of the river of light that is the Milky Way. It's too straight to be called a river and is nothing like the shifting, muddy water that adds and subtracts sandbars from my life. Alec's body is warm and he smells like a pleasant mix of curry and smoke. My mind drifts along the sparkling star river to Colton, who is having dinner with his parents. I wonder what he will say to them after the engagement is over. Lorraine has been enthusiastic about planning an enormous wedding, but nothing has been done officially despite her complaints that we seem to be content to "stay engaged for the rest of your lives." I wonder if I always knew that we were playacting at being mature adults with a future. If Colton always knew.

I think about Saphira and how it would feel to walk away from someone you loved because they refused to believe you loved them. If that, more than reality, has colored her impression of Mom and Dad's marriage. Only she found Mom's journal before she met Flynn. She heard the screaming. She thought Mom didn't want her. That none of us wanted her because she was too much trouble.

Will you love me as much as the baby?

When did the childlike ability to ask probing questions disappear from my life? When did I lose the ability to ask honest questions of people who had potentially devastating answers? Why is love so hard?

I gave my love a cherry that had no stone.

I feel Alec's fingers on my face and I realize I've been asleep with my cheek pressed into his shoulder. The October mists have soaked through my jacket and into my skin. Shivers attack me, and my back hurts from squeezing my stomach into it to stop the shaking. The moon is straight overhead and we've been sitting here for hours. Sitting up, I watch him rub feeling into what must be a numb arm.

"You should have woken me up before now," I say. "Your shoulder will be stiff."

"I was thinking."

"Me, too."

Back at his house, I go inside to use the bathroom. He walks me back out to my car and we look at each other for a long time.

"I don't know where this is going," I say.

"Does it have to 'go' somewhere?"

"No. But most people think on a linear basis."

"Maybe it's time to break free of convention."

"Is it possible?"

"Probably not. But we could fool ourselves in the meantime."

I nod. Above us, the dry leaves of the old burr oak tree rattle in the wind. The clouds are skimming by, high and fast, racing after the moon, and the weatherman on the radio predicted the first real frost, just in time for Halloween. In a couple of months, the longest night of the year will be here again and then the sun will begin its climb back to the warm days of summer. The frozen ice on the river will thaw and the sandbanks will shift and change with each flood. If the world around me is cyclical, maybe my story is, too.

"There's no fool like an old fool, and I feel old right now."

Something about my muttered words must seem funny to him.

He laughs out loud for the first time since I stepped into the bike lane. It's a beautiful sound, as free as the calls of the wild geese that pass by overhead during a winter night.

————

The eastern sky has a grayish cast by the time I switch off the ignition in front of Dad's house. My house. Saphira's house. Our house. I imagine jack-o'-lanterns on the steps and want to thank Saphi for turning the garden into a riot of fall color. I'm climbing out of the car when she opens the front door.

"Where were you? Your cell phone must be off. I called and called."

"Sleeping under the light of the full moon and becoming a lunatic. I really like the mums, you know. I'm sorry I was so angry about them when you dug up the garden."

"Colton had an accident."

I look up. Her arms are wrapped around her. Dread settles in my chest.

"Lorraine and Howard called this evening, yesterday evening, trying to reach you."

"Is—"

"He's at the hospital. Local."

"Did they say how bad . . . ?"

I trail off as Saphi shakes her head. Turning around, I go to the car. Saphi doesn't offer to come with me. In the porch light, her face is gray.

At the hospital, I go to the emergency wing and ask for Colton's location when I don't see anyone I know sitting in the waiting area. I haven't been here since the night I had to go to the morgue and I was lost in body and mind. The padded chairs bring painful memories that crush to dust the spirit inspired by my flight in the vaulted ceiling of College Church. I walk up to the desk and the matron sitting behind it who packs an extra hundred pounds of flesh and attitude.

"He's not here anymore," she tells me. "He's in room two thirty-one."

She looks at my face and the ring on my hand.

"Are you his fiancée?"

"Ye—"

I break off the sentence, then decide to not bother trying to explain, so let the half-finished word stand alone.

"He's okay. A broken collarbone and some bumps and bruises." She purses her lips. "You might want to talk to him about his drinking habits."

Outside room 231, I bump into a doctor who is a member of the Baptist church and sings in the joint Christmas production.

"He's okay, Augustina," he says, echoing the matron.

He pats my shoulder, hindered by a clipboard and a cup of coffee. I think of him singing "*Stille Nacht, Heil'ge Nacht,*" with a deep bass ringing out over the uneasy alliance of Baptists, Methodists, and Catholics who set aside minor and major doctrinal differences every Christmas season.

"I prescribed a painkiller and he's sleeping it off. A broken clavicle, bruised ribs, and a few cuts here and there. He'll live to stand at the altar."

He laughs at his own joke. I smile and silently thank him for his carefree attitude.

Unlike the doctor, Lorraine is frantic. As soon as I step into the hospital room, she grabs my upper arm in clawed fingers, squeezing until my fingers go numb.

"This is your fault. It's your responsibility to be with him, your responsibility to care for him. He shouldn't have been driving home . . . like that. If you'd been with him, this wouldn't have happened."

On the other side of the bed where Colton sleeps, Howard shifts and coughs. I glance at him, then at Colton's forehead, where a bit of dark hair rests over the pale, bruised skin, then back down into Lorraine's face. I put my fingers over hers.

"He'll be all right," I tell her.

"No thanks to you."

I don't say what I'm thinking, not out of consideration for Lorraine's feelings or because I think Lorraine is secretly chastising herself for allowing Colton to drink and then drive home after drinking. Colton is an adult. He knew he was driving. Lorraine and Howard both knew he was driving, too, yet I'm sure the beer and wine flowed as freely as ever. How Colton has managed to survive this long is a mystery. I know Colton's accident isn't my fault and I don't accept the blame. I wish I could say that Lorraine is taking her own guilt out on me, but Lorraine isn't the type. She blames me, pure and simple, because anything else would damage her wall of self-protection. I don't say what I'm thinking, not out of kindness, not because I fear honesty, but because there's simply no point in doing so.

"Would you like a cup of coffee?" I ask her and Howard.

"Yes," she says.

"I'll help," Howard says.

Standing in front of the machine, waiting for the cups to fill one at a time with three different combinations of coffee, sugar, and cream, Howard clears his throat.

"I'm sorry about Lorraine's outburst. She's just upset."

"I know. It's all right."

"Where were you last night?"

"I went to St. Louis."

"Oh. Tutoring?"

"To see a friend."

Howard looks at his reflection in the shiny front of the coffee machine.

"You're not going to marry Colton, are you?"

In the metal surface, our gazes meet. I don't respond to the question immediately because it is an issue between Colton and myself that hasn't been resolved yet, and until it is, I don't think it's fair to tell his father. But I can't lie and pretend everything is candy-sugared sweet, either.

Howard sighs and scratches his nose. The cup in his hand gleams white in the reflection as it moves up and down with his finger.

"Maybe it's for the best."

I don't ask why. He doesn't offer to tell me.

Chapter 18

"I really don't see why the doctor thought you should be released," Lorraine says to Colton.

The fog and chill damp from yesterday's early morning have gone, replaced by brilliant sunshine and what the old-timers refer to as "Indian summer." On days like this, when the oaks glowed red and gold, I used to go over to Jackson Dover's to help him bind up the cornstalks from his garden. After stripping the sweet corn from the stalks over those precious weeks in July, Jackson would leave them to dry in the garden, then bundle them up and sell them for fall decorations. He also grew giant jack-o'-lantern pumpkins, and after a morning spent making corn shocks, he would let me pick out the pumpkin I wanted as payment for my help. After carefully choosing the best and biggest, I would sit in the grass beside the garden and watch him plow up the now-empty space with his team of mules. Jackson always said that Indian summer was the time to plow the garden under, that the garden was too small for his tractor, and the mules were just getting fat and lazy with nothing to do. He was proud of Barney and Andy and he had taught them to nod and shake their heads.

"Should we let her have that big pumpkin? It would make an awfully good pie," he'd say to Andy as he rubbed the mule's long ears and pretended to whisper into them. Andy would nod his head up and down. "What do you think?" he'd say to Barney, and Barney would do the same. I would laugh and hug the pumpkin with one arm and Beaver with the other.

Outside the hospital, the oaks gleam red and gold in the brilliant sunshine as Colton is wheeled out to Lorraine and Howard's SUV.

"I really don't see why the doctor thought you should be released," Lorraine says. "It's Saturday. He could have kept you under supervision through the weekend, at least."

"I'm okay, Mom."

"Be careful. He's been injured, you know," Lorraine says to the long-suffering orderly who is pushing the wheelchair.

"I'll treat him as gently as if he were a baby, ma'am," the orderly says.

Lorraine gives him a daggered look, but his face is serene and honest. Only the twitch beside one eye lets an observant person know that he would love to wrap the metal wheelchair around Lorraine's neck. Or accidentally trip and tip the darling baby boy out onto the pavement. Poor Colton. Everyone always assumes that the chick invites the mother hen to cackle over it and protect it. Everyone always wants to slap the spoiled brat when Mommy rushes in to protect him. I try not to smile, but the orderly catches the repression and winks at me.

"What? What?" Lorraine asks as Colton gets out of the chair and the orderly heads back for the automatic doors at double time. "He's just leaving now that he's brought you out here?"

"There's nothing wrong with my legs, Mom," Colton says.

"Then why did they use a wheelchair?"

"It's required," I say.

She doesn't hear me, or at least she pretends to not hear me. From the moment when she released my arm from her talons, I ceased to exist. On the drive to Colton's house, she puts on her reading glasses—a pretension, since they have clear glass lenses—and looks at the list of instructions and bottles of medicine from the pharmacy.

"You need to rest. And only take this pill with food. And this one twice a day. And don't shower in the cast. I'll come over and help you—"

"I can read," Colton interrupts.

She slaps the paper down into her lap and turns in the bucket seat.

"Of course you can. But the doctor said you might still have some blurred vision, dizziness, and—"

"I'm fine."

"Howard?"

Lorraine looks at Howard and waits for his support. He turns into Colton's driveway, and I'm faced with the same white garage door I faced last Tuesday night when everything was different. The door seems out of place and foreign, as if I'd never seen it before and Howard had pulled into a stranger's driveway by accident.

"Here we are!" he says, avoiding Lorraine's request for backup. "Everybody out."

Lorraine fusses and tries to take the keys from Colton to unlock his door for him. I notice the tension in his shoulders and stay back by the SUV. He locks the keys in his fist and turns on her.

"Mom, stop it. You're acting like I'm three years old instead of thirty-three. It's embarrassing. I'm embarrassed. Dad's embarrassed. You should be embarrassed. Stop treating me like this. Just give me the medicines and the instructions and *go home!*"

Lorraine almost physically staggers. Once, when a horsefly bit his tender underbelly, Barney kicked Jackson in the stomach by accident. Jackson's face had the same look as Lorraine's when he doubled over trying to breathe. The skin on Lorraine's cheeks sags under the shock. She gently places the bottles and the page of medical instructions into Colton's good hand. One of the bottles falls as he tries to keep a grip on the keys at the same time. She ignores the bottle rolling on the cement steps and walks back to the SUV, opens the door, and climbs in. Straight as a stick, face like stone, staring off at the neighbor's porch that is festooned with fake spiderwebs and collapsing, carved-too-early jack-o'-lanterns.

I bend over and pick up the pill bottle. Howard sighs and runs his hand through his hair.

"We'll call and check up on you," he says to Colton. "To see if you need anything."

"Thanks, Dad."

Colton looks over at his father. I watch something pass between them that has passed between them many times before, many times before I ever knew them.

"I'm sorry," Colton says.

Howard nods and opens the driver's door. In the squeak of the hinges, I realize that what Colton and Howard see as benevolence toward Lorraine is actually a kind of cowardice and cruelty. They let her bully and push them six days out of seven; then on the seventh day one of them unexpectedly explodes and hurts her while she is behaving exactly as she behaved on the previous six. The pattern could be broken, but it has gone on for so long it never will be.

"You don't have a ride home now," Colton says to me, as the SUV backs out of the driveway and leaves.

"I can walk."

He looks at me for a long moment. The sound of the SUV's motor disappears into the distance, drowned in the cries of the lake gulls crossing the sunlit sky on their way from the lake to the river.

"Thank you," he says. "For not babying me."

"You act like you need it sometimes," I say, thinking about him driving away from yet another family dinner after having too few drinks to be above legal blood alcohol levels, but too many drinks to exercise decent judgment when a deer dives across a country road.

He gauges my meaning correctly and the frown lines appear beside his mouth, but instead of responding, he opens the door and goes inside, throwing the keys onto a side table with more force than usual.

"You wanted to talk to me the other day."

I wanted to talk to him a lifetime ago. I look around his house and the foreign objects in it. Even the familiar couch has become a stranger. Although, if I think about it logically, the puffy beige couch isn't the stranger in this house. I am.

"Do you want some coffee?" I ask.

"I would love some."

After turning on the machine that does everything but fill itself with water, I sit down and watch Colton peel a banana. His movements are awkward and unfamiliar to him, left to right rather than right to left. The cast bumps the table and he winces.

The clock on the bookshelf chimes the quarter hour, and I feel a moment of suspension. Once, I was standing on top of an overturned bucket and pretending to be a conductor, swishing a trimmed twig of oak at the stereo and bringing in the woodwinds in a wave of nineteenth-century German fortissimo, when Beaver heard the mailman. In his charge to protect the house from wickedness at the mailbox, Beaver swept the bucket out from under me. For one second the woodwinds hovered and I hung suspended in the air. Then I hit the floor with pelvis-crunching force. My conductor's stand rolled back and forth until it hit the stereo and sent the needle skittering across Dad's precious vinyl version of Mahler's Ninth Symphony.

Sitting here across from Colton, I'm hanging suspended and waiting for that pelvis-crunching thump that happens when gravity takes over.

"I don't think I'm ready," I say out loud, my tone more pianissimo than Mahler-grand.

He chews and swallows.

"For what?"

"To get married. I'm not ready for it. It doesn't feel right."

"You mean to me."

"To anyone."

"I can't say I wasn't expecting it."

"I didn't realize before how it was with me," I say. "I haven't felt right—"

"Since your sister came home."

I don't bother to deny it, since it's probably true, but Saphi's homecoming was just the finger that pushed over my domino life. It was just a tipping point. If she'd stayed in Alaska with Flynn or moved to Florida or some point in between, my world might suddenly have been changed by the simple act of dropping an orange at the grocery store or having the post office be out of any stamp but those generic flag stamps or being cut off by some pimple-faced boy in a truck while driving back from St. Louis. I might not have reached the tipping point until I was forty-five and crowded into a corner by marital complications, but when it was all said and done, I would have known, as surely as I know now, that what I was doing was a mistake.

"You want to go have adventures, don't you? Just like your sister."

"Maybe. I—"

"Do you think you'll ever come back—"

"I'm not sure I'm going to leave."

"—to me?"

"You will always be my friend."

The words sound pathetic, because it's obvious that we will be acquaintances who meet each other with a smile, but we will never be friends. We look into each other's eyes for a long time, simply gauging the emotions and the unsaid words. I tug on the ring around my third finger, intending to give it back.

"Keep it."

I look up from the band covered in etched June roses and find him smiling a smile as lopsided and awkward as his cast-hampered banana peeling.

"You're the only person I know who would want a ring that looked like that."

It's part compliment, part complaint.

"It doesn't even have a diamond."

"It's what's in here"—I tap my chest—"that counts. Not the trappings."

"In this case, the trappings matched what was in there."

"Not when we bought the ring."

"Even then."

"If you thought that, why . . . ?"

"Hindsight. Don't you see it?"

I lay the ring on the table, where it glitters brighter than the golden leaves on the oak trees.

"I wouldn't need a *ring*, much less a diamond."

"If you were in love."

Exhaustion swamps me, and I push an annoying, ticklish strand of hair off my face. When was the last time I took a shower? Yesterday? Two days ago? I close my eyes and the swirls of color in the darkness behind my shuttered eyes take on the form of birds flying up on a song.

"Some things should be seen and stored in your mind. Taking pictures either distorts the beauty, diminishes it, or lets you forget what you saw."

"If I were in love," I say out loud, "I wouldn't even need a ring."

"So you admit you weren't ever in love with me?"

"Did you love me?"

"Yes."

At first I feel guilt and draw circles on the tabletop to keep from looking up into Colton's face, but I can't keep drawing forever. When I look up and into his eyes, I notice something I've brushed aside many times and refused to acknowledge. Whether it is because he grew up with Lorraine or for some other reason, Colton is a manipulator. I don't think he means to be a manipulator, but he is so good at it that he has manipulated himself into believing that he is honest. Looking into his eyes, I can see that he wants me to feel guilty. Even if he wants to break off this relationship as much as I do, he prefers to have me do the deed so he can remain emotionally blameless. I can't decide if he is doing this consciously or not, and that makes it difficult to feel anything but a sort of tired regret for what might have been.

————

My junior year of college, I was woken up in the middle of the night by Tallulah shaking my shoulder and holding out the cordless.

"You have a phone call."

It was Grady, sounding distraught and drunk and frightened all at the same time.

"She's pregnant."

I snuggled down into my blankets and yawned.

"Who?"

"Linda. She's pregnant."

"Congratulations."

It wasn't the right thing to say and I knew it. Grady had faded out of my life on the scent of cut grass, and with the ease of distance and youthful immortality, I'd thrown off the ties that bind first loves together and tangled myself up with a variety of decent human beings during the last few years. Because of distance and new tangles, I found myself looking down on Grady for staying put in Stoic and having relationships with safe, familiar people. Not looking down, exactly, but feeling a greater degree of separation from him and his problems than what probably actually existed.

"She wants to get married."

"That's logical."

I reached over and touched the button to light the face of the bedside clock. Three in the morning.

"I love you," Grady said in my ear.

His words cut and stung. I cared about him, but I didn't love him anymore. I didn't think he loved me, either; he was simply confused by the sudden changes in his life. Childhood confidences are a hard thing to shake, so in his confusion, he was calling me in the wee hours.

"You're just scared. Go home, sleep it off, and you'll feel a lot better in the morning."

"You think?"

"Yes."

"Do you still love me?"

"You're my friend, Grady. I'll always love you because we're friends."

"But you don't love me."

"Not like Linda does."

"She wants a diamond."

"Then buy her one."

"You wouldn't need a diamond."

"What does that have to do with it?"

On the other end of the line, he was quiet.

"Nothing, I guess," he said.

"Go home and go to bed. And for God's sake, don't drive yourself."

"Is it really over? Between us?"

"You broke it off, kiddo. Remember?"

"But is it over?"

A car's headlights flashed over my ceiling as I stared up into the cracks and patches that generations of tenants and owners had made to the horsehair plaster. Somehow, either in his confusion or maybe in those times when Linda and he were at odds over something, Grady must have kept our relationship on the back burner of his mind. In a flash of three a.m. clarity, I realized that he wanted me to douse that burner forever because he wasn't capable of doing it himself. And I realized that I still loved him enough to do it.

"It's over, Grady."

A long silence followed during which I could hear him breathing and absorbing this last gift I had to give him.

"Good-bye, Augustina."

"Good night."

"You wouldn't need a diamond."

I look across at Colton and feel a sort of tired regret for what might have been between us if we hadn't even needed a ring.

Chapter 19

The next morning, I do the unthinkable for a pastor's daughter and I skip church. It wasn't premeditated, but when I came in the door yesterday afternoon, Dad looked up from the soup he was making and asked:

"How is Colton?"

"He can get around all right. Lorraine seems to be his biggest problem."

Dad shook his head and sighed. I opened the refrigerator door and took out the nearly empty carton of orange juice.

"Can I finish this off?"

Dad nodded.

"I broke up with him," I said, while the juice flowed into a glass.

The spoon stirred around on the bottom of the pan. Dad was buying time, trying to think of something to say that wouldn't condemn me as an unmerciful dragon lady who would kick a guy when he was down.

"He already knew what was up," I said. "But he wanted me to say it."

"Are you sure that isn't just your conscience fooling you? Because you want to move on without any guilt?"

"Eighty to ninety percent sure."

He reached out an arm and I dropped down beside him for an awkward hug. Wheelchairs make physical contact difficult. In the years since the accident, Dad and I have gone from demonstrative to touching only out of necessity. Maybe that is why the group hug after Saphi came home stands out in my mind as a pole where I can point my compass and chart the recent changes in my life.

"You should still make sure he's okay," Dad says.

"I will."

Thanks to Dad's quiet words, when I woke up my conscience smote me, as the old books say, and I lay in bed thinking about what I could do to cheer Colton up. Those thoughts led to others until I remembered the recipe box hidden in my closet and realized that even though Colton wouldn't take back the ring, I should return the box.

On the way to Colton's house, I stop by the grocery store and choose a pumpkin from among the last of Jackson Dover's precut crop that he hauls to the store early in the month. The store will be tossing them out in a few hours so the stock boys can get busy setting up for Christmas, and Halloween will be forgotten before it happens. From the store's specialty section, I pick up a bouquet and a few five-hundred-piece puzzles, since Colton has always liked the methodical task of turning puzzle pieces right-side up and sorting them by color before putting the pictures together. I'm humming to myself when I reach his house, but the humming stops when I see his driveway is filled with the Morleys' SUV. I almost keep going, but instead I park the car in the street and wipe the sweat from my palms before juggling the recipe box, puzzles, and bouquet.

Lorraine meets me in front of the steps leading to the minuscule entry area. The door to Colton's house is firmly shut behind her.

"He told me," she says. "He told me what you did."

"I thought maybe I should drop by and see how he's doing," I say, ignoring her greeting.

"Praise God. She has a shred of decency in her."

The "shred of decency" bit is a little below the belt, but I shouldn't be surprised, since the dissolved engagement will probably look harsh to most of the people in the town, especially after Lorraine gets through talking about it.

"I suppose I should be grateful to you," she says. "Why should he marry someone whose family is steeped in a lack of morality?"

"Excuse me?"

"The blood that runs so true."

She slams back through Colton's front door and I stare, open-mouthed, at its smooth surface. At the well-taped paper notice that reads, NO SOLICITORS. Then I climb the steps and rap the surface with my knuckles. When no one answers, I turn the handle and walk on in. Colton is scrunched down in the beige couch clicking through the television channels in a brainless, bored way. Lorraine is throwing things around in the kitchen. Down in the basement, Colton's dryer beeps, and the door to the basement slams as his mother goes down to answer the appliance's call.

"Hi," he says. "I was wondering if you meant to stand outside all day."

"Your mom—"

He rolls his eyes.

"—just said that lack of morality ran true in my family. What did she mean by that?"

"Who knows?"

"You obviously do."

And he obviously doesn't want to go into detail, because the channel surfing has slowed to a crawl and he's pretending interest in a show on cake decorating. I set the recipe box, bouquet, and puzzles onto the couch cushion beside him.

"Colton?"

"Your mother . . ." he begins.

His mouth twists a little with something that could be annoyance or that tiny streak of cruelty. I'm not interested in deciding which twist right now.

"Your mother came into the office a few years ago and asked me some questions about getting a divorce."

"Asked you?"

"Asked Alan," he amends, naming his boss. "But Alan asked me to look up the legal issues, so I knew why she was there."

"A few years ago."

"Right before—"

"—the accident," I finish.

"Yes."

He turns off the television and sets the remote on the arm of the couch. As an offhand distraction, he picks up one of the puzzles.

"These are nice," he says.

"You didn't tell me about this. Why?"

"It didn't seem right to tell you."

It doesn't seem right that he told anyone, but of all the people in the world, of all the people in the world who are connected to Colton, I would think I was the one who had the most right to know.

"But you told Lorraine."

"Before I met you."

I stare at the blank television screen. Its reflective surface shows Colton sitting on the couch, looking very small and far away. The image runs a hand through its hair in a gesture similar to Howard's.

"Look," the image says, "I'm sorry Mom brought it up. She's got it in her head that what your mother did is an indication that you would—"

"I have to go," I say. "I'm late. I brought the recipe box back."

"Thanks. Are you coming by again this afternoon? Mom should be gone and we could—"

"No," I say. "I won't be back."

He smiles a sardonic little smile, chuffing air through his nose in a "so that's how it's going to be" way. We both understand that I'm not just talking about this afternoon.

"Augustina—"

My hand on the doorknob, I stop and turn to find him looking at me. Until Alec, I didn't know how sterile and observatory Colton can be when compared to someone who is genuinely interested.

"—it could have worked, you know. Between us."

"For a while, it might have."

I open the door and step out into the sunshine.

———

"You decided to enter the world during the middle of Dad's graduation ceremony at the seminary. I think you were jealous that someone else was getting all the attention."

"I was not."

Mom and I were sitting on the front porch swing while Dad sized up the pumpkin and thought about what kind of face it should have.

"Angry or happy?" he asked us.

"Scary," we both said.

"It's always scary with you two. What if he wants to be a happy jack-o'-lantern?"

The jack-o'-lantern aside, it was a scene repeated many times. Dad sitting on the steps in the hushed sounds of the early evening, Mom and I on the swing, me wanting to hear the story of how I came into the world. This particular story time happened on Halloween. I can still see the knife cut into the top of the pumpkin as Mom said:

"It was a dark and stormy night."

"Rain everywhere," Dad said. "And me in my graduation gown."

"He took off the mortarboard, though."

"Should have left it on for an umbrella."

The pumpkin lost the top of its head and Dad started the process of scraping out the interior.

"Then what?" I asked.

"We pulled up to the hospital's entrance and you decided you wanted to be born in the car," Mom said.

"It was messy," Dad added, pulling glop out of the pumpkin. "Like this."

"Yuck," Mom and I said together.

"The doctor came just in time—" Mom continued.

"—to slap you on your butt," Dad finished, slapping the pumpkin's side.

"He did not!"

"He did!" Mom said. "Then they wiped you off and handed you to Dad and he said . . ."

Dad looked up from the pumpkin and smiled at us.

" 'Now we're a family.' "

Inside, Saphi started crying after her nap.

"Saphi's awake," Mom said, disentangling herself from me and getting up.

Dad looked down at the pumpkin.

"Won't a scary pumpkin frighten the baby?"

―――――

After leaving Colton's house, I drive myself and the pumpkin far out into the wilds around the lake. The tiny clinical, scientific part of my mind that has kept its sanity shrieks in white-knuckled agony as I press the accelerator all the way to the floor and listen to the satisfying crunch of gravel tearing up my wheel wells. Somehow, reading in a journal that a woman wants to go live by herself on the side of a mountain isn't the same as finding out she walked into an attorney's office and asked how she could obtain a divorce.

Were you ever going to bother to let me on it? I ask my memory of Mom. *Or were you going to let me keep on making excuses for you? Were you going to call me up someday and say, "Well, gosh, Augustina. You know all those stories? They were just lies. Have a nice day!"*

Were you going to separate me and Saphi? Choose one of us to go live with you and leave the other with Dad?

Why didn't you tell me?

I skid the car to a halt in one of the unofficial pullout areas made by fishermen who aren't wealthy enough to own a bass boat or who just prefer to fish from the warm, comfortable rocks that ring the lake's shores. This pullout area tops a steep bank filled with rocks and scrub trees. Standing beside the car, I can see—far below, where a narrow path disappears into a tangle of vines—the glitter of the sun on the lake. The sun is an insult. Everything inside of me is black.

"Now we're a family."

Reaching into the car, I pick up the pumpkin and throw it as hard as I can down into the ravine. It smashes on the rocks and smashes the image of Mom smiling at Dad. Smashes all the beauty and warmth and . . . complacency of forever-love under the moon and planets that Mom destroyed with a secret visit to Colton's office.

I slide down the dusty side of my car and sit on the mix of sand, dirt, and rock. The pumpkin bits glow orange and wet in the sunshine. My nose is running. I wipe my wet face and nose on my sleeve.

"Damn you, Mom. Goddamn you, Mom."

It's a whisper. As if I don't want anyone to hear.

"Do you ever wonder," Saphi's voice asks in my memory, *"if Mom died because she didn't think she could find the courage to leave us?"*

I guess Colton and Lorraine answered that question.

"Goddamn you, Mom!"

The echoes die quickly, leaving me frightened that someone will actually hear. Someone who might take me seriously and disturb Gail Fletcher's eternity. I pull my knees to my chest and bury my face in my arms, gulping in breath after breath on the wake of audible tears.

Lacrimosa dies illa, qua resurget ex favilla judicandus homo reus. The words from Mozart's famous Requiem make an absurd appearance in my tear-filled mind. *That day of tears when all humanity shall rise up from the ashes to be judged.* Oh, God, what ashes? The ashes of my childhood? No, the ashes of the absurd feeling of security that came from having a history I could count on. The ashes of the pleasure I took in those stories that were true fairy tales. Stories now made false because of their twisted humanity. Stories judged false. Lies.

"Goddamn your stories, Gail Fletcher," I say into the crook of my arm.

Something wet and cold bumps my ear. I scramble sideways

on a gasp of a scream. The black dog beside me scrambles in the opposite direction and yelps when it puts weight on both back legs. We stare at each other. Me on all fours beside the right front tire of my car, the sand and rocks digging into my palms. It—she—on three legs, her head down, ears flattened slightly, and tail wagging cautiously.

Above us, the wind plays in the leaves, and the wild geese call out to one another as they cross from one portion of the lake to another. Far away in the distance, a fisherman revs up his boat's motor. Heat waves from the sunlit gravel warp the air between me and the dog, altering the impression of the distance that separates us.

"Hi," I say.

I'm surprised the word is audible, coming from my raw throat. The dog's ears come up in response.

"Who are you?"

She gives me a doggy grin that reminds me faintly of Alec's smile.

"Are you the devil, too?"

Limping toward me, she whines. Her left hind leg dangles use- lessly from her hip.

"Did someone hurt you? Or did you run off and leave some- one behind?"

It's common in the areas around the lake where hunting is al- lowed. Untrained dogs hear a gun for the first time and run away in fright, not stopping until they've lost their way.

Sitting back on my heels, I hold out both hands in a welcom- ing gesture. The dog hops the final two steps in my direction, leans into me, and sighs.

Chapter 20

"Another injured stray?" Doc Jones asks me. He brushes the crumbs of Sunday dinner off his shirt.

Mom used to hold my hand whenever I would find another animal to bring to the white-haired vet. He's had white hair since I was six, but he never seems to grow any older. He had white hair when I brought the first of many strays, a howling tabby kitten I'd rescued from an overflowing drainage ditch.

"Is that a kitten?" Mom had asked as I'd run into the kitchen bare chested, the wet bundle wrapped in my good Sunday shirt. She was taking the roast out of the Crock-Pot and everything was ready for the usual after-church dinner.

"He's hurt," I'd said, holding the kitten up for inspection.

We were new to Stoic, and Doc Jones was the only vet who was willing to leave Sunday dinner and go to the office in response to Mom's phone call. She made me put on a shirt before we left and lined a basket with flannel for the kitten. The drainage-ditch mud never did come out of my good shirt, but I still tried to wear it as a badge of honor the next Sunday.

Doc Jones brushed crumbs from his shirt and felt the kitten all over. "Cold, wet, and a few cracked ribs—and he probably has worms," he announced. "But he's alive, thanks to the young lady."

Doc became my childhood hero. He fixed the wing of a great blue heron Dad and I found injured in the river after someone took a few lazy shots at the bird. Technically, I suppose we should have called a wildlife person, but Doc fixed up the bird and we fed it fish until one day it simply flew away on its own. Doc fixed the classroom hamster after it ate a few things it wasn't supposed to eat. He removed a fishhook from Bonzo's lip. "You and your animals get into more trouble. I see you more often than my best customers."

Mom used to hold my hand. And Tiger—the first kitten—lived to a ripe, fat old age, sunning himself on the steps of our porch.

"Another injured stray?" Doc Jones asks me. "I haven't seen you since your mama passed."

He doesn't look a day older, but his fingers are twisted up and they tremble.

"I can't kneel down to see you, doggy," he says to me by way of speaking to the dog. "My knees aren't what they used to be."

I squat down and pick the dog up by slipping my hands under her belly, quietly hoping that I'm not hurting an injury I can't see while trying to protect an injury I can. The old man strokes the dog's head, but the dog buries her face into my shoulder.

"Already your friend for life," Doc says to me.

"She hopped right into my car, anyway."

"Lab mixes do that. Can't resist a car ride. Their only complaint is that the state won't issue them a license to drive."

He chuckles at his own joke as he runs his hand toward the dog's hind leg. My shoulder vibrates as she growls in her throat.

"I don't think she likes that," he says. "Looks to me like she's got a dislocated hip. Probably was bumped by a car or fell a long ways. Let me sedate her a bit and I'll pop it back into place."

Doc Jones doesn't have an X-ray machine or pretty pictures on the wall, but he's felt twenty or thirty animals a day, six days a week, for the last fifty years—and that doesn't include the cows and horses. In a few minutes of touching, he can figure out what it takes a machine and two lab-coated assistants a half hour and one hundred dollars to figure out at any other vet's office.

"You up to this?" he asks me when the dog is on her side and her tail is brushing a mildly sedated thump. "I could go get Nora, but she's watching *The Sound of Music*. I can't tell you how happy I am to be here instead of listening to another chorus of 'Do, Ti, Do.'"

I nod and hold the dog just as he tells me to. The bones grind sickeningly; then it's all over.

"All better now," Doc says. "Put your head down if you feel faint. You're kind of white." He pats the dog's ribs. "I imagine this girl is going to be a new addition to the family."

He looks across the table at me and smiles. His blue eyes are milky, but he sees perfectly when it counts.

"You needed a dog."

————

Doc Jones takes me on a tour of all the animals in his care while the dog comes far enough out of the anesthetic to hobble to the car on her own. I smile and nod at the kittens, cats, and dogs, but it's just a distracting dream. I write an absurdly low check for his expertise and a bag of dog food.

"Bring her back in for her shots before the end of the week," he says. "She may feel a little sick after she comes completely out of the anesthetic, so expect a little something on the floor."

On the floor of my car. Her tail wags apologetically.

"All a bit much for one day, huh? I know how you feel."

The closer I get to home, the more I want to be farther away. Growing up, I can't claim that I had much kinship with Saphi when it came to emotions, but today I understand why she packed a bag and ran away with the monetary contents of the cookie jar. The dog hops out of the car when I open the door for her and climbs the steps as if it were the natural thing to do. Her hip is sore, but she's getting around just fine and making herself at home, exactly as Doc predicted.

"You need a name," I tell her. "I can't keep calling you Dog."

She grins up at me, reminding me of Alec again.

"Don't do that. It gives me shivers."

Sitting down, she waits for me to open the door. The house is silent. I might even believe that it is empty except that the van is here and Sunday afternoon is a strict routine of pure relaxation after the weeklong buildup to morning service. I finally turn the handle and open the door, letting Dog in ahead of me. I'm hanging up my coat when I see her sitting beside Dad's wheelchair, her chin on his knee.

"Who's this?" he asks.

"She appeared out of nowhere."

"Smells like she's been to Doc's."

The vet's office has a particular antiseptic smell that clings to coats and fur.

"Yes."

Dad leans down and is rewarded for his attention by a doggy kiss. I dig my hands into the pockets of my jeans and look at man and dog. The black tail is swishing enthusiastically, batting around a stray book in its wake.

"Saphira's asleep," Dad begins, "but—"

"Was Mom thinking about getting a divorce? Just before the accident?"

A perfect rock of a sentence. It lands in the water of the moment and ripples out and out, lapping at walls and ceiling and my knees in perfect three-dimensional unpleasantness.

Dad's hand stills on Dog's head. The dog turns and looks at me. Her grin is absent.

"What makes you ask?"

Dad is hedging. He resumes stroking the black head and ears. I watch his hand for a moment, then look up into his face and find him watching me. His eyes have lost their . . . What did Mom call it? Starshine.

"Was she?"

"We were having some problems."

"Enough to get her to go to Colton's boss to talk about divorce?"

Dad appears puzzled.

"Did Colton tell you that?"

"Lorraine hinted at it. Colton confirmed it."

He shakes his head and resumes his petting of Dog's ears.

"I'm beginning to think you made a good decision, scamp."

"What?"

"To not marry into that family. Yes, your mother went to Colton's boss to ask about divorce laws. Do you remember Aunt Sadie?"

I struggle to bring my memories into focus through the ripples of confusion. A fuzzy memory of a woman with big plastic glasses who always had a piece of gum in her purse for the pastor's daughter emerges.

"I think so."

"She bumped into too many doors and fell down too many

basement stairs for your mom's taste. When she found out that Sadie tended to be on the receiving end of her husband's temper, she talked to her about it. Sadie thought infidelity was the only reason for a divorce and wouldn't be convinced until a lawyer said differently. In writing. She was too scared to ask for herself, so your mom did it for her."

I stare at a point over Dad's head. On the far wall hangs one of Mom's paintings. It's been there almost as long as I can remember, a dark canvas filled with swirls of color that, van Gogh–like, attempt to catch the feeling of light more than the actuality. I think the official title Mom gave the work was *Star Melange*, but the painting went by the nickname *Planet Blender*, thanks to Dad's teasing and Saphi's inability to work her baby tongue around the word "melange." Mom always rolled her eyes a little, but we were her favorite audience, her most enthusiastic audience, and she forgave us our teasing.

Lorraine is Colton's favorite audience, and Colton knows how to appeal to her. Years ago he gave Lorraine juicy confidential information, knowing she would enjoy it. Today I was his target audience and he used that information again, knowing that, just as Lorraine had done, I would draw conclusions from the hazy truth. Perhaps I should applaud his genius at creating a work of art that brought both pleasure and pain. Perhaps I should have expected his streak of cruelty—he probably feels used and abused by my dissolving our engagement, maybe rightly so—but I wish he'd been honest about those feelings yesterday instead of acting like we could still be friends. Still, maybe he assumed we *would* be friends, until Lorraine started a Christmas list of sins and worked on his self-pity. Or maybe he was looking for a sympathetic audience for his pain, and talking about my genetic flaws helped heal the wounds of yesterday's outburst and bring him back into the loving embrace of his mother.

"Did Aunt Sadie ever get that divorce?" I ask, still looking at Mom's painting.

"Carl had a fatal heart attack and made the issue moot. She's living with her children in Connecticut."

I pull in a chestful of air and close my eyes on the outward breath, shutting out the picture on the wall and my mental picture of Colton and Lorraine. After a few ticks of the second hand, I open my eyes and ask the inevitable question.

"Were the problems you and Mom had serious? Divorce serious, I mean."

Dad sighs and rolls his chair over to the lamp table. He carefully removes his glasses and sets them down, then, equally careful, he picks up his cup of tea, which must be cold but seems to bring some measure of comfort nonetheless.

"Yes."

"Why didn't you tell me?"

He smiles just a little and his fingers wrap tighter around the mug. Dog moves between us and whines, but we ignore her.

"I—we—didn't want you to be upset. And after—"

"Upset? It was that far along? Mom was going to leave us?"

"No, nothing like that."

But he looks away to one side. I can't tell if it is guilt for not being completely honest or an attempt to gloss over something that is a painful memory.

"We were scheduled to see someone in St. Louis. For marital counseling. Then the accident happened and—"

"—and it wasn't necessary," I finish. "Do you know I read Mom's journal?"

He looks up at me and raises his eyebrows.

"Did you?" he asks.

"Do you know that for the last six years I've been making excuses for some of the things I found in there? That Saphi thought Mom didn't want us anymore? So if you were trying not to upset us, you didn't succeed."

"Gusti—"

"You could have told us!"

And for the first time in my life, I see my father lose his temper. He throws the half-empty mug of tea at the far wall. The stoneware breaks and splatters tea over the yellow paint and the floor.

"It was *our* marriage! Between us. Our problems. Not just something else for the entire community to gawk at and gossip about. Not something else for me to smile over and pretend I didn't notice that everyone was talking about behind their hands."

"Saphira and I are *not* the community. We were your children. Your *family!*"

"And Gail was the love of my life. Isn't there something that is just my own in this world?"

"There's a dog in the house," Saphi says from the staircase. "I think it knocked something over. . . . Oh, shit."

She stops at the foot of the stairs, Dog beside her.

"Oh, shit."

"She was our mother," I say to Dad, ignoring Saphi.

"Does that give you the right to know everything that went on between us? Just like everyone else thought they had a right?"

"This isn't about your fucked-up parishioners or your religion!"

Dad pales.

"It's your religion, too," he says.

"No, it isn't. It hasn't been for years. There is no such thing as God."

" 'The fool says in her heart.' "

"Yes, this fool says exactly that."

And Dad slaps me.

We stare at each other. Father and daughter. We can practically read each other's shock. I see the tears on his cheeks before I feel them on my own.

"I'm sorry," he says, touching my cheek. "So sorry. For everything."

I sit down on the floor and close my eyes.

"I've made so many excuses," I say. "I knew something was wrong, but I kept making excuses, because I couldn't . . . couldn't live with thinking all those stories you told us were fake—"

"They were real."

"—but I was wrong just now. Demanding that you—you and Mom—should have told us before you were ready to talk about it."

"Every night I regret the fights Gail and I had toward the last. Why didn't I realize that being a pastor was nothing compared to being with her?"

Saphira hands us both a box of tissues.

"Blow your nose," she says to me. "What do you mean, Dad?"

"Gail was tired of being in a fishbowl. But I was scared. I don't know how to do anything else. This"—he waves a hand to encompass the community—"this is all I know."

"That's not true," I say. "You could have done anything you wanted to do."

"A pretty theory. But it's hard to apply it when you have one kid in college and another getting ready to apply."

"No," Saphi says. "No, you can't blame us for that. You know we would have supported—"

She breaks off at Dad's memory-filled half grin and laughs a little.

"Okay," she amends. "You know that Gusti, at least, would have been behind you all the way. I would have bitched and moaned—"

"Take it easy on the language," Dad says. "I've had my quota for the day."

I blow my nose and throw away the tissue.

"She's right," I say. "It's not fair to blame us. We would have taken out more student loans, gotten jobs. I had good scholarships. This wasn't about providing for the family—it was about fear. Your fear. If you'd talked to us . . ."

I trail off. I hate two things: injustice and hypocrites. Looking up at Dad from my hard seat on the wooden floor, I realize I'm reacting to perceived injustice by being a hypocrite.

"I'm sorry," I say.

Saphi frowns at me, but I ignore her and focus on Dad.

"I'm not really angry that you and Mom didn't tell us," I continue. "Not really. Not now. I'm angry because I'm scared. All those stories about love at first sight and being a family, all those experiences . . . I feel like they're a foundation"—I smile at the memory of that long-ago walk to the river's altered sandbar—"a foundation of sand, and the wind and rain just knocked my little house over."

"All those stories were true," Dad says. "Absolutely true."

Chapter 21

"Your grandma hated your dad as soon as she laid eyes on him."

Beyond the porch where Mom and I sat on the swing, I could hear the late-summer cicadas crying out for love in the humid dark. We were sitting on the porch watching an incoming thunderstorm. Lightning bolted out of the sky to strike the faraway earth.

"One-one-thousand," Dad began. "Two-one-thousand."

"Three-one-thousand," we all said in unison.

Two more counts, and thunder rolled like bowling balls through the dark clouds overhead. Mom bounced Saphi on her knees.

"Isn't this fun?" she asked into Saphi's ear.

My toddler sister crowed and pointed to the next lightning strike.

"One-one-thousand," we began, but this bolt was farther away.

"What did Grandma say?" I asked, prompting a return to the familiar story I had asked to hear again.

" 'You're another one of those shiftless poetry beaters, aren't you?' " Mom said.

It was a perfect imitation of Grandma's voice when she told me to "Get those baby mitts out of the cookie jar or you'll ruin your appetite." Grave and disapproving. Dad's laughter overrode Mom's imitation.

"And I said, 'I've never beaten poetry in my life.' "

"Which is probably why Grandma told me your dad wasn't welcome in her house a second time. She didn't think much of smart-mouths."

"She's the one who said it," Dad said.

"So when your dad asked me to marry him, we decided it would be better to tell Grandma *after* the wedding."

I always got shivers at this point in the story.

"My roommates threw rice at us as we left, even though we hadn't gotten married yet. We were in the VW Bug, driving to the church where one of your dad's friends was waiting to marry us, when I looked up and saw a full moon—"

"And Venus, Saturn, and Mars, all near one another," Dad added.

"—and at least three planets. And I said—"

" 'Pull over Warren, you fool,' " Dad said in a high voice.

Mom laughed, the sound mixing with the hum of the cicadas and the distant roll of thunder.

"Something like that. And we got out of the car and I pledged to love him forever, while standing under the moon."

I shivered.

Sitting on the hardwood floor with Dog's chin on my knee and Dad and Saphi beside me, I push my hand through my hair and try to reconcile my childish vision of a perfect love with life's flawed reality. It's not that I am so naive as to think that my parents' marriage was perfect, but Mom's death created a sense of . . . arrested development, perhaps, leaving their love trapped in my childhood memories rather than seen through my adult understanding of human flaws and vulnerabilities.

"Do you really not believe anymore?" Dad asks me.

I'm so caught up in my family memories and new realizations that it takes me a moment or two of staring into his concerned face before I realize that this question is a matter of theology rather than love.

"I'm sorry I said that. I wanted to hurt you."

His face relaxes. Bitterness trickles in as I realize that having family foundations kicked out from under Saphi and me is less important to him than my continued belief in his God. I look down at the floor as honesty battles with my desire to not hurt him. Alec is right about honesty in relationships. Sometimes honesty is just an excuse to lash out. Sometimes it is just a pretense, and the true reason for being honest has more to do with wanting to hurt the other person and "get even" than as an open expression of feelings and thoughts. I'm not sure whether my desire to tell Dad that my unbelief goes far, far back to the afternoons at the lake with Grady is a desire for the truth or just a way to hit back in revenge for his secrets about Mom. So I look at the floor and wonder how to respond.

The phone rings and Saphi stands up. Dog lifts her chin from my knee. From the other room we can hear her low voice as she talks to someone. The longer she talks, the more both Dad and I relax, realizing that we won't be called upon to provide some falsely cheerful sentences at a moment when neither of us feels much cheer.

"I'm sorry you had to find out about . . . your mom and me that way," Dad says.

"Lorraine was angry. And I think Colton was, too. He had to know Mom wasn't asking for herself."

"Without knowing, you can't really assign blame, though."

I laugh a little.

"Oh, I *can*, it's just a matter of whether or not it's the right thing to do."

Dad laughs with me; then his chin droops a little as he rubs his forehead.

"I think I fooled myself, Gusti."

"How so?"

"Thinking that you weren't giving anything up to stay here with me. I was selfish. I thought that since I never *asked* you to give anything up, I was blameless because it was all your decision."

I reach out and lay my hand over his, catch his fingers in mine.

"You didn't ask, but I wasn't going to say, 'Sorry about the accident, Dad. Hope you make out okay,' and just go my merry way, leaving you by yourself."

"You could have."

"Could I?"

He looks at me and smiles. All the afternoons spent on the river, all the dancing to records, all the songs to chase away the shadows roll into one smile shared between us.

"I thought, when you and Colton . . . I thought you were happy."

"I'm just stalled a bit. I have some thinking to do. I wouldn't have been happy with Colton. That was just . . ."

"Desperation?"

"Thanks. No, frustration maybe."

Dog pushes her nose into my face and wags her tail.

"We're going to need a name for this stray of yours," Dad says. "How about Philomena, patron saint of lost causes?"

"Can you imagine yelling, 'Here, Philomena,' out the back door at night?"

"We could just call her Philo or Mena."

The dog wags enthusiastically.

"See?" Dad says. "She agrees."

I roll my eyes and shake my head, giving in to the inevitable.

"Okay, okay. Philomena it is."

Dog—Philomena—dances around us and barks before trying to climb into Dad's lap. When the confusion has died down and Mena has been convinced that fifty-five pounds of wriggling dog and chairs with wheels are a difficult combination, I finally say something that has been nagging to be said.

"I'm sorry you've had to live in a fishbowl all these years. I knew about it. I've even played the game—the 'everything is okay in the pastor's family and we're always open to suggestions for how to be more spiritual' game—but I didn't think how hard it would be to . . . just *live* and to have problems like other married people while being watched every second. Even by people who care."

"It's a give and take. I was supposed to watch out for them, you know."

"That's not what I mean, and you know it."

He looks away from me and out the window where the sun is sinking into midafternoon.

"Lots of things in life are difficult. Maybe I feel safer in the fishbowl than out in the wide world."

As he says it, I can hear Mom's voice in the words, and I know this is one of those final arguments he's turned and polished in his mind during the long nights when he lies in bed, unable to feel the blankets covering his toes. I wonder how it feels when your last memories of the person you love more than your own life are tinged with the unhappy scuffles of daily living. Looking at the lines around Dad's eyes and mouth that are highlighted by the sun's reflection off the window glass, I know Mark Twain was right and that there's no need for a hell to punish sins after death. People do an excellent job of that on their own while they're still living on this earth.

"What are you going to do?" Dad asks.

I look up and find him still staring out the window. There's a peculiar tension in his body, and it takes me a moment or two to shake my thoughts of self-induced hell and realize that he believes I am going to leave everyone behind and, as Colton put it, run off to have adventures. If adventures leave a person as busted as Saphira seems to be, an adventure is the last thing I want.

" 'Two roads diverged in a yellow wood,' " he continues.

"And I took the fork in the road."

It's an old joke between us and not even funny, but it shakes him out of his morose musings on things unseen out the window.

"You're asking me about something I don't even understand yet," I say when our smiles fade. "Last week I was preparing to marry Colton and have in-laws and some kind of cookie-cutter future that I thought was the normal progression of things. Today . . ."

"You could go back to school."

"I don't know. Maybe. I've certainly thought about it. But I don't have to decide right now."

"It's important—"

"Dad. Stop."

He frowns.

"You don't have to fix me. Or counsel me. Or make up some way for me to . . . recapture my youth or something."

"I'm not—"

"Please. Let me process this on my own for a while. I'm not broken and I don't need glue this very second."

"That's up for debate."

"No, it isn't."

He shakes his head. I squeeze his hand to let him know that this has nothing to do with anger over the past or over our recent fight. It doesn't. It has to do with my being able to make a decision after the dust settles. I've made a lot of decisions in the heat of the moment or in the throes of emotional upheaval, and I've let those decisions continue to dictate the pattern of my life long after they have ceased to be the right decisions.

"I want to take my time for a change," I say out loud. "Take it slow. Think."

He frees his hand from mine and pushes gently at my forehead.

"For all the book learning up here, you have never spent much time thinking about anything. Mom used to lie awake at night and ask me where you got that 'jump first and look second' attitude."

"And?"

"Who do you think? You don't see me jumping, do you?"

"If that was a joke, it was awful."

"You've been jumping a lot lately."

"I know. And maybe now I need to stop and look first."

"You've already done the jumping. I don't see a change in the pattern."

"Dad . . . you're starting to piss me off."

———

"Hold my hands."

I reached out and up and caught Mom's hands. We were standing on the bouncy, inflated "moonwalk" trampoline at the fair. All around us, children, teenagers, and the few adults brave enough or indulgent enough to accompany frightened first-timers leaped and fell and staggered like drunks in a bad TV movie.

"Now jump!"

She hopped and I followed several beats too late so that we staggered into each other. She grabbed me and hugged me close, my ear just under her heart.

"We have to jump together. Here."

Catching my hands again, she held me at arm's length and smiled. I smiled back up at her and thought the sun coming through the white canvas overhead made her look as glowing and beautiful as Mary looked in the old nativity story pictures in my children's picture Bible. Pretty and gentle like the scene from a Christmas card.

"You're beautiful," I said.

"Say that again thirty years from now."

"You'll always be beautiful."

Shaking her head, she laughed.

"Together this time. One, two, three."

We jumped and bounced, higher and higher until we couldn't hold on to each other's hands and fell apart into the inflated floor, laughing and sweaty in the canvas-tinted sunshine.

———

I smile up at Dad's rueful face.

A warm beam of autumn sunshine floats through the open window and sets the air around the wheelchair on fire. I'm sitting on a solid floor, but I feel like I'm walking on the inflated rubber moon, reaching for a guiding hand and falling down laughing.

Chapter 22

"Once upon a time, on a Halloween night just before Augustina was born, your father and I went trick-or-treating."

Mom took the pins out of her mouth and looked up past my pirated person. I smiled down at her because I'd heard this story before and knew she was telling it for Saphi's wide-eyed benefit.

"But you were grown-up," Saphi protested.

She was wiggling in her pink tights and fluffy tutu. Leave it to my baby sister to like pink. We were going to look pretty silly together. Captain Blood and Tinkerbell. Everyone would ask to see my hook and I'd have to explain the difference between Rafael Sabatini and Walt Disney. Disgraceful. I sighed in a fit of eleven-year-old nostalgia for the good old days when Saphi wore a baby pumpkin outfit.

"Yes, we were grown-up," Mom said. "But we were broke and didn't get paid for two more days."

"Broke?"

"We didn't have any money. And I was pregnant and in desperate need of chocolate."

"Pregnant women need chocolate?"

"They live on it," Dad said from the door.

"Look, Dad!" Saphi said.

She twirled in a puff of pink and waved her star wand.

"I'm Tinkerbell."

"Didn't Tink wear green?" Dad asked.

Mom groaned. "War-ren."

We all stared wide-eyed at Saphi, whose lips had come apart while her chubby chin quivered with the beginning of tears. We stared wide-eyed while Dad rushed in to cover the gaffe.

"No, no. Definitely pink. I'm sure she had a pink outfit."

"Definitely," Mom and I said together, nodding vigorously.

Saphi's smile was restored. Dad grabbed her hand and twirled her around in a pirouette until she laughed and fell down, dizzy.

"Smooth move, Ex-Lax," Mom muttered to him when he came over to inspect Captain Blood. "Pink was all we had."

"Sorry. It slipped out."

Mom straightened my vest and greatcoat.

"Not bad. Try not to move suddenly or the pins will jab you."

She caught my elbows and made me look at her.

"Are you sure you will be all right trick-or-treating on your own?"

"Mo-om."

Rolling her eyes, she looked up at Dad and shrugged.

"Okay. But take care of your baby sister. And if you need help, remember the Barghest."

"Have you ever thought it might be better to say 'phone home' or 'pray'?" I heard Dad whisper to Mom after the obligatory Polaroids.

"It's Halloween, Warren. Don't ruin the atmosphere."

She pinched him and gave him a kiss, then waved to us as

Saphi and I set out to look for pirate treasure in the form of chocolate coins and candy. Trick-or-treating in a small town steeped in tradition is a child's delight. The neighbors' porches were filled with scarecrows and leering jack-o'-lanterns, courtesy of Jackson's pumpkin patch, and to complete the mood, a barely full moon skimmed along the Milky Way on a boat of cloud. Saphi and I wandered from porch to porch until we couldn't cram any more candy into our bags. I looked up and wasn't sure where we were, but I remembered the house with the green-eyed witch hanging from the tree on the corner.

"Come on, Saphi," I said.

Saphi's lips were ringed with purple from the sucker she had in her mouth. I wasn't sure she should have a sucker in her mouth while walking, but I knew she'd scream if I tried to tell her so. I took one of her sticky hands in mine and walked back toward the witch. At the corner I didn't know which way to turn, but a glance up at the moon told me to go right. We walked and walked. The houses beside us grew darker as the moon sailed right on into a fleet of clouds. An owl called from a patch of woods off to our left.

"Gusti?"

"What?"

"I'm scared."

I stopped. I was scared, too, but Captain Blood wouldn't have been afraid of anything. I took a deep breath and knelt down in front of Tinkerbell, ignoring the stab of the pins.

"Let's call the Barghest," I said.

Not that I thought a Barghest would get us home, but if Saphi lost it, I was going to lose it, too. Saphi took the sucker out of her mouth.

"What's a Barghest?"

"It's a big black dog. Like Beaver. And when you feel afraid on a dark road, you can call him. And he'll follow you and make sure you get home."

"Okay."

"We have to say it together. Can you do that?"

She nodded.

"We have to say: 'Good dog, gentle dog, I'm on my way home.'"

"Good dog, gentle dog, I'm on my way home," Saphi repeated.

I stared at her and realized I didn't remember the rest of the rhyme, so I thought about what we needed and made one up, trying to sound like it was the right thing to say.

"Guard me, walk with me, to my front door."

"Guard me, walk with me, to my front door."

"Now we have to shout the last part," I said.

"Barghest, Barghest, walk with me home," we yelled, Saphi one word behind me so that the word "home" had a childish echo.

She let out a long breath and we looked at each other.

"What happens now?"

"We keep walking."

"When will the dog show up?"

"You might not see him. But you'll hear his paws."

We'd reached a porch that held a guttering jack-o'-lantern and a white cat when Saphi squeezed my hand.

"I hear him!"

I stopped, heard the soft footfalls, and felt my heart fall into my pirate boots. Saphi tugged on my hand.

"We have to keep walking."

Running! I thought, but merely walked a little faster until Saphi tugged on my hand again.

"I can't keep up!"

I turned around, and the Barghest was on top of us.

"Woof!"

I screamed. Saphi screamed. And Dad wrapped an arm around both of us, tickling us until we laughed our way out of our fright.

"Did two lost girls call a Barghest?"

———

Standing at the east window in the living room, I wrap my arms around myself. The midafternoon sunlight refuses to let any secrets hide in the hollows of Jackson Dover's fields or the rim of trees on the far side of the world from me. Everything beautiful is stripped away in the harsh light of the sun beating down from a cloudless sky.

I called a Barghest today.

It wasn't until a college myths and legends class that I discovered a Barghest was rarely considered some kind of savior for the dark road. Usually, in stories, it was an evil omen, a dark phantom come to steal the nighttime traveler's soul and drag it to hell. As always, it is impossible to separate pagan fiction from Christian fiction. Impossible to separate which old gods and spirits were merely capricious and which were demonized by a young religion trying to dominate the old ways. Mom chose to meld Beaver and the Barghest to create something that would help soothe my childish fear of the dark and the shadows that lurked there. But sometimes, just like Dad's soft footfalls behind Saphi and me on that Halloween night seventeen years ago, the Barghest was equally frightening in its possibilities.

I called a Barghest today in the form of requiring the truth. I was scared when I came home with Dog—Philomena—and I came to Dad and wanted a protecting spirit that would walk me safely to the door of the truth I have decided to believe in during the years since Mom died. Only instead of bringing comfort, the

Barghest of truth turned on me and made my fears real. And unlike that Halloween night when Dad made Saphi and me laugh and turned our fear into a delicious memory to be rehashed at the supper table every Halloween for years to come, this time no spirit guide has appeared to turn the truth into a mere pleasantry.

I wrap my arms tighter around myself and watch Jackson's distant figure as he goes out to the barn and corral to check on Castor and Pollux, the generation of mules that came after Andy and Barney. Behind me, I can hear bare feet on the floor and smell the scent of Saphi's bath powder. She never returned from taking the phone call and she's been in the shower for a long time.

"Is Dad taking a nap?" she asks.

I nod, still looking out at the harshly lit fields.

"You were right," I say. "About Mom and her wanting to leave."

"Just because they were having trouble doesn't mean she wanted to abandon us. I overstated things the other day."

A wheeling arc of starlings and blackbirds, massed for migration, lands on the field. They fly up and land in a rhythm reminiscent of the ocean waves. Just a few days ago Saphi was the one tossed by the wind, and I was the firm shore of reason. Today our positions have been reversed.

"And now we're just going to the opposite ends of the equation," I say.

"Lorraine always was a bitch. And Colton is definitely her son."

She says it with such viciousness that I turn to look at her.

"My little sister is being protective?"

"It was a cruel thing to do."

I watch her profile for a moment. Something has happened to her. A feeling of great age and emotional exhaustion is coming off her skin along with the scent of her powder.

"Are you all right?"

"Do we have a pumpkin? We should carve a jack-o'-lantern."

"I bought one, but I threw it down a ravine."

"Why?"

"I needed to break something and it seemed like the cheapest and most satisfying thing to break."

"Was it spectacular? The break?"

"Very."

She doesn't want to talk about how she's feeling. I turn and look at the fields again. Orange patches among the brown and green catch my attention, and I realize that Jackson has pumpkins dotted throughout his garden. It's been a good year for pumpkin growers, and he obviously has a lot left over. I can see him lead the mules out for the annual garden plow-up and I have a brilliant idea. One that will require the cooperation of two determined sisters if the brilliant idea is to become a reality before Halloween night is over.

"Let's go get some pumpkins from Jackson."

———

It's not easy to carve some fifty pumpkins into jack-o'-lanterns in a few short hours, but it's even harder to get them into a car.

"We'll never sort out which lids go with which," Saphi says.

After laying out my plan to Jackson and Saphi and waiting for them both to stop laughing, we filled up my entire car with pumpkins that Jackson helped us cut free from the trailing, frost-nipped vines in his pumpkin patch. We drove away, waving, while he hitched the mules to a plow and prepared to turn the garden under.

I look up at the nearly full moon sailing through the skiffs of dark cloud. Each time the clouds cover the moon, its light turns their edges into a silver lining.

"What time is it?"

"Eightish."

I open the car door and Mena jumps in. I steer around a jack-o'-lantern sitting in my lap, and Saphi holds Mena as we drive to the old cemetery on the edge of town. It's one of those Italian-horror-film cemeteries, filled with obelisks, crypts, earth-covered mausoleums, and the traditional arched tombstones decorated by carvings or river shells, depending on the wealth of the family. We drive slowly through the graveyard, stopping every few feet to place and light jack-o'-lanterns in among the gravestones and in the trees. I set the pumpkin down, Saphi lights the candle with a lighter, and I put the lid on top; then we jog back to the car where Mena waits for us, her front feet on the window's edge. We creep through the graveyard until the whole area facing the road is filled with ghostly grins and scowls.

"It's a good thing there's no wind," Saphi says as we drive back through the gate, our lights off just in case there's someone in the graveyard office.

"I wonder if this constitutes vandalism," I ask when we've reached the corner and I can turn my lights back on.

"Enjoy your misbehavior. It makes the best memories. Besides, the worst they'll do is fine us."

We park the car a block away, slip a rope around Mena's neck for a leash, then sneak back to the edge of the graveyard to hide in some shrubs along the edge. Crisped oak leaves crackle under our butts and Mena's paws, releasing their distinctive, dusty, earth smell.

"Look," Saphi says.

A car driving up the street slows, then stops altogether. Costumed goblins pour out of the car, pointing and shrieking in delight. They climb up and hang on the wrought-iron fence around the graveyard while the adult with them snaps pictures. We hug Mena's neck and giggle, and her tongue hangs through a doggy grin. Twenty minutes and fifteen cars later, a local TV station and a newspaper photographer show up.

"We're famous!" I say.

Mena barks, and we both grab for her nose. The photographer looks our way, then shrugs and goes back to taking pictures.

Around eleven thirty the excitement dies down, and we stretch our cramped knees and lean back to look at the fast-lowering moon. The jack-o'-lantern nearest to us gutters in a breeze, casting eerie shadows across the grass and leaves just under its glower.

" 'The moon's the North Wind's cookie,' " Saphi says.

I smile at the memory of Dad teaching me the children's poem about the continual competition between the North Wind and the South Wind to bake and eat the moon. I was shivering and cold after a church function where I had fallen asleep with my head pillowed in Mom's lap. Dad carried me out to the car and said, "Look, Gusti, the South Wind has baked a brand-new moon cookie for the North Wind."

Mena yawns and turns a few circles before lying down with her chin on my thigh.

"Do you think Philomena is a Barghest?" Saphi asks.

I look down at the black dog who came to me when I shrieked my outrage at having the past torn to pieces.

"She came to show me the way home," I say. "But I claim not to believe in the supernatural, so whether or not she's a Barghest will have to be a mystery."

"No supernatural. Not even life after death?"

"Especially not."

"But what about the people who die? Don't you want them to go to a better place?"

"It seems like most religions rejoice in sending people to a worse place."

She snorts.

"But when it comes to people," I continue, "Mom, for instance . . . I think she would miss us. And somehow it's easier to be the only one who feels pain. It feels less lonely if she is just gone. That she can't feel any emotion. That the only one who is sad is me."

"If that's what you think, why do you care so much about the stories being true?"

I sigh and watch the jack-o'-lantern's candle sputter and go out. From the woods behind us, a barred owl calls out a hoarse, barking cry. Another owl answers as the moon slips in and out of the clouds.

"Selfishness," I say at last. "I wanted to remember things a certain way, and that wasn't the way things were. All the stories . . . Dad and the wrong color of paint. Mom promising to love Dad forever under the moon. Eloping. The way they would look at each other when they told me the story of me being born in the car at the emergency room's door. I wanted all of that to still be real even in the adult world of irreconcilable differences."

Saphi pulls her knees to her chest and rests her chin on the living shelf. A car without much of a muffler pulls up and a too-young driver gets out.

"Let's take a few," he says.

"Get back in the car, dumb ass," someone inside the vehicle yells.

A siren wails up the road.

"That's probably a cop," says the voice from inside the car. "Come on."

The driver shakes his head, but he gets back into the car and they drive away. The siren comes from the nearest fire station, not the cops, but it saves a few jack-o'-lanterns from being stolen and smashed somewhere up the road.

"Flynn died today," Saphi says.

It takes a moment for the full impact of the words to register. I reach out and touch her hair. Hesitantly, as if she might jerk away and reject any comfort. Now I understand why she seemed so aged after her shower. I remember times without number when I used the shower as a solitary, wet world where I could curl into the tile and sob while the falling water beat the sadness out of me.

"Saphi . . . it must hurt so much."

The words are inadequate. Both she and I know exactly how inadequate, but we also know the meaning they intend. She lays her cheek on her knees, and I stroke the hair away from her moon-lit face.

"What scares me," she says, "is that I don't feel the same."

"I don't understand."

"The same as when Mom died. I feel sad, but there's some part"—she touches her chest—"in here that isn't . . . doesn't feel the same kind of grief."

She wipes her cheeks on her jeans, then looks out over the graveyard and the jack-o'-lanterns that are winking out one by one as the candles inside burn up the remnants of wax.

"I think Flynn was right. Maybe I didn't love him so much as want to care for him. And when I couldn't care for him anymore and came home . . . maybe . . . I don't know. I can't believe he isn't there. I can't believe that we never talked to each other again. I tried to call but he wouldn't pick up the phone or call me back. I miss him. But it doesn't feel the same inside."

I wiggle out from under Mena's nose, but when I try to put my arm around Saphi, she hunches her shoulder and pushes me away.

"Don't. I'm sorry. Just . . . please. Don't."

I nod, remembering how raw my skin felt when I finally realized that Mom wasn't coming back. How much every hug following the funeral burned my skin.

"Will you go back to Alaska?" I ask.

Carving and setting out jack-o'-lanterns helped distract her from her grief this evening. Now I'm hoping to distract her further by asking concrete questions.

"There won't be a funeral."

"Friends aren't getting together?"

"Nothing. He hated people making a fuss, and his body is going to science."

She laughs a little at some memory I can't share.

"He always was a stubborn bastard. Margie said he filed the divorce papers the minute the dust settled from my passing."

I don't know if I should tell her that I'm sorry or if I should stay silent. I decide to follow the old adage and hope keeping my mouth shut is golden. She doesn't seem particularly destroyed by the speed with which Flynn went after the divorce, more rueful and amused, as if at least Flynn did what was expected of him rather than something that might have told her he regretted his decision or had changed his mind.

"Are we going to pick up all those pumpkins before morning?" she asks.

"I suppose we should."

"Is this going to be a new tradition?"

"I have blisters from carving pumpkins. Maybe it should just be a mystery. A memorable event."

" 'It was night in the lonesome October,' " Saphi begins, quoting Poe.

" 'Of my most immemorial year,' " I finish.

"Let the mystery begin," she says.

Chapter 23

It's nearly one in the morning when we pull into the driveway in our coach smelling strongly of candle-cooked pumpkins. The moon is dipping into the mists floating above the trees, testing the water with one toe before jumping in. Above us, the stars play peekaboo with the last shreds of cloud. Saphi wraps her jacket around herself and shivers.

"It's cold!"

"It's supposed to frost tonight."

We enter the house as quietly as two stiff, cold humans and one toenailed dog can enter, but Dad is sitting near a lamp, reading a book. *The Brothers Karamazov*, I think, but he closes it before I can be sure and lays the book in his lap.

"I woke up to find a house haunted by the smell of cut vegetable matter," he says. "At first I was confused, but then I found and read this cryptic note."

He holds up the scrap of paper we left on the kitchen table before loading the pumpkins into the car.

"I presume this"—he looks down and reads—"'Dad, we're

off on a mission but will be back in a few hours.' I presume this has something to do with all the thumping I heard earlier and the pile of pumpkin innards out by the squirrel feeders? The squirrels are going to turn orange with all that beta-carotene."

Saphi and I shuffle like two naughty teens.

"Did you watch the local news?" I ask.

Dad has to bite his lip not to smile, and I know that he knows. Glancing sideways at Saphi, I see her grin.

"Spooks apparently invaded the graveyard," Dad says, trying to be serious. "The next thing you know, they'll be calling on Harry to perform an exorcism."

Harry being the priest of the Catholic church.

"I don't think the Church performs exorcisms anymore," I say. "But I got that from *The Exorcist*, so who knows?"

"They could always call Max von Sydow," Saphi says. "In a pinch."

Looking beneath Dad's smile, I see something else. A kind of sad nostalgia. This is the sort of stunt he would have been a part of when we were eleven or twelve or even twenty. He was the Barghest, sneaking up on us to give a lasting Halloween thrill. The creator of practical jokes like snap pops that would go off when we would pick up our plates to carry them to the sink on April Fools' Day. The one who dyed pancakes green on St. Patrick's Day and hid Easter eggs over and over for two little girls until the eggs cracked and fell apart from use. And while he is still the person he was before and does many of the same tricks and jokes, he is limited. Not only by his legs, but by the loss of Gail Gilbert Fletcher. In his life and also in his memories. Because without the chance to prove that no problem between them was too big to conquer, he has lived the last six years in a state of doubt over whether she would have stayed with him. He has lived with doubt, just as I have lived *without* doubt by forcing myself to pretend there was no possibility of any problems to begin with.

"We've decided that Philomena is a Barghest," Saphi says. "Well, Augustina isn't sure she believes—"

Saphi cuts off the sentence before she can resurrect the specter of my unbelief. She can feel the emotional barometer falling as my gloomy thoughts mingle with Dad's nostalgia and sadness. Her mouth opens and closes, and I know she is struggling to find a way to bring things back to a cheerful balance. Saphi has never, in my experience, been the kind of person who would be both sensitive to the emotional atmosphere *and* try to alter the balance. She was always the one who used every available means to get her way. Even if it meant doing something she didn't want to do, she would still pretend to desperately want an unattainable something in order to be the child in the limelight. Whatever it took to be special. For the first time, I realize how much she has changed since she left home and how much I have to learn in order to get to know her as she is now. I realize how much I have to learn about her *and* myself. Because she's not the only one who has constructed a sham stage for herself. I was—maybe still am—the daughter who sought the limelight by being her sister's opposite, by being the smart girl who never did anything wrong. In public, anyway.

"I'm not sure Philomena's big enough to be a Barghest," I say, jumping in to save the conversation. "But she did show up at an awfully auspicious time for a spirit. It being Halloween."

Dad pretends to consider the issue. Philomena rolls onto her back and rubs her face with her paws, enjoying being the center of our triple concentration. She looks up at Dad with her tongue lolling so far out of her mouth that it drags on the floor beside her ear.

"Well, Saint Philomena is known for interceding when there is unhappiness in the home," he says.

It is the first and last time he mentions the unpleasant atmosphere that invaded the parsonage with Gail Fletcher's departure. Maybe, years from now, I will find the newspaper article with its picture of the jack-o'-lantern-haunted graveyard slipped between the pages of his Bible commentary along with a photo of Philomena. *The Fletchers strike again,* will be written in Dad's handwriting under the picture of the graveyard, and on the back of Philomena's photo: *The dog who taught us to how to be a family again.* Maybe I will find these mementos, just as I've found lots of mementos over the years, but I know Dad will never talk about them.

Saphi stretches and yawns, only partly faking.

"I think I'll go to bed."

She looks at me and then at Dad, and I expect her to tell him about Flynn, but then I see that this is something she is going to leave until the future. Maybe she will leave off talking to Dad about her marriage and Flynn's death until the pain is less. Maybe she never will talk about it with Dad. Saphi has always held her secrets closer to herself than I have. My secrets tend to not be secrets for very long.

"Me, too," Dad says.

His smile draws all of us in to the warmth.

"Happy Halloween, although it is past the witching hour."

Saphi laughs, gives him a hug, and climbs the stairs, calling a "good night" over her shoulder. Dad puts his hands on the wheels of his chair, but he doesn't move. From the kitchen I can hear Mena lapping water and crunching the dog food she disdained in all the excitement of loading the pumpkins.

"Will you let her out to go to the bathroom before going to bed?" Dad asks.

I nod. He pats the wheels a little, but still doesn't move away.

"I've been thinking," he says at last.

"Okay," I say when he doesn't continue. "Does it hurt?"

He doesn't respond to the tired joke, although he does look up from his knees to my face for a moment.

"I'm worried that I'm trapping you here," he says. "That you won't fulfill any of your dreams because you waste away taking care of me."

"That sounds suspiciously like self-pity rather than concern for me."

He frowns and we look at each other for a long moment. He had this speech prepared, and now I'm questioning his motives. At first he looks frustrated, then thoughtful.

"You think?"

"What did you expect me to do?" I ask. "Even if I had known what my dreams were—dreams beyond the thrill of the prestige of going to Johns Hopkins, I mean—was there really any choice after the accident? Can you even know if I wanted another choice or felt resentful? Especially when I hardly know myself?"

"To tell you the truth, I didn't think you were resentful, but when Saphi came home . . . you seemed so angry at her."

I sit down on the arm of a nearby chair and try to figure out a way to put my recent irrational behavior into rational words.

"Familiarity breeds contempt," I say when no words present themselves.

"You think I take you for granted?"

"Not you. Not exactly. It's just . . . for the last six years, I've been adjusting my expectations of myself to fit boundaries. I'm not saying they were real boundaries, but I saw them as real. I guess I expected people to notice that I was doing this adjustment and think . . . think I was being someone special, someone extraordinary. Then when Saphi came home, everything that went before, everything I did . . . Well, suddenly, I've been boring the choir with no Bach all these years. I've been a stick-in-the-mud who won't change anything. It's not a matter of being taken for granted—it's a matter of pride. My pride. My *hurt* pride. So I've been feeling sort of like the prodigal son's older brother. How come no one ever killed a fatted calf for me?"

I smile a little as I say it. And I realize that I no longer feel as if the boundaries are so high or so wide. I no longer feel that things will always stay the same just because that is how they have been or just because that is how they've come to be. The resentment I felt when Saphi came home . . . I guess I should have expected it . . . but the core of the resentment had less to do with Saphi and more to do with the dam I had built across my life to hold in my real self until I was ready to burst. All the Sundays of pretending to believe in a God I no longer believed in. All the dinners with Colton's parents, pretending that their way of life was a good one for me. All the doubts I pretended I didn't have about Mom's journal entries. All that pretense was just a dam keeping me from asking questions about where I wanted to go in the future.

Dad and Mena are both watching me and the emotions that must be crossing my face as I consider my feelings.

"Have you thought about the future?" Dad asks. "What you want?"

"I'm just now learning how to live in the present. Maybe I'd better leave the future until tomorrow."

———

Climbing the stairs, I hear the music box. It brings back the feeling of cold noses pressed against glass as Saphi and I, hard-saved allowances—and the little extra Dad had slipped into our pockets for Christmas buying—clutched in our hands, pressed our noses against the old-time glass counters at Brecker's Jewelry. Behind the glass, special for Christmas, were music boxes of polished wood.

Dark mahogany, teak, oak, cherry, and walnut. We finally picked out a red cherrywood box from the very back that was small enough for us to afford and that had curves gentle enough for Saphi's chubby fingers to encircle.

"What tune do you ladies want in the box?" Maurice Brecker, son of Calvin Brecker, grandson of Owen Brecker, asked us.

We didn't like most of the tinkling themes until Mr. Brecker pulled out the last mechanical.

"Here's one just right for a lady who lives by a river," he said as he wound the key.

"It's 'The Blue Danube Waltz,'" I said to Saphi when the familiar music began. "The Danube is a river. Just like the Mississippi. Only in Europe."

"I know," Saphi said, even though she didn't. "I'm not a baby."

Climbing the stairs, I hear the swishing sounds of the waltz that call to mind the diaphanous dresses, the dashing uniforms, and Audrey Hepburn's long neck in the movie version of *War and Peace*. I stop at the door to Mom and Dad's old room, where Saphi is sitting on the bed and has the music box open in her hands.

"It's 'The Blue Danube Waltz,'" I say. "The Danube is a river like the Mississippi, only in Europe."

Saphi smiles at me through the wetness in her eyes.

"I know, stupid."

She holds the box up until the red wood glows in the soft light from the lamp on the dresser.

"Can I take this with me to my room?"

"Of course."

"Do you remember when Mom opened it? On Christmas morning?"

"And we waltzed around the wrapping paper on the floor?"

Saphi shuts the lid of the box and the music stops, taking the memory with it.

"It's okay," she says. "It's okay."

I'm not sure what she means, but I say, "Good night," as she slips past me and down the hall to her room, Philomena trailing along in her wake. After a moment or two I hear the music begin again. She's left the lamp on and I move forward to turn it off, then find myself sitting on the edge of the bed and looking at the open door of the closet. I don't remember opening the door, but maybe Saphi did. Mom's robe is still hanging on the inside hook, where she hung it up after that last shower just before the Singspiration service. I've never been able to wash it or fold it away. For years I imagined that it still held the scent of her soap, but summer dust collected on the maroon terry cloth and wiped the scent away. It's an old robe, frayed and ratty around the edges, "but too old to give up," as Mom used to say.

I stand up and unhook the robe from where Mom hung it six years ago and sit down again with it in my lap. The scent of her soap surrounds my imagination and I can feel her arms around me just like they went around me when she hugged me that long-ago "Blue Danube" Christmas morning.

And somehow I know, as if someone had told me the path of an alternate future, that Gail and Warren Fletcher would have worked it out and that the vows made in the moonlight beside the Beetle would have remained true. I know that the stories are true.

————

I wake up in my own bed after only a few hours of sleep. It's still dark outside, but the sounds are different. Just before dawn, the chorus of die-hard grasshoppers and crickets slows to a stop, and the wind brushes the house with a gentler touch after playing with the fog hovering over the river and fields. I place both hands on my chest and breathe in, feeling the first touch of the harvest month before breathing out. Slipping out from under the blanket, I tie Mom's old bathrobe around me and tiptoe down the stairs and past Dad's closed door. Someone has already made coffee. I pour a cup and step out onto the porch, toes curling on the cold wooden floor.

"Hi," I say to the blob on the porch swing.

"Hi," Saphi replies.

I sit down next to her, petting an enthusiastic Philomena and fending off a concerted doggy attempt to spill my coffee by bumping into my cup. Saphi pushes a toe into the floor and the swing begins to rock. An early bird complains and a few oak leaves scrape over the cement as the wind pushes them down the road.

"Is that Mom's robe?"

"Yes."

"Where did you find it?"

"In the closet. Hanging up. I never took it down after the accident."

I find myself saying the words without the usual catch in my heart. Saphi pushes at the floor again and the swing picks up speed.

"You can have it if you want it," I say.

"No. That's all right."

"I mean it."

"So do I."

I wait for the swing to slow down enough that I won't risk scalding myself with hot coffee when I take a sip. Just beyond the trees that border Jackson's hay field, the sky is turning pink.

"Someday I want to find a little house," I say, "with a porch and a view of the sunrise."

"Here?"

"Here. There. Somewhere."

"What about this house? There's a porch. And a view."

"It's not mine."

She nods. "We all need something that belongs to us."

"It doesn't have to belong to me. It just has to be my own."

Above the pink clouds, the deeper reaches of the universe are purple-blue, studded with stars.

"But I think I'll stay here for a while."

"Me, too," she says. "Me, too."

"Once upon a time . . ." I begin.

I stop as the familiar words that Mom used to begin a story come out oddly when said in my voice. I clear my throat.

"Once upon a time, Mom and Dad moved to a small town named Stoic. They had a little girl named Augustina and a dog named Beaver. They named the girl after a saint and the dog because he slapped the water with his tail when he swam. Everyone worked together to make the new parsonage into a home. Well, Mom and Dad worked while the little girl and the dog mostly got in the way. Things went along the same for several months. Then you were born."

I put my arm around her and she lays her head on my shoulder.

"And Dad said, 'Let's name her Sappho!' And Mom said, 'Warren Fletcher, you will not name our baby after a lesbian poet. I don't care how historical she is.' And Dad said, 'How about Saphira, then?' And you smiled at him."

Saphi's breathing is softer and I know she's fallen asleep on my shoulder. I sip my coffee. When the sun climbs over the trees, I don't look away. I look into the light and dream about the future.

Author's Note

For the sake of the story, I have taken a few minor liberties with St. Francis Xavier or College Church on the St. Louis University campus. The church restricts weddings to Saturdays, so as not to interfere with normal proceedings, but I have a newly married couple step through the doors on a Wednesday. The music of complines that Augustina and Alec attend springs completely from my imagination, but it is based on the rich musical ministry of the church. However, the "haunting" by the devil/demons and the resultant exorcism are a part of actual pop history, and the events that supposedly occurred around the church in 1949 did, in fact, provide the basis for William Peter Blatty's novel *The Exorcist*.

Photo by Sears Portrait Studio

The daughter of American missionaries, **Karen Brichoux** grew up in the Philippines, but now calls the Midwestern United States home. After receiving a master's degree in European history, she began writing fiction full-time and is the author of three previously released novels: *The Girl She Left Behind, Coffee and Kung Fu,* and *Separation Anxiety.* For information about future releases, excerpts, or to sign up for her monthly newsletter, visit Karen's Web site at www.karenbrichoux.com.

Falling into the World

KAREN BRICHOUX

This Conversation Guide is intended to enrich the
individual reading experience, as well as encourage us
to explore these topics together—because books,
and life, are meant for sharing.

A CONVERSATION
WITH KAREN BRICHOUX

Q. Tell us a little about yourself.

A. My parents were American missionaries working in the Philippines. I was born in the Visayas—the central region of the Philippines—and lived at home until I was twelve years old. After that, I went to boarding school in Manila. I came back to the United States for college and tried a number of majors: secondary education, theater, humanities, creative writing, literature. I eventually graduated with a degree in art history and English literature, but my graduate work was in European history. Everything interested me. Well, everything except math, but I think the uninterest had more to do with frustration because math is almost never taught as a discipline that should be *understood* rather than merely practiced.

Q. You say you majored briefly in creative writing, but you obviously didn't continue with the degree. What happened?

A. I had a number of wonderful professors. The best was Dex Westrum, who made me circle all the adjectives and adverbs in a (painful) short story I wrote for his class. He also lent me a book called *On Fiction* by R. V. Cassill that I forgot to return and found about six years ago in a box at the back of my closet. I feel guilty about virtually stealing this book (it was a result of careless youth!), but rereading the selections and commentary caused me to reconsider writing. Dex was the kind of prof who would find that bit of confluence enjoyable.

But I think the purpose of your question is to discover why I didn't realize I was destined to write fiction earlier in my life. The simple answer is that at the time I was taking those classes, I wasn't destined to write fiction. My fiction writing was—to be blunt—horrible. I thought good fiction contained pain, sex, death, suicide, cigarettes, and maybe a little sadism thrown into the mix. While I confess that I've read good fiction that deals with some or all of those topics, I think the main goal for this kind of writing is to get the reader to look at the author and think s/he is worth looking at. Since this kind of writing is also what most creative writing profs see, I never stood out from the other students writing about pain, sex, death, suicide, cigarettes, and sadism. With no encouragement, I drifted off to other majors where I felt I had some degree of talent.

Q. Shifting the focus to your work, Falling into the World *is a story about a woman in her late twenties. Given that most work classified as "women's fiction" seems to focus on issues facing women in their forties, is this an attempt to reach younger readers?*

A. A while back, I read about a panel discussion between publishers and women readers in their twenties and thirties where the focus of the discussion was to determine what would appeal to these readers. One frustrated woman stood up and said, "Good books interest me." Her implication being that lifelong readers rarely read a book because it is supposed to appeal to their age group or sex. Lifelong readers read good books. I don't intentionally write books geared toward a specific age group or sex. I try to write good books and I hope that readers will enjoy them.

As for choosing the ages of my characters, I write the stories of the characters that come to me and want me to tell their stories. If a seventy-year-old man shows up on my mental doorstep with an interesting story to tell, I will listen and write it down.

Q. *Augustina, the protagonist in* Falling into the World, *has been described as "unlikable." Do you think this will adversely affect how readers react to her as the protagonist?*

A. Not at all. How many of us are genuinely likable at all times to those people who are privy to our innermost thoughts? Humans are complex, emotional beings. In a day's time, we go through all kinds of situations that create all kinds of emotions. Likability tends to be a function of how well we hide the darker, more complex emotions. There's a reason why we have the saying "Laugh and the world laughs with you; cry and you cry alone." Because I write in the first person, readers are privy to Augustina's innermost thoughts. Some of those thoughts will be laughter; some will be tears.

Q. *Falling into the World uses the Mississippi River almost as another character. Is there a reason for that?*

A. Have you noticed how little contact most people in this country have with nature? Houses are climate controlled, windows are covered with curtains or blinds, offices have few or no windows at all, electronic devices are constantly blaring. Most people experience nature in that thirty-second walk between leaving a building and entering their vehicles. Yet nature is the most powerful force around us. Sure, it has been beaten into submission by our ability to cut, kill, alter, and destroy it—and the seeming willingness of many to do just that in the name of profit—but it still changes us in subtle ways. And for those people who are willing to embrace the natural world and allow it to work its magic, nature *does* become another person in their lives. Augustina has always run to the natural world as a means of comfort, as a source of excitement, and as a place where she can hear herself think. So, yes, the river, the fields, and the birds and animals around her are as much a part of her family as her father, mother, and sister.

Q. *You obviously have strong feelings about the environment!*

A. It's closer to a sense of bewildered amazement that people can endure harried, hurried lives that don't allow them a quiet moment to notice the sunset or the changing whirl of the stars above them. And a profound sense of discouragement when I realize that many deliberately embrace that harried, hurried life and couldn't care less about the sunset or that Orion is back in the winter sky. They say that the modern conveniences that should have brought us more leisure time have only managed to make our lives more hectic by increasing expectations for how much we are able to do in a single day.

Q. Is your life harried and hectic? What is a typical day like for a writer?

A. I think each writer has a different schedule. Some of my friends who are published authors juggle so many responsibilities that I can't figure out how they keep all the balls in the air! My life is less hectic than most because I don't have any children, but writing is still a six-days-a-week job. I spend my mornings on creative work; my weekday afternoons on the business work. I think writers are a lot more involved in the business side of things these days. Or maybe I'm just fooled into thinking these days are different because of the pop culture image of the writer sitting at his typewriter, a glass of whiskey and overflowing ashtray at his elbow, his greatest fear being that he won't overcome his writer's block. I don't know any authors who worry about writer's block. Usually we are wishing we could ignore our business and family responsibilities long enough to write down at least *one* of those insistent ideas that are pounding at the door!

Q. Speaking of the pop culture image of the writer, have you seen the T-shirt that reads "Just researching my novel"? Do authors really see the people around them as fodder for their next book?

A. I've seen the T-shirt and threatened to draw and quarter anyone who buys it for me! I can't speak for all writers, but my family and friends—even casual acquaintances—do not need to worry that they will suddenly appear in my books. I don't research my novels. I mentioned earlier the example of a seventy-year-old man appearing on my doorstep with a story to tell. That is actually an accurate way of describing how stories come to me. I'll hear a bit of song, see a candy wrapper folded into a triangle, smell the wet-leaf smell of fallen oak leaves, and suddenly a person will appear in my mind and say, "When I was a little boy, my father taught me how to fold a paper boat out of a candy wrapper. I floated it down an overflowing gutter on a Saturday morning. That morning changed my life." I'll ask him why it changed his life; he'll answer; and the answer leads to more questions. Eventually the whole story will come out. The paper boat might never appear in what I write, but it is still part of my understanding of the boy or man who has told me his story.

Q. Who are some of the authors who inspire you?

A. I read a lot of books in a year, and just when I start to think I've exhausted the well and won't find a single new author I love, I'll find one or two new ones who overwhelm me. The list of authors who have inspired me by their writing or

their courage to write in uncharted waters is long and var-
ied, but a few of them are: Mark Twain, Ernest Hemingway,
Willa Cather, Kate Chopin, Terry Tempest Williams, Silas
House, Monica Wood, Margot Livesey, Gretchen Laskas,
Neal Stephenson, Penelope Williamson, Mary Jo Putney,
John le Carré, Patrick O'Brian, Laura Ingalls Wilder, and
C. S. Lewis. Some of these are old, old friends; some are new
discoveries. All inspire me to never be content with my own
writing.

QUESTIONS
FOR DISCUSSION

1. Trace the influence of Gail Fletcher on her family from the time she and Warren met. How has she continued to be a part of her family's life since her death? Is her continued presence a help or a harm?

2. In chapter 17, Alec says that there is "no such thing as a completely honest relationship" because we "weigh the hurt to the other person versus the gain." Is there a point when communication—genuine communication—can break down because we choose our words too carefully? At what point does the Fletcher family begin to communicate again? Is it healthy communication, honest communication, or just the beginning of communication?

3. Augustina accepts Colton's proposal because she feels like a runner who has fallen behind in the race of life. Have you ever made a bad decision in a moment of desperation and later regretted it? Did you try to justify the decision to yourself rather than taking steps to change the situation?

4. Augustina has a different relationship with each member of her family. Are you or were you closer to one parent than to the other? Did your relationships with your parents change as you grew older? If you have siblings, how has your relationship with them changed over the years? How do these different relationships affect the interaction in your family?

5. Do you believe in love at first sight? Have you ever had an instant connection with another person? Did you have trouble defending this connection to skeptics?

6. Saphira's husband forced her to leave because he thought she was staying with him out of pity and because she needed to work out her guilt for abandoning her father. Do you think he was right or do you think Saphira really loved him? Would the relationship have worked out if he had never contracted cancer?

7. In chapter 18, Augustina realizes that what Colton and Howard think of as benevolence toward Lorraine is actually a form of cowardice and cruelty. Do you agree with her? Would it be possible for the Morleys to change?

8. In the final chapter, Augustina seems to feel her mother's presence. Do you think this was merely wishful thinking? Were you surprised that a person who didn't believe in the supernatural would feel this way? Will Augustina's beliefs change?